DEMONS RISING

Return of the Damned

MELVINA HAWKINS-PATTERSON

PAGE PUBLISHING, INC.
New York, NY

First originally published by Page Publishing, Inc. 2016

ISBN 978-1-68289-651-8 (pbk)
ISBN 978-1-68289-652-5 (digital)
ISBN 978-1-68348-110-2 (hardcover)

Printed in the United States of America

CHAPTER ONE

Satan had defied God, and he and a multitude of angels were cast out of the kingdom of heaven and into the fiery pits of hell. Two angels were sadly mistaken and put on earth to reside the remaining of their immortal lives. Their names were Time and Oblivion.

Time had went on into priesthood and practiced at Saint Sandreas Cathedral in Mexico. Oblivion had become homeless on the streets of New York, eating out of garbage cans and dumpsters. Two men living in two different worlds.

Father Time knelt down on the pew and prayed. "Father, forgive them, for they do not know what they do."

The main door of the church slammed shut. A nun approached him by the name of Sister Mary Claire. "Father, a storm is coming. Would you like me to chain the doors?"

"I don't think we should be having any more trouble out of them tonight, Mary. Thank you."

Trouble out of who? The undead? The streets weren't safe, and a colony was born. Father Time walked toward the back of the church, into his room, and picked up a bottle of scotch. He poured it into a glass and drank, pouring more of it into the glass until he drank himself into a stupor. He lay down on his cot and went to sleep. He had those same reoccurring dreams. The room got dark, like a black cloud was hovering over him. A shadow came out of nowhere, and a weak, eerie voice spoke out, the Angel of Death.

"Are you God's favorite?"

"I have done no wrong." Father Time shook his head side to side.

"This war is not over, Time."

"I never expected it to be!" He snapped his holy rosary from his neck, beads rolling across the floor. Sweat ran down his forehead as he cried in his sleep.

Gazing at the ceiling, a cockroach ran across it. Father Time picked up a Bible and read it. He whispered to himself each part of the scriptures. "Hear me when I call, O God of righteousness." He glanced up toward the ceiling at the cockroach. "Thou hast enlarged me when I was in distress," he continued, still glancing at the bug. "Have mercy upon me, and hear my prayer." Gazing back up, the cockroach turned into a human cockroach with eight legs, crawling on all eight and leaping from the ceiling in an attack position. Father Time immediately dove off the bed onto the floor, avoiding the cockroach from killing him.

He then reached for a can of Raid sitting on the dresser and sprayed it into its eyes. By the time the mist in the air cleared, the human cockroach was still standing and breathing. "Damn, that sure feels good!"

"You evil demon from hell, I'm going to send you back where you came from!" Father Time then ran toward the closet and sought out a cross-shaped sword encased in brown leather. The human cockroach chased him. He snatched the sword from its case and waved the tip of its blade at it. The human cockroach snapped at him with its clawlike jaws. Its long antennas glared at him. Father Time struck at its hideous figure, cutting it down in size and separating it in parts.

Father Time placed his sword back into its case and proceeded out of the room. The phone rang. He was already shaken up. It was Sister Lucy on the other end of the line. "Hello?"

"Father Time, my name is Sister Lucille Reeves. We met some time last month at the church, and I mentioned that I had a child who was, well, uh, possessed. You said that you could possibly help me, and I was wondering if we could meet somewhere?"

"Where?"

"I don't know. I guess at the café on Rio Drive?"

"I'll be there."

"Thank you, Father. I was worried that you wouldn't."

The café is a small shop that sat on the corner of Casa Drive. There they serve fresh baked bread, bagels, muffins, and coffee. Sister Lucy was sitting at a table. Her prescription eyeglasses were lopsided across her face as she sipped a hot cup of tea. Father Time walked into the café and immediately captured her attention. To her, he was drop-dead gorgeous and then some. Just the thought of him sitting at her table made her very excited.

"I have something that I would like to show you, Father," she said, reaching into her purse. She pulled out a picture of the possessed child. "His name is Kyle. Kyle Craven. He's a new one that came into our orphanage. His eyes, his eyes are evil. They pierce you like a knife, Father. It's almost like he can see straight through you. Like he can read your mind." She glanced at the picture. The boy's eyes were fiery red.

"Take me to him."

Father Time had his sword with him and approached the boy's bedroom. Slowly, the door creaked open as he pushed it.

"I've been waiting on you, Time," an eerie voice came out of the boy's lungs. The child's face was disfigured, and his hair had a touch of gray.

"Who are you?" Father Time drew his sword at the child.

"Father?" The nun became afraid that he would kill the boy.

"I am Cedillius, demon of all demons. I have been sent to you to deliver a message."

"And what might that message be?"

Sister Lucy grabbed Father Time's arm.

"We are coming for you, Time!" The boy began to laugh, and the laughter shook the house into a frenzy.

"Leave here now!"

The child attacked Father Time by flying in midair. His fingernails, long and sharp, were savagely clawing at Father Time. The nun grabbed her Bible and began to pray for the boy. Father Time grabbed a hold of the child and threw him across the room. The boy struck his head at the edge of a dresser drawer. Bleeding profusely, the child crawled up the wall to the ceiling. He leaped upon the priest, pounding him with his fist, growling like a wild beast. Father Time held the boy down onto the floor and grabbed a medallion around his neck. Shaking black ashes onto his finger, he smeared the sign of the cross on the boy's head.

"In the name of the Father, the Son, and the Holy Ghost. Amen!" Repeatedly, those same words blurted from his lips. The possessed child tried pushing Father Time off him, but it was useless. Suddenly, its demonic figure came bursting out of the boy's mouth and stood before him. Father Time got to his sword and swayed it side to side at the creature, trying to kill it. A battle went on in that room, a battle between good and evil. The child came through upon the floor, and Sister Lucy snatched him by the arm to get him out of harm's way. Toys and schoolbooks flew at the priest, hitting him.

Father Time swung his sword at the demon, which was flying at him. He slashed its flesh and clothes into pieces. He then cornered the beast and said, "Get out!" He tossed holy water at the beast, which disintegrated into tiny pieces upon the floor and disappeared.

"Are you all right, Father?"

Sweat and blood dripped from his chin, soaking the rug in the boy's bedroom. "I think so. How about you and the child?"

Sister Lucy embraced the child and wrapped a sheet around him.

Kyle began to shiver from the chillness in the air. "I'm sorry, Sister Lucy, I—"

"That's all right, child. This man here helped save you."

Kyle walked over to Father Time and grabbed his hand. "Thank you."

"My pleasure. I really must go. I'm needed at the church."

Sister Lucy smiled. "Father, you think we'll ever meet again. I mean, soon."

He turned around and could feel that she liked him a lot. Kyle ran over to hug him. Father Time lifted him up, embracing him in his arms. "You're welcome, young man. Now, I want you to always pray and listen to Sister Lucy, okay?" Father Time put the boy down, and proceeded to walk away. Kyle stood there, staring from behind.

"Hey, mister, what is your name anyway?" the child asked.

"They call me Time."

In the slums of New York, an angel had plucked his own wings. Drinking at a bar, the place was closing for the night, and he was the only patron who hadn't left. The bartender was irritated and tired for the day and would like to go home.

"Hey, buddy, I believe this is your last drink."

Oblivion attempted to stand up and fell to the floor. The bartender grabbed him by the collar and tossed him out the back door. Oblivion lay there sleeping in his own piss. Suddenly a gleam of light shined down upon him. It was the Almighty.

"Oblivion? Oblivion?"

Oblivion heard his name being called and lifted his head up high toward the stars in the sky.

"Remember what you promised."

"Why me? Why me, Lord?" he cried out loud to himself and stood up on his feet.

He staggered all the way toward a rehab center for alcoholics. There, they fed, clothed, and rehabilitated him back to good health. He received help for his drinking, and in three months, he was able to get back on his feet and hold down a steady job. Oblivion became a new man, a man of God. Deep in his mind, he never forgot. He never forgot what happened.

"What seems to be the matter?"

She wiped her eyes and glanced at him. "My old man left me. He just left. No reason for leaving, just gone!"

Oblivion placed his hand upon her shoulder, and she felt a sense of warmth from the touch of his hand.

"What is your name?"

"My name is Oblivion."

She wiped her eyes, laughing. "You say that as though you aren't human. You're somehow different."

"I am, and you are somewhat different yourself. I never met a woman as beautiful as you. Men should appreciate women like you, but unfortunately, they're lovers of themselves." She smiled at him. "What is your name?"

"Lori, but you can call me Lo. Say, would you like to go for a cup of coffee or something?" she said, gently placing her hand on his knee.

He got nervous and took it off. "I'm sorry, but it's been a long time since I . . ."

"That's all right. I'm used to it. Look, I got to go. I hope we meet again, Oblivion. It's been real nice talking to you. I all of a sudden feel better," she said, inhaling, exhaling, and smiling at him.

"Don't worry, we will."

The beautiful woman walked away from the man who was soon to be her husband.

Oblivion heard voices in the night. The trees spoke to him. "Oblivion? Oblivion?"

"Who is that?"

It started to rain, and a brisk breeze blew through his hair. He got up to go back to the center. His clothes were soaked, and his hair flopped over his eyes.

"Oblivion? Oblivion?"

Suddenly, dark shadows appeared before him. Oblivion ran as fast as he could to get back to the center. An open window allowed the rain to flow freely inside his room.

"You think you've escaped hell, but you haven't—at least not yet!"

Oblivion slowly turned around to face his oppressor. "You don't scare me," he said, backing away.

CHAPTER TWO

Oblivion backed up against the wall. "Who are you, and why are you here?"

"I am the Messenger. I was sent here to deliver you a message, and the message is, a great earthquake will come and release the demons from the fiery pits of hell. Blood will shed upon the innocent, and the earth will churn, crumble, and sink away, cracking into huge tilted blocks. Trees will fall, and houses will rip in two or upended. The violent shaking will trigger landslides and hurricanes. Tall buildings will creak, tremble, and groan, falling into the sea. Great chunks of buildings will crash to the streets. Highways buckled, sending twisting railroad tracks curled in steel. Whole waterfronts will vanish, surging away from the city. The twitching of the earth will go on lasting for weeks until you are both destroyed!"

"I'm sorry? Us both? Who?"

"You and Father Time." The messenger attempted to walk away.

"Wait a minute! Wait! Where can I find this Father Time?"

"Don't worry, he will find you." The messenger disappeared into thin air.

The next morning, a woman at the rehab shelter walked onto the front porch and noticed Oblivion sitting on the steps. Sitting in a sleeping position. Her name was Vivian Anderson.

"Oblivion, Oblivion, are you all right?"

He was slightly drunk. "It's starting up again."

"What? What's starting up again?" She rubbed his shoulder.

"The dreams, they're starting up again, and I can't stop them!" He attempted to stand up and fell. Vivian helped him up on his feet and into the center. She slowly eased him down on his bed. She walked over to the sink, rinsing a washcloth in the faucet and running cold water onto it, freezing the tips of her fingers. She then walked over to the edge of his bed and placed the rag on his forehead.

"That's cold. Take it off."

"What?"

"I said take it off!" He swung the washcloth onto the floor. His forehead was dark pink, looking like a first-degree burn.

"What seems to be the matter, Oblivion?"

He grabbed a hold of her sleeves. "The end of the world . . . the end of the world is near!" He was sweating profusely.

Vivian picked up the damp cloth and rinsed it under cold running water. She placed it on top of his forehead. "Look, child, I can't save you. Only God can save you."

Oblivion was wearing a rare cross around his neck. He tugged it with his fingers.

"Hey, where did you get that?" Vivian reached over to touch it.

He pushed her hand away. "Don't touch it!"

She gazed at him in a frightened sort of way. "You say that as though you have something to hide. What is bothering you? Maybe I can help or—"

"You can't help me. Nobody can help me!" He began to cry in a fetus position. Tears ran down his face and soaked his pillowcase. "I'm gonna die, Vivian, and there isn't a damn thing I can do about it," he said, sobbing his heart out. She embraced him in her arms.

He aimed it at the open window. The window slowly closed on its own. He realized that he still had a halo. He was an angel with torn wings. "Oh my god, oh my god, I'm . . . I'm still an angel," he sobbed, gazing up at the ceiling. "You never forsake me. Thank you, Lord, thank you." It echoed into the hallway of the center. Vivian overheard his cry for help and began to weep, leaning over the sink.

Walking away, Sister Claire turned to face Father Time in an angry way and ran to the women's restroom sobbing. She gazed up at the ceiling. "I'm sorry, Father. I know that I have to control these feelings that I have for him, but . . . but I can't help myself," she said, crying.

Father Time approached the women's restroom and stood by the door. "Are you all right, Sister?"

"I think . . . I think so, Father," she said, wiping her eyes. She slowly paced her way toward the door, leaning her ear against it.

"I'll be here if you need me."

"Thank you, Father." She smiled.

Sister Mary Claire was eating with a group of nuns at the Catholic Mission of Christ, an old Catholic school for nuns. The nuns' names were Sister Alice, Sister Rachel, Sister Elizabeth, and Sister Ann.

"So tell me, how's that new priest, Father Time?"

Sister Mary Claire blushed to herself. "Well, it's hard to say. The church congregation has grown since he's been there, and financially stable. I think he's a good man."

"Oh, come on, Mary. Everybody knows you've got the hots for him. Every time you're around him, you are always blushing like a sixteen-year-old virgin." The nuns began to laugh.

"I-I can't help myself. It's as though I've lost my mind or something. I think I'm falling in love with him."

"Oh, come on, girl. You can't possibly expect that priest to fall in love with you, do you? I mean, after all, he's a man of God."

Mary chewed on her turkey sandwich. "Yeah, maybe you're right."

Sister Elizabeth had always been envious of her. "Besides, Sister Claire, you would be breaking your vows before God." Sister Elizabeth ate the peas on her plate.

"You're wrong, Sister Elizabeth. I have the highest, utmost respect for Father Time."

"The only thing high right now are your panties, dear." The nuns burst out in laughter while Sister Elizabeth smiled in a vindictive sort of way.

"My panties aren't all you would have to worry about, Sister." Sister Claire stared into Sister Elizabeth's eyes, slamming her tray of food down onto the table, and left her supper there for someone else to clean up. The nuns were in shock as she walked away.

"Well, the nerve!"

In her room, Sister Claire was kneeling over the edge of her bed, praying. She repeated the Hail prayer fifteen times before she turned in. She slipped off her panties and put on her nightgown. She loosened her long red hair. She was exceptionally beautiful.

She slid the patio doors open for a breath of fresh air. A breeze blew her hair off her shoulders. What stood before her, gazing at her from a distance in the woods down below, was a demon, watching her. Its eyes were bloodshot red. It had sharp fangs, pointed ears, a tail, and feathered brown wings. Mary was very much afraid. Shocked, she ran out of her room, proceeded to run down a flight of steps, and bumped into Father Time.

"Oh," she gasped. "Father Time, I didn't see you. I'm sorry."

"That's all right, Mary. What seems to be bothering you?"

Mary looked behind and turned back around to face him. "Oh, nothing, Father. I . . . well . . . I guess it was nothing."

Father Time realized how beautiful she was with her hair down and smiled at her. "Mary, I never realized how beautiful you are until now," he said, holding her hand.

"Thank you," she said just as she looked up and gazed into his eyes.

He embraced her quickly into his arms and kissed her passionately on the lips. She got lost for a moment and found herself. Father Time immediately pulled back.

"I'm . . . .I'm sorry."

Sister Mary Claire placed her finger up to his lips. "Shhh, you've done nothing wrong, Father. I felt the same way. I was wondering when this moment would come, and now I know. I love you, Father Ti—"

"I really must go." He ended up walking away.

After mass, Father Time gathered in the company of clergymen.

"Father Time, what type of new ideas do you have in mind for our ministry?"

"Rescheduling the children's Bible studies on weekdays, organizing a group of church members to visit the sick, and later, land development. I also have an engagement with a personal friend in New York."

"Oh, and who might that be?"

"I'm sorry. I can't say." Father Time crossed his legs and smoked a pack of Drop Dead.

The clergyman smiled. "Father Time, as you know, the church is not fond of secrets."

"The church isn't asking. You are." Father Time gazed at him in an angry way.

"When are you leaving?"

"Oh, I don't know. Three days from now, I suppose."

"Do you plan on ever coming back to Sandreas Cathedral, Father?"

"I don't know. I certainly hope so." He went back to his room.

Father Time was packing his clothes in a suitcase. Sister Mary Claire, careful not to wake the others, secretly tiptoed into his door. Father Time overheard her footsteps and turned around to face her. She was wearing a beautiful white robe with nothing on underneath.

Father Time was startled. "Mary, I'm sorry, I didn't know you were here. How can I help you?"

She untied her robe, and it dropped to the floor, exposing her every curve.

"Time," she said, walking up to him, placing her arms around his neck, "why don't we skip the bullshit. I am in love with you. I was the very first day we met." She was drunk and trying to kiss him.

He unwrapped her arms from around his neck. "Mary, what happened this evening was a mistake," he said, pulling away from her.

A tear ran down her right cheek. "The first time I met you, I was sure then that you were the man for me. I've waited so long for a man such as you to come into my life, and now that I have you, I won't let you go. I heard that you were leaving Sandreas. Is that true?"

"I'm afraid so. How did you hear about it so soon?"

"Word gets around, Father Time. Time, what has happened to us?" she sobbed her heart out. "These feelings I have for you—"

"I couldn't give you the life you want, Mary. Not even if I tried."

She smiled at him, caressing his cheeks with the back of her hand. "Why do you say such words?"

"Because it's true."

As she gazed into his eyes, she saw fire and the screaming souls that never made it, burning in the fiery pits of hell. Mary was in shock, gasping for air.

"Are you all right?"

Mary nearly fainted as he helped her to his bed. "I think so. Who are you? What are you?"

He went to get her a glass of water. "I'm Time, a fallen angel from heaven who was never condemned and sent to hell. I am a demon slayer. A curse was lifted off me, but not freely. The hand of God is still upon me, and that's why I came here." A tail appeared from behind him. Mary gasped in horror.

"This is part of the curse that never left, and I'm fighting so hard to get rid of it. This is why we could never live a normal life together, Mary."

"You're crazy . . . you're crazy. I'll do whatever I can to help you, Father."

"Thank you. I would appreciate it if we could keep this between ourselves. In the meantime, I'm leaving for New York, and you really must go before the others find out."

Mary proceeded to leave his room. "Will you write me?"

"I'll try."

A plane was arriving in New York, and the passengers were leaving the airport. The luggage area was packed, and Father Time pushed through the crowd to get his luggage. He saw his luggage roll around the belt and proceeded to reach for it. A strange fellow grabbed it and proceeded to walk away.

"Excuse me, but I'm afraid that's mine."

The man turned around, and he was missing an eye. A black patch was covering the wounded eye. "Father Time?"

"I'm sorry. We've met?" he said, surprised that anyone knew that he was coming.

"We are old friends. My name is Hans Ozack. We've been waiting for your arrival here at the cathedral. It's not far from here, and it would be an honor to drive you there, sir. Follow me."

A limousine was waiting for them outside. Entering, Father Time noticed a glass bar. "You mind if I have a glass of scotch?"

Hans poured him a glass of scotch and handed it to him.

"Thank you," he said, sipping it down slowly. "You've mentioned that we were old friends?" Father Time sipped his drink.

"Oh, yes, I met you a few years ago at a conference in Chicago. You probably wouldn't recognize me. I was sitting next to a beautiful woman named Ms. Cheri Melendez. Does any of this strike your memory, Father?"

"Not quite. Go on." Father Time crossed his legs, sipping his scotch. He remembered this beast. He was not a man.

"I was interested in your theory, from beyond the grave. Where did you get your information from?" His skin was different from any man he'd seen before, and Father Time knew he was here on a mission.

"From years of research. Who told you I was coming?"

"Sandreas notified us about your arrival. I thought I would get to the airport in time to welcome you. New York is no place for a man such as yourself to be alone, Father. The homeless population has grown, and thieves have been known to attack their victims."

"The thief isn't the one you would need to worry about." An hour had gone by, and the limo had pulled up in front of St. Peter's Cathedral. It was an old tall church built in the early 1800s.

"Uh-huh. We're here!"

A young boy ran out to the limo to greet them. "Hans?"

"Pedro, I would like you to meet a friend. Father Time, this is Pedro. Pedro, this is Father Time."

Father Time stooped down to shake his hand. "Hello, Pedro, and how old are you?"

"Nine. Nice." Time was wearing a silver medallion around his neck, which stood out like a sore thumb.

"Thanks."

Hans escorted him around the premises, while the child carried his luggage up to his quarters. "This here is where we eat brunch, and a library is located next door for your leisure. The church is surrounded around three acres. Those who have been buried here since the Civil War are still here."

"Interesting. You mind if I smoke?" he said, pulling out a pack of cigarettes.

"Be careful where you put your cigarettes out, Father. They may very well be your own." Hans Ozack walked away. Father Time gazed at him in a peculiar way. He lit his cigarette, puffed it, and blew out smoke.

CHAPTER THREE

His suite was groomed with satin sheets, vintage-style curtains, and stained glass windows. Time stepped out of the shower and dried his hair with a white towel. He heard a knock on the door. It was Pedro. He was shaking in fear of something.

"Pedro, how are you this morning?"

"Senior Time, I didn't mean to disturb you, but—"

"But what, Pedro?"

Pedro tiptoed into his room and closed the door. "There are demons among us, Senior Time."

"What?"

Pedro signaled for him to place his ear next to his lips. "They can hear us. They may look human, but they are pure evil, Father."

Father Time gazed into the boy's eyes. "Is Hans one of them?"

"I must go." Pedro pulled away from him and proceeded to step out.

"Pedro, if you need to talk about anything, I mean anything, I'm right here, okay?"

"Sure."

That morning, Father Time went for a run. He sweated under the hot morning heat. Smog engulfed the city of New York, and Central Park was barely empty. Dog owners walked their golden retrievers, and the homeless were scattered among the park benches, sleeping. Oblivion went for a walk that same morning, not realizing what was to come. Father Time continued on running, checking his watch, and ran past an old oak tree. The fog blurred his vision until he accidentally bumped into Oblivion, knocking him down onto the hard pavement.

"I'm sorry, I didn't see you. Are you all right?" Reaching down to help him up, Father Time felt electricity surge through his veins and immediately snatched his hand away. "I'm . . . I'm sorry." He began to feel weak and dizzy and sat down on a bench. "I feel so weak its as though."

"Would you like for me to call an ambulance, sir?" Oblivion was standing over him.

"No, that wouldn't be necessary. I'm just glad you're all right."

Oblivion sat next to him and handed him an unopened bottle of fresh springwater.

"Thanks. I appreciate it." Father Time opened the bottle to drink. "What's your name?"

"Oblivion."

Father Time gazed at him and rubbed his lips dry. He had a white towel wrapped around his neck.

"Oblivion, seems though I've heard that name somewhere before."

Oblivion got up to walk back to the center. "It's been nice meeting you."

Father Time knew this man was different than any man he'd ever met before. He got up and followed Oblivion to the rehab center. Oblivion crossed the street and entered the center. A young lady by the name of Alice White greeted him at the door, carrying a basket full of clean laundry up to her room. Oblivion ran to help her.

"Let me help you with that."

She handed him the basket. "Thanks. What's your name?"

"Oblivion."

"What?" She stood in front of him and placed both hands on her basket.

"My name is Oblivion."

"Have we met before?" She gazed at him real hard. She didn't have a clue who or what she was dealing with.

He handed her back her basket and proceeded to walk away.

"Oh, I'm sorry. It's just that you look familiar. My name's Alice, Alice White," she said, setting her basket of clothes down on the floor and attempting to shake his hand.

He grabbed a hold of her hand and saw sudden flashbacks of her life before him. He could see that she was a recovering crack addict. She was strung out on drugs and trying to kick the habit.

She snatched her hand quickly away from him. "Are you . . . are you all right?"

"Such a beautiful girl. Don't you realize what you're doing to yourself?"

"You're weird!" Alice turned around to unlock the door behind her. She stayed at room 13. She slammed the door from behind.

Oblivion walked back to his room and undressed, slipping out of a pair of jocks, and stepped into the shower. He turned the shower stall knob on. Warm tap water tapped onto his skin. He reached over to grab a bottle of shampoo and lathered his hands. He caressed the soap into his hair, scrubbing his scalp gently with his fingers. There was a small ceiling fan, which ventilated cool air from above. He could feel a slight breeze on his skin. It felt comforting, so he kept staring up at the ceiling. He closed his eyes, and suddenly, small objects fell from the ceiling fan onto his face. It felt cold and slimy. He opened his eyes, and they were snakes.

"I know now why I was sent here."

"Who are you, and how did you get in here?" Oblivion got scared and pointed his cross at him.

"I'm sorry you had to see that, but it was the only way I could get you to believe me."

"It worked."

Father Time placed a cigarette up to his lips and lit it, blowing smoke into the air and coughing. "I'm trying to quit, but after seeing you like that—"

"You don't have to explain, Father. I'm just glad we've met."

Oblivion sat down on a love seat and rubbed his wet hair back. Water dripped from his hair down his back. He got up and walked into the kitchen. "Would you like a bottle of beer?"

"No thanks. You ever heard of a man named Hans Ozack?"

"Ozack? You've got to be kidding me." Oblivion recognized his name and walked back into the living room. His hand shook and shivered. He knew what he was facing, but it wasn't human. "Hans Ozack isn't his real name. His name is Olarim. One of the most notorious men you'd ever want to come across. He has inside connections with drug smugglers and the mob. Families were destroyed because of this man. He ain't no one to mess around with. You know him?"

Father Time smiled, blowing smoke into the air. He paced the floor back and forth. "He's not human."

Oblivion gazed at him in shock. "What did you just say?"

"I'm afraid he's one of them, a demon. We're under attack, whether you know it or not."

"What do you suppose we do?"

A knock came to the front door. Father Time walked into the restroom and hid behind the door. Oblivion answered the door. It was Vivian Anderson. She looked worried and tired for some odd reason. As soon as the door opened, she fainted in his arms. Oblivion carried her to the sofa and laid her down upon it to rest. She suddenly awoke and panicked, trying to scratch Oblivion's eyes out with her fingernails. He restrained her arms away from his face as she calmed down. Gasping for air, she was frightened.

"Are you all right?"

"No, no I'm not." Vivian slowly sat up on the sofa. "Something or someone came to see me last night. It was getting late, and I went to bed. The first thing I knew, something was putting pressure onto my left shoulder, leaning me hard against the sheets. I couldn't move, budge. I felt like . . . like I was suffocating, Oblivion!" She began to cry upon his shoulders. "It had a voice and told me to deliver you a message." She gazed at him in a strange way.

"Me?"

The white around her pupils turned yellow, green gums, and sharp fangs.

"You're dead meat!"

Oblivion immediately pushed her away from him and gazed at her once more. She went back to her normal state.

"You . . . you all right?" Vivian wiped her eyes. The air sat still, and Oblivion wasn't sure what he really saw. Father Time overheard the whole discussion from inside the bathroom. He knew what had just happened.

"Oblivion, what do you suppose it meant?"

"I'm not really sure, Viv. I'm expecting company in a few minutes. I'm gonna have to ask you to leave." He stood up from the sofa, and she got up and walked over toward the front door.

"You watch your back, dear. There are forces out here stronger than us," she said, rubbing the back of her hand across the side of his face. He gripped her hand and kissed it, and she left.

Father Time walked back into the room, and Oblivion shut the door. He then walked over toward the closet and checked the upper shelf. There he retrieved two silver crosses and gave one to Father Time.

"Thank you, but I have one of these."

"Hold it in your hand. It's not your ordinary."

"What?" The two crosses evolved into swords before their very eyes. Father Time was shocked and placed the sword against Oblivion's Adam's apple. Sweat trickled down his forehead. "You know, you're full of surprises. How do I know that you're not one of them?"

"If I was one of them, do you think I would take a chance on showing you my secrets?"

Father Time put the sword down slowly. Oblivion sat back down on the sofa and picked up a pencil. He drew an Egyptian hieroglyphic on a piece of paper. "You've seen this before?"

"No, I don't reckon I have."

"The one who wears this has it written on his forehead. He is the main demon that we would need to look out for when the earth opens up and releases them. He will be the one to lead them. That will be the time for us to change."

"I'm sorry, did you say 'change'?"

"I know that you're not one hundred percent human, Father."

Father Time paced the floor. "You . . . you don't understand. If I change, there's a good chance that I will not be able to change back. I must continue my practice here as a priest."

"By the time they get finished ripping your soul apart, you'd wish you weren't one. Don't' forget, Father, we are at war. The chances of us both surviving this extremely crucial. Our faith will be put to the test. These things won't let up till we are both dead, in which others will be sacrificed."

"You're right. Our faith is all we have to go on. God will protect us and guide us in the right path. We must stay strong, my son. We must stay strong," Father Time said, gazing out the window.

CHAPTER FOUR

At Saint Sandreas Cathedral, Sister Mary Claire was called in to see Sister Elizabeth in her office. Sister Claire was nervous and sat down.

"You have disgraced the sisterhood here at Sandreas, Sister Claire."

"Pardon?"

"You've fallen for a priest! Do you understand, Sister? You've fallen for a priest!"

Mary was shocked and ashamed. "I-I can't help the way I feel."

"Did you have sex with him, Sister?" Sister Claire ignored her. "Did you . . . did you have sex with him?"

Sister Claire covered her ears with the palms of her hand. "I won't listen to such rhetoric!"

"I have put in for you to be transferred to Saint Opias, Sister Claire."

"What . . . what?" She began to cry. Tears flowed down her cheeks. "Oh, please, Sister, please don't dismiss me from here! I'm so happy here at Sandreas. I don't want to leave, Sister!"

"Tell me, why should I let you stay?"

"I have so much here to learn, Sister Elizabeth." Her lips were dry and cracked. Her skin was pale. Her piercing eyes captured the rays of the sun. Shivering, a shadow stood behind her. Sister Elizabeth walked over to the desk and retrieved a long stick.

"Sister Claire, approach the desk immediately."

Sister Claire got up off her knees.

"Don't get up! Crawl!"

MELVINA HAWKINS-PATTERSON

Sister Claire crawled over toward the desk slowly, for she knew what would happen next. She knew the consequences of her actions. Her eyelids felt heavy as she faced the desk in front of her.

"Sister Claire, you have violated the rules of the church. Fornicating with a priest is against God's law. Therefore, the punishment shall be by the stick. If you should decide to stay here at Sandreas, place both your hands upon the desk."

Suddenly, Sister Elizabeth smacked her fingers hard onto the wooden desk, breaking open the flesh on her hands and bruising her fingers. Her scream could be heard throughout the hallways of the dormitory as the others placed the palms of their hands against their ears, trying not to imagine the excruciating pain Sister Claire endured.

Sister Claire passed out onto the floor. Blood ran from her delicate fingers and soaked into the wooden floor. Her eyes were bloodshot red. Tears ran down her cheeks. She fell into a deep sleep. Within a few hours, she awoke on her bed, wondering how she ever got there. She realized that she had been beaten for falling in love with an ordained priest.

She slowly got up and sat at the edge of the bed, thinking. All sorts of evil thoughts ran through her mind, but reacting on them was another. She tasted revenge in a strange sort of way. A tear trickled down her cheek, and she licked it off her dry lips. It was salty. Her face turned flush red as she sat there thinking.

The sisters held a mass at the church that afternoon. They all gathered up front. She knelt down on the podium, praying. Gossip about the beating spread like wildfire. Sister Rachel whispered to Sister Alice, "Did you hear what happened the other day?"

"Yes, it sounded awful. I hope she's okay," she said, gazing over to her right at Sister Mary Claire, who was praying. "From the looks of things, I think they're going to transfer her—"

"Transfer her?" echoed loud into the church. Sister Claire overheard their conversation and walked over to them. "Are you talking about me? He who has not sinned. Cast the first stone."

The sisters suddenly got quiet and continued praying among themselves, ignoring what was said. Sister Claire stormed out of the church. Sister Ann followed her.

"Sister Claire?"

Sister Claire stopped walking and proceeded to turn around to face her.

"May I have a word with you, please?"

Both sisters walked on soft white sand that smothered their feet. The wind blew their silky hair off their shoulders and their prescription lenses against their brows. The dolphins swam up toward the shore and the seagulls hovered over their heads while the sun rose over the ocean. Sister Claire and Sister Ann walked over to the dock to sit.

"I heard about what happened the other day. Fortunately, I wasn't there to witness it, and I thought Sister Elizabeth was way out of line. I know how you must feel."

"No, you don't know how I feel right now! He's not like any of the others I've met. He's different. He makes me feel whole again—free! I can't begin to tell you how I feel right now, but the things that I know about him cannot be revealed among any human." Sister Claire gazed down.

"You're human. Why would he share it with you?" Sister Ann took off her lenses.

"Because we love each other."

Deep in the pits of hell, an army of defiant demons gathered in a rally. The decision was to destroy the chosen two. Their eyes were filled with hate and envy, their hearts with vengeance. They walked with a hunchback and toes curled like goats' feet. They were thirsty for blood in their minds. They were a legion of lost souls. Satan had released a plague of destruction upon them. "I want them both killed—killed!"

Father Time was in church, dismissing the congregation. "May the body of Christ be with you all."

The doors opened as the crowd of believers approached their vehicles. Suddenly, a loud, horrible, screeching noise penetrated the air. The people gazed up toward the sky. There, a migratory swarm of locusts surrounded them. They ran and ran as fast as they could toward their vehicles, only to be greeted by danger. Father Time tried to be of some assistance, snatching children back into the church. "Over here!" he yelled from the chapel.

The locusts were devouring them one by one to the bone. "Aaaahhh!" Terror was in the air. The agony of watching and not being able to help. It forced him to kneel before God. "Dear God, please, don't forsake me now!" It echoed in the wind and brought on a new hem for Time. His cross evolved into a sword, and his body into a legend. A black cape draped from his side. Father Time and the children were amazed and ran outside. The locusts were suddenly gone, and carnage painted the streets and the pavement before him. The congregation that he once worshipped with were attacked by an old enemy.

He'd seen a newborn infant covered in a bloody blanket and slowly walked up to it. He opened the blanket, and inside, the infant was murdered. "Noooooooooo!" He knew then he had a score to settle, and getting even was difficult. Father Time wept and wept. The infant was dead, and so was his mother. A crowd of passersby surrounded the area. Sirens from miles away could be heard approaching. A new hero was born, and his name was Time.

A small child approached him and yanked his cape. "Who are you? You're not a priest."

"I'm what you want me to be."

The little boy smiled and wrapped his arms around him. Authorities had finally arrived at the bloody scene and slowly picked up the pieces that were left behind. The children were questioned and stood beside Father Time, embracing his waistline. Family and children services workers escorted them one by one toward their vehicles while Detective Chow Ho observed the area. He was from Hong Kong, and sharp. He walked up to Father Time and took notes.

"So you're Time . . . uh, Father Time, of course?"

"Yes, I am."

"I'm sorry, but you don't exactly look like a priest. What happened here, Father?"

"I don't know. I wish I could be of some help, Detective, but I don't know."

"Do I look stupid, Father?"

"Pardon?"

"I asked, do I look stupid to you? You have at least forty-five bodies sprawled out, mutilated in front of your church, and you don't know what happened?"

The children, who were members of the congregation, were sitting in the vehicles, staring at Father Time, wondering if he'd be charged with their parents' murders.

"The children are saying huge, giant locusts flew down out of the sky upon them and tried to kill them. In return, deliberately making them orphans, Father, and you don't know why? This type of thing naturally wouldn't happen. It's not normal, Father! I'll tell you what, this case is still under investigation. Don't bother leaving town, Father. A man of your stature wouldn't get very far."

Sister Mary Claire pointed at the sun. Her fingers were swollen, wrapped in gauze. "When a fallen angel was spared to prove he is worthy to God and slaughtered his way to salvation, that man is the chosen one."

"Who are you speaking of, Sister Claire? There aren't any fallen angels that I know of."

"Oh, but there are! The sun's beautiful, isn't it?" Her skin glistened under its warm rays, and her hair wild like red dandelions.

"Sister Claire, I don't think that it would be a wise decision to see him again."

Sister Claire paused for a moment and thought about what she said. She just stood there, glancing down at the sand. She knew then that Sister Ann was no friend of hers.

"I see."

"Father Time isn't coming back, Maria."

"It's been a long time since anyone has called me that." A tear fell from her cheek.

"He was transferred. He was transferred because of you. I'm sorry."

Sister Mary Claire ran as fast as she could to the dorm and into her room, slamming the door behind her. She stood there, staring into a huge vanity mirror that sat on the floor. She then gazed into the closet and snatched two bags. She stuffed them with clothes, shoes, a Bible, and a holy rosary. What she couldn't bring, she left behind. She then sat down behind a desk and wrote a note, addressing it to Sister Elizabeth: "I'm sorry, but I feel that my stay here at St. Sandreas Cathedral would not be beneficial to me."

A plane was now departing from Mexico to New York City. Sister Mary Claire was on it, while Sister Elizabeth was reading the note that was left on the dresser: "Please accept my apology. Sincerely, Sister Mary Claire."

The trip to New York was long and tiresome, and Sister Mary Claire sought through a folded newspaper inserted into the flap of the seat in front of her. On the front page was an article about the killings at a local church. Father Time's face appeared on front, standing next to the victims' children. "Oh my god, this can't be," she gasped in horror. A nightmare had come true. "I must go to him. I must—"

A fellow passenger who was sitting next to her gazed over her shoulder at the front page of the paper and commented on the incident. "Those poor children. They have to face a maniac like that!"

"I'm sure there must be some logical reason behind this," she said, placing her prescription glasses over her eyes.

"Sure there is, he's a maniac priest."

Sister Claire froze in dismay. She couldn't understand why this had happened. All she knew was that she needed to find the church, and fast. All types of thoughts ran through her mind. She hoped and prayed that the man she was in love with was innocent. She carefully read the article: "Giant locusts supposedly attacked the church congregation, leaving the church. Priest is under suspicion of murders."

"Time." She folded the paper back up and tucked it into her bag.

The guy who sat next to her wanted to read it too. "You mind if I read that?"

"Yes, yes, I would mind if you read it," she said, folding her arms.

"Well, excuse me."

Arriving there, the streets were cluttered with white-collar workers, pimps, children, homelessness, and prostitution. Sister Mary Claire was accompanied out of the terminal with a bellman, who was rolling her bags out on a cart. She tipped him ten dollars, and he waived down a cab. He helped her load her bags into the trunk of the vehicle.

"It's been real nice talking to you, Sister Claire. Put in a good word for me, will you?"

She placed the palm of her hand on his forehead and said, "God be with you, my child."

Getting into the backseat of the cab, she waived good-bye to him. The driver was a chain-smoker, and she began to choke, inhaling the polluted fog in the air and coughing. He had his radio up high, the beep bopping to rap music.

"Do you mind turning that down, young man?" she said, rolling down the window.

"Oh, I'm sorry, Sis," he said, turning down the dial on his radio. "So where are you headed?"

"I'm looking for a church chapel named Saint Hosea Ministries. Do you know where that is?"

"Saint Hosea . . . isn't that where all those people got killed by that crazy priest? Everybody's talking about it."

"Yeah, well, it's still under investigation, and besides, I don't think he's so crazy. Sorry."

"What brings you to New York?"

"I'm here on business."

"Business," he chuckled to himself. "Yeah, well, we don't see your kind around here too often," he said, gazing up into his rearview mirror, admiring her beauty. "Are all the nuns beautiful like you where you come from?"

She blushed. "Thanks for the compliment, but beauty is only skin deep," she said, gazing out of the window.

"Then yours has certainly surfaced. Hey, what would a woman like you want with a man like that anyway?"

The cab sped down a busy street. A glimpse of a demon could be seen standing on the sidewalk in the midst of a crowd of pedestrians. Sister Mary Claire gasped in horror. She covered her mouth from screaming with the palm of her hand. "Stop the car!"

"What?"

"Stop the car, please!"

By the time the vehicle stopped, the demon disappeared. She glanced across the street, wondering where it went. The heat from the sun caused her to perspire. Sweat rolled down her forehead and onto the seat.

"Are you . . . are you okay, ma'am?"

She grabbed her chest, panting, and wiped her forehead with the back of her hand. "I think so. I thought I saw some, well, never mind. You can continue as you were."

The driver continued on driving her to the church. "What's your name, if you don't mind me asking?"

"Maria, Sister Mary Claire, and yours?"

"Carlos. Carlos Sanchez. I was raised in the Bronx. New York is a big city, Maria. You will soon find that out."

Thirty minutes went by, and Carlos pulled up in front of Saint Hosea Chapel and got out to allow Sister Claire to exit out of the back. He then walked over to unlock the trunk and handed her bags. "This is a big church, Maria. I hope we meet again. Give my regards to the priest." He got back into his cab and pulled off, leaving her standing in front of the church. A priest by the name of Father Joseph welcomed her arrival and helped her with her bags.

"Welcome to Saint Hosea! My name is Father Joseph, and you are?"

"Sister Mary Claire. Is Father Time here?"

"I'm sorry, Sister. Father Time is not available at the moment. I'm sure you've heard about the killings here at Saint Hosea."

"Yes, I have. How tragic. How is he taking it, Father?"

"Not good. The people here are asking him to step down."

"Take me to him, please?"

Father Joseph walked her over to his quarters. "He's inside. Sister?"

Sister Claire attempted to walk. "Yes?"

"Try not to worry him. I'm looking forward to seeing him this Sunday."

She smiled and walked over to the door to knock. Suddenly, she heard weird, strange noises coming from inside. She could hear her heart rapidly beating and beating. She lost consciousness, suddenly fainting. The door opened, and a man lifted her up, carrying her over to a sofa. Deep, dark visions of a holy war raced in her mind, sending her into another dimension, another time.

She was there when Satan denied God's perfection and was cast out of heaven into the lake of fire. "Two . . . two angels. What—"

Fallen angels were left behind and put on earth to exist. They were marked for death. She suddenly awoke and saw Father Time sitting next to her, smiling. "Hi, are you all right?"

"I think so," she said, rubbing the knot on her forehead.

"I'm . . . I'm so glad to see you. Um, would you like me to get you some hot tea?" Sister Claire leaned up. "No, no, no, no, you rest. Looks like you have a bad bump on your head there from the fall." He got up from the sofa and proceeded to walk into the kitchen. Sister Claire glanced around the room and noticed old relic Bibles, burned candles, and crucifixes lying on the coffee table. A warm fireplace embraced her skin. He then came back with a hot cup of tea and gave it to her.

"So how do you like it here in New York?" she asked, leaning back on a fluffily pillow, sipping her tea.

"It's okay. Father Joseph sure keeps me a lot of company, and my work here seems to keep me busy. I'm happy here, Mary." He was smiling, but she could see that he wasn't being honest to himself. He wasn't happy at all. In fact, he was lying. The expression on his face was pale, sort of sad. Part of himself was lost. She glanced into his dreamy blue eyes as he sat down beside her.

Their lips slightly touched, and he backed off. "I'm sorry again."

Suddenly, she couldn't hold back the passion she felt inside and quickly wrapped her arms around his neck, pulling him closer to her. "I've got to have you," she said, kissing his cheek and taking off her headpiece.

"No, Mary, I can't—"

"Father, please forgive me, but I've got to have you," she said, unbuttoning her robe.

"Mary, please don't," he said, slowly pushing her away.

"Ouch, I love a man who's hard to get," she said, ripping open his shirt. The buttons popped off one by one and landed onto the rug. Their lips suddenly locked, and he proceeded to grab her hand, placing it on the hard bulge in his pants. Their clothes quickly hit the floor, and they had intimate relations.

A bright and sunny morning arrived, and the rays pierced the curtains. Scrambled eggs, sweet rolls, and ham was cooking over a hot oven. He made it as close to home as he could make. Feeling the guilt inside, after setting the table, Sister Claire got up and walked into the bathroom. She dropped her robe to the floor and sat next to the tub, running warm tap water against her silky skin. She let down her curly red hair, which draped past her shoulder. She then walked over to the sink and picked up a toothbrush to brush her crowns. The mirror was steamed, and she slowly wiped it by the palm of her hand. Until suddenly, an angel appeared before her, the Messenger. He was dressed in a tight gold outfit. Gold wings hung by his side.

Startled by his presence, she accidentally dropped the toothpaste and toothbrush upon the floor.

"Please, please don't hurt me . . ."

"I come here with a message. Time and Oblivion are in great danger."

"Who? Who is Oblivion?"

"He was a lost soul who was given another chance to live by the Most High. You will know him when you see him." The Messenger disappeared before her eyes.

"Wait, wait!" Sweat ran down her forehead.

A man living without fear, walking the earth in squander, Oblivion walked the alleyways and streets of New York, searching through dumpsters for food. He then found a half-eaten burger in its wrap and finished it off. There wasn't a dime in his pocket, but a rosary hung from around his neck. Suddenly, dark shadows flew down before him. A mist of fog engulfed the air. Oblivion wasn't sure who stood there, but someone did. Razor-blade-sharp nails screeched, scratching the brick walls of the buildings. Oblivion knew it meant trouble.

"Oblivion." He could hear his name being whispered into the night. "Oblivion, come out, come out wherever you are." Nails scraped the concrete off the walls.

"Who's out there?"

He then walked out into the middle of the fog. He was surrounded by a swarm of demons standing on fire escape steps. Their wings were dirty and plucked like sick pigeons. Their leader approached him.

"Hi there, lost soul."

"Who stands before me?" Oblivion stood face-to-face with a demon, holding onto the crucifix around his neck.

"I am the evil one."

"What . . . what do you want from me?" Oblivion got nervous. Sweat trickled down his forehead.

"You think you are saved. A fallen angel, only to be forgiven by the grace of God. You and I know that you should have went to hell too! How did you bargain with him?"

"I don't know who you are talking about."

"God, the one who put me in bondage. I am a slave to him, and there isn't a damn thing that I can do about it! My days are numbered, and I can't seem to stop the clock from going off inside my head."

"You defied God, and now you want me to suffer! I don't think so. You and your entourage better clear out of here, or."

"Or what, you'll destroy me? No one can destroy me, not even you."

Oblivion's skin suddenly turned purple. His eyes were sharp like an owl's, and huge wings extended out from his side. He held his crucifix, which transformed into a sword. The angels engaged in war within the alley. Blood spilled onto the pavement while a legend was born.

CHAPTER FIVE

He impaled the hearts of those who came after him. The earth shook as the carnage grew. Oblivion sliced and diced them with his sword. He ran, leaping off high vehicles and the side of buildings. They kept coming as though one would succeed more than the other.

The warlords chased him as he flew from building to building. He swung his sword, amputating their skulls from their bodies, cutting his way toward victory. Revenge was in his eyes when he heard the loud growling of the demons' thirst for blood, hungry for flesh. The friction from the swords smacking against one another sparked. Oblivion got slashed open from behind. His skin popped open like broken stitches.

The more they slashed open his flesh, the angrier he got.

"Aaaaahhh, noooo!"

Their eyes followed every move he made. He was surrounded by hundreds of abominating gargoyles, their swords drawn, that came from deep within the bowels of the earth. He was wounded from the battle. He slowly changed back to human, profusely bleeding upon the ground. Their leader walked slowly over to him to finish him off.

"Now give me your soul willingly or die!"

"No, no I can't," he said, sliding his elbows back, pushing his weight away from the demon.

"I'm not asking you. I'm telling you." The evil one kicked Oblivion's shoulder blade.

"Aaaahh! I won't!"

"You will. You see, we're going to win this war, not God."

"I don't think you will," he said, spitting blood onto the pavement. Oblivion was in great pain.

"Join me, Oblivion, and I will give you eternal life," he said, extending his claws out toward him, but Oblivion was resistant.

"Where, in hell?"

"Enough of this shit. Do you take me as a joke? I will rip your heart out and feed it to my beasts. I will kill you!"

"Mister, mister, are you all right?" A young girl named Meredith Montgomery saw Oblivion lying helpless in a pool of blood and dropped her book bag. She wasn't able to see the evil spirits standing before her. She immediately ran to Oblivion's aid and dialed 911 on her cell phone. The sound of sirens roared in the air.

"Are . . . are you okay, mister?"

He passed out in her arms, only to wake up to another day in Patterson General Hospital, a prominent trauma unit facility in New York City. Most of the worst cases in New York were sent there.

IVs had been inserted into both arms, a nurse was checking his temperature with a thermometer, and thick-wrapped gauze was glued to his chest. Oblivion slowly opened his eyes. He had blurred visions of the little girl who helped him, who held his wounded hand. She was with her mother, Julie Montgomery. Her eyes were hazel blue like the sea, and her hair was blond. Meredith was so happy to see him awake. Then she smiled and chuckled. Her mom was a little nervous, not knowing how he would react seeing them there. She didn't want Meredith to disturb his rest.

"Mister, mister, it's me, Meredith." He eventually leaned up and sat up in bed. "This is my mom, Julie."

Oblivion took one look at her and fell totally in love. "Hi, I'm sorry. My name is Oblivion. It isn't everyday I'd meet such a beautiful woman in the hospital. This is your daughter?"

"Yes, my daughter, Meredith, found you."

"Hello," he said, shaking her hand. "Hello, Meredith, and thank you."

"What happened to you out there?"

He scratched his head and nose. He wanted to lie, but it would only lead up to another, so he would rather not say.

"Nothing, nothing happened out there." He strayed away from answering the question.

"That's funny. From the way she described it, you were cut up very badly, found in a pool of blood. Is that true?"

"I guess you can say that."

"So what did happen out there? I'm sure the authorities would like to know."

"I'm sorry, but I can't. I can't share that with you. Besides, you wouldn't believe me if I told you anyway." A nurse came in and checked his pulse and temperature and left the room. "Try me."

Dr. Tihaji Li Wang entered the room. He had a worried, confused expression on his face. Oblivion was very concerned.

"Hi, my name is Dr. Tihaji Wang. Are you his wife?"

"Oh, no, I'm not. This is my daughter, Meredith."

"Hello."

"My daughter found him on her way from school. I was supposed to meet her at the park, until this happened."

"So you are the young lady that I've been hearing so much about?"

"Yes. Is he going to be all right?"

"We hope so. Meredith, would you and your mother mind if I had a few words with him alone?"

"Sure. We'll be right outside, okay?"

"Okay."

Oblivion smiled. Dr. Wang closed the door. "Have you've been feeling dizzy, tired all the time?"

"No. What seems to be the problem, Doc?"

"Besides this incident, you have a rare disease. Unlike any disease I've ever seen before."

"Am I gonna die, Doc?"

"I don't know. In fact, we don't even have a medical terminology for it. We would need to run more tests to find out. In the meantime, we will do all we can to help you," he said, embracing his hand on his shoulder.

"Dr. Wang, you are needed to room 103. Dr. Wang, you are needed to Room 103," an emergency page came from the PA system.

"Excuse me, I'll return soon."

Julie knocked on his door.

"Come in."

"I hope we didn't disturb you, but Meredith and I—" She noticed that he was putting on his shirt. "Leaving so soon? Don't you think you need time to heal?"

"I have to go. I've been found out."

"Found out? What do you mean?"

"Would you like to come home with us? I can show you my goldfish."

"Meredith, that wouldn't be necessary. I'm pretty sure he has a place to stay." He kindly reached over to grab her hand. A warm feeling brushed over her, enough to change her mind. "Do you . . . do you have somewhere to stay?"

A Land Rover pulled off from in front of the hospital. Oblivion hid behind the driver's seat and sat up. Along the interstate, the ride was long. Meredith listened to her Walkman and beep-bopped to a hip-hop sound. Oblivion gazed out the window. A group of geese flew over a lake. He imagined them as angels watching over him. Julie smiled behind the wheel, curious about the fellow she was taking home. Meredith began bouncing up and down on the seat, dancing to a new sound.

"Meredith?

"Aw, Mom, I can never enjoy my music!"

"You do realize we have company?"

"Sorry," she said, turning down the volume to her headphone.

"That's okay. You are only being yourself."

"Do you have any children?"

"No, I'm afraid not," he said, gazing out the window.

"Why not?"

"Do you have to ask such questions?"

Along the interstate, Julie drove farther out than she expected. The trees were thick, and a harvest of flowers covered the hillside. Julie drove over a small bridge that crossed over a huge creek, leading to an old mansion hidden beyond the hills: the Montgomery Estate.

"You have plenty."

"I'm sorry, what did you say?" A brisk breeze blew through her hair.

"God has blessed you with plenty."

She kept staring through the rearview mirror, which focused on his blue eyes. They were somewhat strange, beautiful. Julie was definitely attracted. The first time she laid eyes on him, she knew he was the one, the man she would someday marry. The Jeep slowly pulled into the driveway.

"We're home!" Meredith jumped out from the backseat and grabbed Oblivion's hand, leading him up the porch steps. Ringing the door bell, the butler answered, a very tall man dressed in a black tux. His name was Edger.

"Dragging in another one of your stray cats, Meredith?" Insulting, he was, and very obnoxious.

"No, but if you're curious, his name is Oblivion."

Oblivion held out his hand to shake, and suddenly the butler backed off. It was as though he could see through him. Edger's eyes bulged out, and he began to shiver. He sensed that Oblivion was not of his planet, planet Earth.

"Have we met?"

"I'm . . . I'm sorry?"

Julie stood at the front door, angry. Meredith forgot her schoolbooks in the car. "You forgot something, young lady?"

"Sorry, Mom."

Julie approached Oblivion and smiled. "Let me show you to your room." She led him to the attic. The shelves had old figurines, wooden ships, a telescope, and books. An overgrown deceased stuffed bear stood along a brick wall. Fire burning in the fireplace kept the room warm.

"This is a room? More like a suite. Thank you." Oblivion limped his way toward the room. "You are a kind woman. Thank you."

Julie smiled and went downstairs to fix dinner. The maid was gone for the day, and she prepared a table for three. A bouquet of flowers sat in the middle as she cooked a pot roast smothered in vegetables and potatoes. She then put on some soft music as Meredith walked into the kitchen, grinning.

"You like him, don't you?"

"He's nice. Don't get any crazy ideas, young lady. I'm still in love with your father. It's just that . . ."

"It's just what, Mom? You and Dad been divorced for five years now. Get over it!"

"Yeah, five long years."

Oblivion sat on the bed and laid his head onto the pillow. Dark visions raced through his mind. Dark shadows fell from the clouds and plummeted into the lake of fire. Lost souls were screaming out in agony.

Oblivion could hear them scream. He could feel his flesh burning, peeling from the bone. This dream was unlike any dream he'd had before. He wanted to awake, but something was holding him there. Something dark and evil.

"Oblivion, Oblivion, remember me?"

"Yes, yes, I do remember. You are Lucifer, the deceiver!"

The evil one approached him and grabbed his chin, pacing his steps slowly around him. Oblivion became afraid and began to shiver uncontrollably. "I don't exactly know who you are fucking, but it's not me! You think God gave you another chance?"

"I know he has. God loves me, and you can't change that!"

"We'll see about that." Suddenly, a cloud of smoke surrounded him. Demons charge at Oblivion at full speed, tearing his flesh apart with their sharp claws. Dozens more came to devour his soul, until Meredith woke him up from this deadly dream. "Aaaaahh!" His clothes were soaked in sweat, and his eyes were bloodshot red.

"Are . . . are you all right?"

"I think . . . I think so."

She glanced at him in a sort of strange way. "You don't look very good. Would you like us to call you a doctor?"

"No, that wouldn't be necessary, thank you."

Meredith smiled. "Dinner's almost ready. It's hot too."

He wiped his forehead. "I'm sure it is."

He sat at the table as Julie smiled, wiping the side of her mouth with her handkerchief, laughing. He could sense she liked him. Meredith ate her potatoes.

"So tell me, where are you really from?"

"I come from a place where many wish to go, where men die to be resurrected, only to be free, live, and prosper. A place where no man can ever grow old or be sick."

"You mean heaven?"

"Yes, Meredith, heaven. God sent me here and gave me another chance to live again."

"Now wait a minute, I've heard a lot about ghosts and goblins, but angels? That's a little hard to swallow."

"What, you don't believe in God?"

"I didn't say that, but what you're saying is that you are not of this earth. My daughter and I haven't been to church in a while now."

"Perhaps you should go. We are living in the last days. The demons will soon unleash themselves from the bottomless pit of the earth, and all those who are wicked shall be removed from the earth."

"Just . . . just where did you hear that?"

"It's in the Bible."

"Mommy, may I be excused?" Meredith said, wiping her mouth with her handkerchief.

"Sure, hon."

Meredith stepped away from the table and ran out the back door. She gazed up at a huge oak tree house, which her grandfather built years ago. Juicy red apples hung in the oven, and as she closed her eyes, something happened. Something went terribly wrong.

A woman was jogging along a park. Sweating profusely, she wiped her forehead dry. It was dark, and she wasn't alone.

"Anyone out there?" She continued her morning lap around the park, but it was too late. Demons came out of nowhere in numbers, attacking her devouring her alive.

Meredith quickly opened her eyes and ran into the house up to her room, slamming the door. The thought of seeing death before her made her suddenly feel unclean. She immediately ran into the restroom and turned on the shower faucet. Warm water ran across her fingers. She could see small glimpses of that same woman screaming in agony. She then stripped naked and got into the shower, shivering. Her hands huddled under her chin. She held her head up while she cried.

"Hail Mary, full of grace, the Lord is with thee. Blessed is he amongst sinners, and blessed is the fruit of thy own Jesus. Holy Mary, mother of God, pray for us sinners. For now, and the hour of our death. Amen." She repeated that prayer over and over again. Her eyes got flush red staring into space.

The next morning, Dr. Robert Stein paid them a visit, and Julie was worried. Meredith was sick and had to stay home. Oblivion sat by her side, holding her hand.

"I don't know what's wrong with her, Doctor. She went outside to play, and now this."

"We'll keep an eye on her for now. Make sure you give her these pills twice a day."

Julie was holding a deadly prescription and wasn't aware of it. Dr. Stein was working for the enemy and wanted Meredith dead.

"Thank you, Doctor."

He left with a smile, holding a bag of poison. Julie went upstairs and prepared her daughter's medicine.

Oblivion gazed at the little angel and smiled at her. "I won't let anything happen to you" was softly spoken as she opened her eyes.

"Oblivion?"

"Sssshhh," he said, placing his finger up to his lips. "You need rest, Meredith."

"I'm all right. I-I had a bad dream."

"Oh?"

"I'd seen a woman jogging in the park. She was wearing a pink tank top and pink shorts. Her hair was brown, and her eyes were blue. She was alone and very scared. The fog came in closer and swallowed her shoes, and suddenly . . ."

"Suddenly what, Meredith?"

"The world was being attacked by demons. They were everywhere, flying down from the sky, ripping into her flesh, tearing at her clothes!" That vision never left her mind, and probably never will.

Oblivion knew that she knew. He knew then that he had to protect her before it was too late.

"Oh, I don't want to see those things. Every time my eyes open, I wonder what I'll see next!"

Oblivion embraced her while she cried on his shoulders. The crack of thunder roared across the sky, and the rain came. Julie closed the patio doors and curtains. Meredith went back to sleep. She went up to Meredith's room to check on her. While peeping through the ajar door, she could tell that Meredith liked Oblivion very much.

Oblivion exited the room. Julie approached him and smiled. "Seems like she took to you great. I'm sorry. It's not every day that I would take a man home with me and my daughter likes him. You see, she's young, and you can't be too careful, you know."

"I understand. Children are precious, aren't they?"

"Yes, yes they are." He attempted to walk back to her room. "Thank you for being there for her."

"No problem. Meredith was there for me, and I figured that I would be there for her."

"No, although I wish I had, but the good Lord has ways of working that out."

"I'm sure he does." Oblivion turned to walk up to his room. Julie noticed how fit he was, and she was very much impressed at what she saw.

"Nice," he said, lying on his bed. He fell into a deep sleep.

A great storm occurred, and the angels fell from the heavens. Damp feathered wings snapped in the wind. Oblivion could see his fate. He was desperately gasping for air, choking on his sweat. He could feel the heat gazing down from above. He could see those who were condemned. He could hear them yelling out in agony, "Oh, dear God, please forgive us!" It echoed in the great storm, but it was too late. Some were impaled upon their own swords. Others were cast into the lake of fire. The look upon their faces spelled death. Those who defied God and laughed at him became flocks of lost souls, those who took the wrong path.

By the hand of God, Oblivion suddenly felt the bottom and landed safely on soft soil. His wings were broken as he stood up on both feet. He gazed up high at the heavens. A bright light swooped down upon him. God had forgiven him as he cried tears of joy. He was given a new lease on life, another chance, another day to prove himself worthy. He could feel his burden lift from his shoulders and discover a life he'd never known.

Sister Mary Claire sat at the altar and prayed, praying for the return of their fellow church members. "Please, dear Father, bring them all back home. The church is safe now." She heard noise coming from one of the rooms at the back of the church's chapel.

Slowly, she paced her way to look. The hallway was dark, and Sister Mary Claire tried clicking on the light switch. It didn't work, and the room was cold and gloomy. Every step she took led down a different corridor. As she entered a room, a presence was among her. The Messenger delivered her a message.

"Who . . . who's there?"

"I come in many faces. Those who have seen me turn away in sheer terror. I am not pretty, nor want to be."

"Why are you here?"

"I am here to deliver to you a message."

"But this is the house of the Lord. How did you—"

"It was not easy, and my time here is limited. The message is, two angels were delivered. Two angels are marked. The two that were chosen are to be destroyed. You yourself know of one of them."

"I-I don't understand."

"Are you, in fact, in love with Father Time?"

"I don't see how this would have anything to do with—"

"Do not fall in love with a dead man, Sister, for the dead don't stick around long." The Messenger disappeared, and Sister Mary Claire ran to the bathroom and rinsed her face under warm running tap water. Gazing into the mirror, a hideous decrepit old woman was staring back at her. The old woman was on crutches, grinning at her. Her face was frail, and her scalp was bald. Moles, cold sores, and dark blemishes appeared on her body. Her teeth were missing, her lips tucked into her jaw.

Her eyes sunk in, and her skin was extremely wrinkled. The old woman began to laugh hysterically. She kept laughing and laughing until saliva flew out of her mouth into the mirror, and Sister Claire got angry and punched a hole into the mirror, shattering the glass everywhere, cutting her right hand and wrist in return.

Blood splattered onto the bathroom floor, and she immediately rinsed her hand under the faucet. Cold running water penetrated the wound as she cried out in pain.

Sister Madeline entered the restroom behind her and was stunned by what she'd seen. Blood splattered on the sink, broken glass, wall, and floor.

"Sister Claire, are you—" She rushed to her aid to cut off the bleeding with a towel.

"I'm sorry, Sister Madeline. I don't know what came over me!"

"What happened here?"

"I'm not sure. I'm not sure at all." Sister Claire slid down the wall and cried. "I'm cursed, Sister, I'm—"

"Now, now, Sister Claire. You are not cursed. You, young lady, just had a little visit from the devil himself."

Sister Claire wasn't quite paying attention to what she was saying. "What . . . what did you say?"

Sister Madeline disappeared in midair before her very eyes. Gone just like that. Sister Claire was frightened to death. *Who was that nun who came into the restroom? Was it really Sister Madeline?*

Father Time approached the altar and took off the holy rosary from around his neck and kissed it. His fingers trembled in fear. His eyes were focused on Christ nailed to the cross. Flashbacks of Christ being crucified came back to him. He could see the nails being driven into the palm of his hand. Each blow was intense, and Father Time felt each spike penetrate his flesh. Father Time yelled out in agony.

"In the name of the Father, the son, and the holy ghost. Amen!"

His collar was soaked, and sweat ran down his forehead. Father Time wiped his face as Bishop Dan Richardson approached him. "Father Time, I got your message."

"Bishop Richardson, I'm glad you made it. May I have a word with you?"

Father Time and Bishop Richardson walked into the conference room and sat down at a table. Father Time had a worried expression on his face.

"What's bothering you, my son?"

"I don't know where to begin."

"Why don't we start at the beginning."

"The beginning, right." A pause. "Bishop, what I am about to tell you might sound puzzling, but it is the truth."

CHAPTER SIX

"Where I come from is a world of beauty. My father governed his country well, and it was different. No crime, killing, stealing."

Bishop Richardson gazed at Father Time in a strange sort of way. "Sounds like heaven."

"Our love was stronger than anything that you can imagine. Then, something happened. The Slanderer and all his angels laughed and called my heavenly Father a liar and were cast out of the kingdom and into the fiery pits of hell. My father continues to reign in glory, Bishop Richardson. There's only one thing holding me back."

Bishop Richardson smiled. "And what is that, my son?"

"This." A forked red tail extended from his robe. It twisted and curled like a caterpillar. His wings began to spring out from his shoulders. Bishop Richardson was stunned and shocked, wiping his head with a handkerchief. Sweat drizzled down his forehead. His eyes bulged out, and his jaws dropped, amazed at what he'd seen. "What on earth . . . What is this, Father Time? What are you?"

"This is why you're here, Bishop. This is the beginning of time, a time when angels were disobedient to God and went astray. We are at war, Bishop. Good against evil. This is to make sure that I keep my word. This curse has prevented me from having relations or even marriage."

"Are you trying to say that you were once one of those angels, Father Time?"

"I don't know how to explain it, but if I could go back in time, I would have done it different. Now I'm not too sure that I can. I can only hope that God continues to forgive me, Bishop Richardson."

"Father Time, this is a little more than I can handle. What is your main purpose here?"

"Saving souls, Bishop, saving souls." Father Time gazed out the window. It was getting late, and the sky was dark. The stars drew clippers. "Soon, they will come, and when they get here, I will be ready for them."

"Who are they, my son?"

"The lost souls that didn't make it, Father Richardson. I am a marked man, Father." Father Time's forked tail moved and curled around a lamp. The Bishop swallowed in disbelief. *Gulp!*

"Isn't there anything that I can do to help you, Father Time?"

"God is my salvation, Bishop."

The rain and a storm came about. The trees blew, and some were uprooted from the soil. The wildlife among the woods hid within abandoned logs. Suddenly, the earth shook beneath their feet, and small creatures flew into the air. They were gargoyles, destined to find the two that were chosen. Their reptilian army had huge wings that carried them, and their claws were sharp like razor blades. Their eyes pierced the moon, and their skin was as thick as stone, with saber-toothed fangs that could rip a man apart. Horns extended outward from the top of their skulls while the night embraced the madness. They were called the Legion of the Damned. They had killed many, and those who had seen them remember their fury. Their eyes had turned men into stone, and their voice would make a man's flesh shrivel. Many were aware of their legacy. Others who didn't died finding out.

The candles that were lit blew out from the storm, and Bishop Richardson quickly relit them while Father Time knelt down on the pew, praying.

"They'll soon be here, Bishop, and when they do, this place will look like Hiroshima. If you want to leave, I'll understand."

"Of course not, my son. I'm in this fight all the way. How do you know for sure that they'll return, my son?"

Suddenly, the power went out, and the rain stood still. The stained glass windows immediately blew out into the building. Shattered pieces of glass blew into Bishop Richardson's eyes. "Aaaaaahh!" The rain brought in cold air. Every breath Father Time took became visible to the naked eye.

"Come out, come out wherever you are, Time!"

"Come out, Father Time!"

Bishop Richardson ran to his side and whispered, "What would you request me to do, Father?"

"Nothing." Father Time walked into a room and took off his holy rosary.

Bishop Richardson walked in on him. "Who are you really?"

"To you, I am Father Time. To them, I am a demon."

His cross transformed into a sword, and a black cape draped over his legs. Somewhere, a legend was born. An angel had fallen. A man who would stop at nothing to rid the world from sin and destruction. A man destined to eternity. A man they called Time.

The Legion screeched their sharp claws across the church building, hoping that Father Time would appear. Suddenly, Time flew out on top of the roof. The dark angels leaped high into the air and angrily hissed at him. Green saliva drooled from their lips. The night sky attracted an owl hooting, and the light was on.

He drew out his sword one by one. They came in a rage, ripping into his robe and tearing at his flesh. Father Time flipped high into the air, amputating arms and legs with his mighty sword. Blood splattered onto the pavement, and a stray cat ran behind a rolled-off dumpster.

Father Time kicked a demon into the chest and quickly spat out acid into the demon's eyes. The gargoyle exploded into a ball of fire. A gargoyle attempted to choke Father Time from behind until Father Time retrieved two daggers from his cape and jabbed it into its skull. Blood splattered into the air. He was surrounded by a brood army of demons hissing and gritting their teeth, testing his faith. Defeated by a priest, the demons jumped high into midair, pouncing on top of Father Time. Time threw them off one at a time, cutting skulls and hands off. A demon scratched him on his chest. Another slugged the priest into his jaw, knocking him to the ground. He waved his sword high into the air. A red ruby was attached to the cross, and it lit up before them.

The gargoyles gazed into the red beam of light, fixating their eyes on the ruby. Suddenly, they burst into flames, exploding into a huge ball of fire.

Rooooaar!

Father Time shed a tear. "Praise be to the Father, the Son, and to the Holy Ghost. Amen."

Bishop Richardson helped him onto his feet as Time limped his way to Bishop Richardson's car. They were on their way to the hospital.

"How do you feel, Time?"

"Not good. Can you deliver a message for me?"

"Yes, Father, anything. How can I be of help?"

"I would like you to notify a dear friend of mine."

Oblivion folded a blanket on the bed and then headed for the shower. He had wrapped bandages around his waistline. He placed his towel over his left shoulder as he turned on the shower knob.

"His name is Oblivion. The message is, the time has come."

Warm tap water caressed his skin as he lathered the soap across his chest and underarms. A red robin flew to the windowsill and ate a spider connected to its web. While in the shower, Oblivion could see visions of those who were condemned. It was dark, and it was sucking him in to no return, a place no man would want to be. He could hear them suffering. "Forgive me!" Men were beaten, raped, and stripped down to nothing. A scorching lash for every sin was inflicted upon them. Slaves were condemned into eternal damnation, working themselves to the bone, and the women were whores that lusted after burned flesh and who walked over hot, burning coals of fire.

Every corner was sin, and it seemed that every time he gazed around, misery was staring at him right in the face. He walked even farther and soon came to an end. Demons were all around him. They came together for revenge. "He's one of us!" they chanted out loud before they could reach him. Oblivion came back to his senses. He'd dozed off for a second but wasn't aware of it. He cried and yelled, "Why me, Lord? Why me?"

Passing his room, Meredith could hear him and slightly pressed her ear against the bedroom door. She could feel his pain and frustration reaching out to her but didn't understand why. She immediately ran to her room and went through her dresser drawer to get her diary. In there, she'd kept secrets hidden away from her mother, deep, dark secrets she'd never revealed to anyone. "Meredith, breakfast is ready!" her mother yelled.

Meredith ran downstairs and sat at the dining room table with her mom while the maid prepared her meal. Her name was Ms. Dumplings, a gray-haired, seventy-year-old woman. She would tell Meredith grim stories of the past that would make a paraplegic stand up straight, stories of how her father would beat her mother every time he got drunk and the times he would lock her in the closet, forcing her to eat off the floor. Too many nights she heard her mother cry, and those lonely moments, she'd spent sleeping in the dark.

Meredith placed her diary on the side of her dish. Oblivion came down and sat next to her. He'd looked distraught, drained. Julie was worried over his appearance. He hadn't shaved, and his hair wasn't combed. Crow's feet sagged beneath his eyelids. He wasn't himself.

"Are you okay?"

Ms. Dumplings sat a tray of muffins down on the table.

"I think so. I had a bad dream." His hand began to tremble vigorously.

"Oh, what about?" Julie drank a glass of orange juice.

"I don't know exactly. Demons, angels, I don't know what to think of it. All I know is that the dreams are so vivid, so real. I could almost reach out and touch them."

"Touch who?"

"The lost souls that were cast out of the kingdom, souls that will never return."

51

"You mean you can actually see them?" Julie glanced at Meredith as though he was insane. "Oblivion, what exactly is happening to you?"

"I don't . . . I don't know what's wrong with me."

Suddenly, the breakfast table, chandelier, and house began to shake. The tremors went on for three minutes.

"Meredith, get under the table quick!"

Meredith and her mom rolled under the table while large pieces of the ceiling tile chipped off onto their plates. The dishes shook off the tablecloth onto the wooden floor. Ms. Dumplings leaned against the kitchen sink and pressed the palms of her hands against her ears. Soon the storm ended, and the sound of birds chirping relieved them. Everything seemed all right, but it wasn't. In fact, Oblivion wasn't afraid at all. Just sitting there, his body never moved a bit, even during the whole commotion. He suddenly leaned over his plate and laid his head upon the naked table. Julie and Meredith knew then that he was different. For this was the beginning of a new day, a day of unrest.

Children were playing outside. A dog ran to fetch a Frisbee thrown by a stranger. That stranger's name was Professor Gabe Ruso, a sweet-smelling, Italian-cologned hunk that never got hitched. That was Gabe, born in Italy and raised in the United States. Gabe had studied on angels and demons for a long time now. Latin was a language unknown to him. His fascination was extreme, and he would very much like to encounter the supernatural. He taught astrology. Two stars had fallen from the sky, and he was reading from a book in a one hand, with a Frisbee in the other.

"All right, Rusty!" *Woof!* Rusty was Professor Ruso's brown shih tzu.

The name of the book was *Angels and Demons, Truth or Phenomenon?* Professor Ruso read about the two angels who never went to hell and often wondered if the story was a myth. Little did he know that he would ever actually meet one. "Time to turn in, boy!" he said, whistling for Rusty to come. Rusty ran, slobbering at the mouth. Professor Ruso bent down to kiss him. Huge amounts of saliva wet his face. The sun was bright, and the flowers bloomed deep pastel colors. Rusty hopped into the back of his Ford Explorer as Professor Ruso got in and drove home. On his way home, he passed by the cathedral and made an immediate stop in the middle of the road. He stared intensely at the beautiful cathedral. Suddenly, he could hear angels singing. Their voices sounded like harps. Professor Ruso parked his vehicle to pay the priest a visit.

"Wait here, boy. I'll be right back." Professor Ruso approached the church and entered. A huge crucifixion of Christ hung on the wall. Professor Ruso knelt down on one knee. "In the name of the Father, the Son, and the Holy Ghost. Amen."

Several nuns walked past him as he stood up. Slowly, he walked past the podium. There were old women dressed in long dresses. Their heads were wrapped in scarves, and their shoes dated back in the early nineteen hundreds. Every wrinkle in their faces could tell you a story. Sagging lines across their foreheads hid their emotions—emotions about what was really happening. Professor Ruso approached one of the parishioners.

"Yes, is Father—"

"Time? Yes, he's here, and you are?"

"Professor Ruso. He probably doesn't remember me. We'd met a while back at the cathedral convention."

"Oh, of course. Well, if you wait here, I'll get him for you."

"Thank you."

An injured man dressed as a priest came out, limping on one foot. A cane held up the other. His eyes were somewhat tired. "I'm Father Time, and you are?" he said he held out his hand. Deep scars surfaced his skin.

Professor Ruso reached out his hand to shake. "You probably don't remember me. We'd met a while back. My name is Professor Ruso. I teach astrology at the university."

"Oh, yes, I remember. Nice to see you again. What can I help you with, Professor?"

"I'm doing research on angels and demons and am very interested in learning about your ministry here. This church, it's beautiful and angelic. I was always fascinated with the biblical ages,

Revelations, and the coming of Christ. Would you have the time to talk about it, Father?"

"As a matter of fact, I do. Follow me." Father Time gave Professor Ruso a tour through the cathedral. The sun beamed upon the bright colors of the stained glass windows, and the angels danced in oils across the ceiling.

"When Christ lived on earth, he lived as a man. The anointed one, appointed by God himself. Born from virgin Mary. She was beautiful, untouched. The Bible foretold the coming of the one whom God has chosen as the Messiah to rid the world from sin, to pay a debt that man owed, and now that the debt was paid. Satan refuses to acknowledge everything else. A deceiver, confuser, and a slanderer. If you are weak, he will try or do whatever he can to destroy you, Professor. He even tried tempting Christ but did not succeed. Christ was humbled toward the needs of others and faithful to the end, teaching us great news of the coming of the kingdom."

"Whose kingdom?"

"God's heavenly kingdom. He healed the sick and resurrected the dead. A whore washed his feet with her tears and no longer worked as a woman of the night. He even overturned a corrupt government that taxed the people needlessly. He walked miraculously on water, fed the hungry, and was baptized by John the Baptist. In the end, many men, creatures, will bow down to him when he returns and stands at the right hand of God the Father Almighty. You will then want to pray, if you can't. For when it is all said and done, only through Christ that you shall see God. God will prevail."

"You are fascinating, Father Time. I would like to write about your life, if you don't mind."

"There isn't much to know about a man who was once condemned, Professor."

"Pardon?"

Father Time walked away.

A café sat at the corner of Luxington Road. The aroma of cappuccino coffee filled the air. Cab drivers would stop by to buy a cup and gawk at the streetwalkers that sold their bodies for a nickel and a dime. A group of nuns met there every Wednesday for a slice of cherry pie and a cup of coffee. Sister Mary Claire strolled down what she thought was a lonely sidewalk and noticed the ladies of the night. One woman dressed in fishnet stockings, hooped earrings, red lipstick, spaghetti-strap heels, a red miniskirt with a matching jacket, a long blond weave, and an imitation fur around her neck approached Sister Mary Claire in a rude manner, with an attitude that would attract Charles Manson.

"Hey, baby, you got a light?" she said, holding a cigarette up to her lips.

"I'm sorry, I don't."

"What, you think you're better than me?"

"I beg your pardon?"

"Look, I know your kind. The wannabe-virgin type. I used to be a virgin back in nineteen . . . nineteen . . ." The woman just stood there and paused, thinking to herself. "Oh, well, anyway, I use to be one," she said, snickering.

"If you don't mind." Sister Mary Claire attempted to skirt around her.

"Uh, going somewhere, Sis?"

When Sister Claire gazed at her face, the strange woman held a loaded gun to her back and coerced Sister Claire into an alleyway. "Okay, Sis, take off all your shit, and hit the dirt!"

Sister Claire got extremely uncomfortable and began to cry. "Please, please don't do this. I beg you."

"No, no, Sister. You see, I need a fix, and I'll do whatever it takes to get it. You hear me?"

"Please don't. I don't have any money."

"Sister, I don't have all day. Now I'm gonna tell you one more time. Take your shit off, and hit the ground!"

Sister Claire carefully knelt down on her knees, gently placing her Bible onto the pavement, and covered her eyes, praying silently to herself, "Our Father, who art in heaven. Hallowed be thy . . ." She had said that prayer a thousand times now, and each word carried power—power beyond your wildest dreams. Sister Claire slowly opened her eyes, and the woman was gone. Gone just like that. Sister

Claire didn't see a thing. She was amazed at what had happened and shocked. A little dirt smudged onto her cheeks and nose from the palms of her hands.

"Where did she . . ." She immediately ran to the diner, distraught and relieved at the same time. Sister Mary Claire made it there safe and sound in one piece. Sister Williams sat there, sipping a cup of coffee. Sister Claire entered the café.

"Well, it's about time you got here. What . . . what happened to you?"

"It's a long story. I really would rather not talk about it."

Sister Lopez sat across them. A waitress approached them as Sister Claire skimmed through the menu. "What will you have?"

"Yes, I'll have a coffee and donut please."

The waitress left and Sister Claire began to nervously bite her nails. The waitress came back with her order and left. Sister Claire began to devour it quickly.

"Boy, are you hungry. Are you okay?"

Voices inside the diner got louder, making the atmosphere uncomfortable, overpowering Sister Mary Claire to the point that she couldn't hear herself speak.

"No, no, I'm not. No, I am not!" A pin could have fell and you would've heard it. It was quiet as a mouse. All eyes were on the woman dressed in black and white.

Sister Williams smiled at her and chuckled. "So what exactly happened to you, Sister Claire?"

"I-I was on my way here, and this woman came out of nowhere and . . ."—Sister Claire had a worried expression on her face—"she held me at gunpoint and demanded that I strip off my clothes."

"Oh my god. Are you all right?"

"Oh my!"

"I was so afraid, I . . ."

"So what did you do?"

"I prayed, and she . . ."

"She what?"

"Yes, tell us!"

"She disappeared."

"She disappeared?" Sister Williams reached into her pocket and retrieved a cigarette, placing it up to her lips. "You got a light?"

Those same reoccurring memories of the street hooker's speech pattern flashed before her. "You know, that's a bad habit. You really ought to give it up."

"Sister Claire, people don't just disappear just like that unless they've been kidnapped or killed. In your case, she knew you were a nun. Maybe she got scared and ran."

Suddenly, Sister Claire had lost her appetite for lunch and stood up at the table.

"Where are you going?"

"I'm sorry, but I'm really not that hungry," she said, leaving the table.

The winds blew hard that evening as wildlife scurried deep into the forest. Within the earth surfaced two condemned souls, two warlords craving for blood among the two that were chosen. They were jealous of the fact that their lives were spared and anxious to get even. Their names were Tobias and Zantor, archangels of deliverance, destined to destruction. They were leaders of the Legion of the Damned. Their vision was sharp. They were nocturnal and sleep at the crack of dawn. They were determined to stop at nothing to fulfill their promise. They were men by day and demons at night.

"Tobias, how do you know if they made it?"

"They did."

Their skin was dry and wrinkled. Their nails were long and curled. Their teeth were cracked and decayed. Black leather gripped their frail figures. Black capes embraced their sinful souls.

"When I find them, I'll suck the life source from their veins."

Death embraced the night. They came without hope and reason, leaving behind a trail of carnage and tragedy. They took hell by storm. Some have felt their fury. Others endured their wrath, searching for new victims. A revolution had been born.

"You sure you want to do this, Zantor?"

"I didn't come all this way for nothing, Tobias. Besides, if we kill the chosen two, we shall reign in glory! Victory to the Damned."

"You do understand there is no turning back?"

"I do."

Suddenly, they had transformed themselves into huge gargoyles soaring into the night sky.

Sitting at his desk, Father Time had written Oblivion a letter, hoping that it will reach him.

Dear friend,

It won't be long before we will be under attack again. They will soon come in numbers, and each attack will be different. We need to stay alert at all times. God be with you, and hope to see you again.

Father Time

He folded the letter and inserted it into a white envelope. He placed his hand upon it with a prayer, "Please, dear God, allow him to receive this message of hope. Amen."

Sister Mary Claire entered the room. Sadness overcame her, but the comfort of his presence made everything seem fine. She smiled sweetly as he placed the envelope into his pocket and turned around in his chair. "May I have a word with you, Father?"

"Yes, Mary, do come in."

She sat down and grabbed his hand, caressing the palm of his hand across her left cheek and kissing it gently. She gazed into his dreamy blue eyes. "I love you, you know that."

"Mary, we—"

"I came all this way to be with you, Time. I wouldn't have done that for anyone."

"Mary, for God's sake, I'm a priest. There wouldn't be much of a future for us, not while I'm like this."

"Time, I love you with all my heart!"

"You . . . you love me the way I am? Well, it's about time we found out now!" he said, stripping his clothes down to nothing. He exposed his naked figure. Huge wings extended out from his side. His skin got slightly dark and wrinkled. He levitated himself from the floor. His eyes got dark and went deep into his head. He was half-man, half-gargoyle, sweeping his tail into the air. Sister Claire was amazed at what she had seen.

"You still want me now?"

"When I first laid eyes on you, there was little doubt if I would accept you or not. I knew then that you were the man for me. I fell in love with someone that I wasn't sure of. I would go to the moon and back for you, Time. You know that, but I refuse to let you go."

He then transformed himself back to a human. "You don't know what you are getting yourself into, Mary. What type of life do you think we would have?"

She quickly walked over to him, throwing her arms around his neck. "Love, so much love. I could give you that, if you let me. Oh, please, oh, please let me in, Time!"

He began to kiss her until there was a knock at the door.

Deep in the fiery pits of hell, the Legion of the Damned resided. Where one came, came many. A multitude of condemned angels organized into a vicious militant attack of demons. Some practiced jousting themselves off black mares. Others flew into the darkness and would soon return to stomp a man into dust. Their eyes were burning windows of lost souls. Souls of those who didn't make it and those who just didn't give a damn. More blood was shed, but then a new life began. Sister Mary Claire was expecting and didn't know it. An army of gargoyles marched into a pit of anger. Heavy footsteps from the soles of their feet crushed hot coals into black diamonds.

Among an angry mob of heathens echoed millions. "Kill 'em!" they yelled to the top of their voices. Slime drizzled down their jaws, gritting their teeth tight like pit bulls.

"Time!" a name that stood out intensely, a vendetta to pay when they meet. A divine wrath was soon to come within the earth's surface, and two marked angels awaited their presence. Hell is no place for any man, for every one that was enslaved came a fierce lash from a hand that carried no emotions, no remorse. Shackles clenched around their ankles and pulled at their throats, cutting off the oxygen. They paced across hot, burning coals that led nowhere. The sound of whips tore into their weak flesh, and the cry of agony wreaked. They were soldiers of injustice, soldiers of no mercy, soldiers of vengeance. The war between good and evil was evident. The soldier's name behind the anger was Tiberious.

"I want the chosen two destroyed!" The sound of voices roared. "I want the blood from their heads on my hands and taste the sweat from their deceased bodies on my tongue. When you catch them, I don't want them caught breathing. I want you to devour them both alive!" They cheered an evil cheer. After all, it was war, it was payback, and it was Time.

After the storm, it became a sunny, clear day. Julie and her new family decided to go for a hike into the mountains. Oblivion stood at the top of a cliff. Staring down, he kicked a rock over to see how long it would take to hit the bottom. The rock hit a couple of boulders and splashed into the running rapids. Julie unexpectedly approached him from behind.

"What are you doing?"

"I don't belong here."

"What?" she said as she moved in to touch him.

"Stay back!" He signaled his hand for her to stay back.

"Oblivion, you don't have to do this!"

"You know nothing about me."

"I do know this, that you are a kind and gentle man. You don't have to do this!"

"The doctor said I had a rare disease."

"What? I thought . . ." She began to cry but tried to hold back the tears.

"It's not a disease, Julie." He began to expose his true self. His complexion was light purple, and the force of the winds plucked his transparent wings beyond the trees. "I am an angel. I am one of the chosen." Suddenly, black clouds blew powerful winds across the sky. The trees bent over like weeping willows as the rain began to fall, casting hail the size of rocks down upon them. The girls ran and screamed.

"Hurry, they're coming. You've got to get back to the house!" Oblivion stopped running and observed his surroundings. No one was there, and he proceeded to run. Until footsteps were heard from behind treading through the leaves. Oblivion glanced from behind and saw no one there. Zantor and Tobias stood there before him as he glanced forward.

"You have a high price to pay, my dear friend."

"What do you want from me, Tobias?"

"You remember my name?"

"How could I forget something as evil as you? You have destroyed those who have tried so hard to honor God."

"There is no—"

"God? Well, I'm sorry to say, but you're wrong. Without God, there is no hope, for man has sinned while sin is no longer acknowledged."

"Tiberious has put a hit out on you two," he said, pacing slowly around Oblivion. Oblivion kept a close eye on him.

"Oh?"

"We know about the other, and after I'm done killing you, I'll kill him too!" Tobias and Zantor suddenly transformed into angry, vicious demons. Horns extended from their skulls, saliva drooled from their fangs, and their eyes glowed fiery red.

"God be with me," he whispered.

They swung their razor-sharp claws at his clothing, tearing at his flesh. A holy rosary hung from Oblivion's neck. He immediately snatched the rosary from around his neck, snapping the beads apart as they rolled across the dirt. The crucifix evolved into a sword. Flawed huge wings extended from his side as he levitated into midair. The demons fought him. Oblivion swung his sword, slashing them across their chests. Blood spurt everywhere while he fought in victory. Zantor slashed him across the forehead, and Oblivion tumbled to the ground, making him bleed above the eyebrow. Tobias leaped upon him and attempted to strangle him. Oblivion grabbed him from around his neck as they furiously fought. Oblivion managed to get up and sucker punched Tobias three times in the jaw. Zantor lifted a huge boulder and tossed it at Oblivion, missing him by a couple of inches.

Dirt, pine needles, and tree limbs kicked up into debris. Oblivion double kicked Tobias high into a tree, snapping his vertebrae in half. Tobias, unconsciously, fell to the pavement. Zantor triple kicked Oblivion into the chest as he fell backward into the weeds. He then punched Oblivion into the jaw. He grabbed ahold of his hair and shoved his head into a stump. Oblivion grabbed his arm, swinging him around several times. Over the cliff to his death. Julie slowly approached him from behind and touched his shoulder.

CHAPTER SEVEN

Oblivion quickly turned around. "I thought you were home."

Embracing him, she said, "I know." They passionately gazed into each other's eyes and kissed. "Are you all right?"

"I think so," he said, checking to see if Tobias's body was still lying near the tree. His body was gone. "They'll be back soon. I must leave before I put you and your daughter in danger."

"Why? You just got here. You can stay in our den. It is safe there."

"You don't understand. There are more where they come from, and they'll stop at nothing until we are both defeated. I must go and forewarn my friend Father Time."

"Must you leave so soon? I mean, you just got here, and——"

"Ssssh," he said, caressing her lips with his finger. "We have a lot of time to be together."

"Can you stay with me tonight? It's been a long time since I had a real man."

The night was toasty near the fireplace. The spark of the flames popped. Julie loosened her hair as he unbuttoned her blouse, slowly slipping her blouse down her shoulders. She then placed his fingers into her mouth, sucking on his fingers as he caressed her nipples with his warn breath. She panted for him to enter her chamber in the bondage of love. He kissed her belly button and then her moist lips. He pinned her hands against the carpet. Meredith could hear her mother passionately yelling from the living room downstairs. She immediately sat up on her bed and put on her robe. The yelling stopped, and she suddenly realized what was going on and went back to bed, pressing her pillow against her ears.

The next morning, scrambled eggs, bacon, toast, and the aroma of hot coffee seeped into the air. Meredith got up and got dressed for school. She could hear them downstairs laughing. As she approached the kitchen, Ms. Dumplings sat a tray of sweet rolls onto the table. A bowl of sliced grapefruits sat next to it.

"I wish you didn't have to go."

"The same here, but if I stay, it could very well cost you your life."

Meredith could hear them talking and leaned against the dining room wall, eavesdropping.

"You don't understand. I am one of the chosen."

Ms. Dumplings stood next to the table, listening.

"The legion will stop at nothing until I am dead."

Julie began to weep, getting up from the table. Wiping her eyes, she ran toward the backyard. She gazed up at the clouds.

"What is it you want from us? Haven't I given you enough of me? I deserve to be happy."

The screen door opened, and Oblivion exited.

"It has nothing to do with you, Julie." He walked over to her and wrapped his arms around her waistline. She weeped, leaning her head upon his chest. "This fight is not your fight. It is God's fight."

"A man walks off the streets into my life and turns out to be Mr. Right. This . . . this is not right."

"If I could change things, I would, but this is one thing that I cannot change."

"I-I understand. When I take you back, will you promise me one thing?"

"And what's that?"

"Will you promise me that when this is all over and you are spared once more, you will come back to me?"

"I promise."

Julie smiled sweetly at him. She suddenly saw the world differently, and it was changing.

A woman walked into the church with her son. Her son showed signs of possession: abrupt change in personality, suicidal depression, extreme rage, withdrawals, hearing voices, and violent aversion of the scriptures. He began developing eating disorders and panic attacks. A complete mess had walked in and knelt down on the pew next to his mother.

"Father Time, the woman and her son are here to see you."

"Tell them that I will be right there," he said, tightening up his collar behind the wooden doors of the sixteenth-century chapel. Father Time was embattling an ancient nemesis. He was armed with a vial of holy water, a sterling-silver crucifix that evolved into a sword, and a book containing the rites of exorcism in Latin. The boy was strapped down in a chair. He had cracked, dry lips dripping with saliva. His eyes were sunken in from long nights of no rest. Deep lesions surfaced from his flesh. His skin was badly bruised from the rope and strappings. An exorcism was about to take place.

"Renounce Satan!" shouted Father Time. "Renounce the evil one!"

The boy's body went into a serious convulsion. "No!" A deep baritone voice emerged from his lungs. Other voices in Latin emerged. The chair started shaking furiously. Books flew into the air. Lit candles flickered out, and some stained glass windows suddenly shattered into pieces. The chair rose into midair and levitated off the floor, spinning around in circles. "No, I hate you!" The boy spat into the priest's face.

"Renounce Satan!"

"God is—"

"God is not dead!" Father Time wiped his head with a handkerchief. The boy's eyes rolled up into his head, exposing the white of his eye. "I hate you, Priest!"

"The power of God is in charge of you!"

"You fucked your mother last night!" The demon inside the boy laughed at the priest. "Your tricks don't work, Priest!" Holy water was thrown into the child's face. "It hurts! It hurts!" The sign of the cross was gestured upon the boy's chest.

"In the name of the Father, the Son, and the Holy Ghost. Amen."

"Stop it, you faggot!" The boy's tongue extended two inches from his mouth, slithering like a serpent. "Mommy, help me!" His mother reached out to her son.

"No, don't touch him. He's not your son!"

"Help my boy, please!" Tears ran down her cheeks. "I beg you, help my boy, please!"

"Get away from me, you old hag!" She clutched her mouth with the palm of her hand and backed away from him. "You slut! You old slut!" More holy water was sprinkled at the boy. Steam sizzled from his skin.

"You fucked the Virgin Mary!" The boy laughed out loud, echoing into the corridors of the hallways.

"Lord compels you!"

"You're a freak, you know that?"

Hymn books, chairs, and tables slammed into the walls. Pens and pencils dislodged themselves into the Sheetrock of the ceiling, knocking off figurines and nativity statues from the windowsills.

"You can't get it up, Priest! You're one of us, and you know that!"

Horns pushed up from his scalp. The priest saw no way out for this lost soul. The child began to hysterically laugh and laugh. Father Time kissed his crucifix and placed it slightly on the child's forehead. The cross burned a deep gash into his flesh. He then wiped it and put it away.

"This is not my child!" The boy's mom took out a .45 and aimed it at her son.

"Please, miss, don't do this!"

"He belongs to Satan now. I must put him out of his mi . . . sery. I'm sorry, Pocito, but you are no longer mine."

"This is what he wants you to do. Please, don't do this. Now, you came here for my help. Now let me help you."

"Go ahead, bitch. Pull the trigger," he said, laughing.

"This child does not belong to you. This child belongs to God."

"Shut up. This bastard is coming with me!" he said, laughing and drooling green slime from his lips. "His soul is damned and ready for the taking!"

"I rebuke you, Satan. In the name of the Father, the Son, and the Holy Ghost. You leave this child, and you leave now."

"I know you. You're one of us!" the boy said, laughing out loud.

"The power of the Lord compels you, evil one, and all that you stand for!" he said, throwing holy water upon the child's face. The boy went into another convulsion and shivered. His heart suddenly stopped, and his breathing slowed down. The chair eased down onto the floor. Father Time unstrapped the child from the chair and pounded on the boy's chest, trying to start his heart back up and giving him CPR. "Dial 911!"

One of the parishioners ran to get help. His mom cried, "Pocito! Pocito, I'm sorry!"

Paramedics, the police, and detectives surrounded the church. Detective Jack Rio and his partner interrogated Father Time in his office.

"I've seen this type of thing before. You had spoken to his mother sometime earlier, and it was evident by other Orthodox priest that an exorcism had to be done to rid this boy's body of an evil force that had possessed it. Now you tell me that this child and his mother came in around eight p.m. His mother was still saying that her boy was possessed by the devil and you had given him an exorcism."

"That sounds about right."

"How long have you been a priest, Father?"

"For as long as I can remember."

"That's funny, I couldn't find any records on you being born. Worst, not even when you were first sworn in." The detective slowly paced around his chair. "Who are you really, Time?"

"I am a priest, Detective Rio."

"A priest. That's a strange crucifix . . ." Detective Rio said, observing the cross Father Time was wearing. "You mind if I take a look at it?"

Father Time carefully handed it to him. Officer Rio glanced at it.

"Where did you get it?"

"What do you mean where did I—"

"I've never seen a cross like this anywhere around."

Father Time crossed his legs in a sophisticated manner. "I'm not at liberty to say."

"Locals around here say you're some kind of superhero. An angel dressed in black saved them from a swarm of deadly locusts that came down from the sky. Is that true?"

"Some might say so."

"You even made headlines: 'Priest performs exorcism on boy possessed by an evil force.'"

"The child was possessed by the devil."

"And how would you know that, Father? That boy almost died here tonight!"

"He showed signs of extreme paranoia, rage, and even schizophrenia."

"Father Time, my own son has shown signs of all those symptoms, and he appears to be a normal twelve-year-old boy as long as he continues taking his ridlin."

"Pull him off of that drug, Detective, and you'll see what you've got."

"Is that supposed to be a joke?"

"I'm sorry you took it that way, but this is very real. Two nuns came to me one evening and told me that one of the sisters had shown signs of possession. We had to examine her first before I could practice. She had a sick eating disorder, which left her with open wounds from eating her own flesh, bleeding from her eyes and nose. She had partially eaten her own tongue. A beastly growl came from a voice that didn't belong to her. Losing control of her muscles. Urinating on herself. I immediately performed an exorcism, which in return left her paralyzed. The next day, she was found literally climbing the walls on her hands and feet. There is no explanation for it except possession, Detective."

"I suppose so. I'm not much of a religious person, Father. So forgive me, but how many of these cases have you seen on a day-to-day basis?"

Father Time stood up and approached him. Placing his hand on the detective's shoulder, he said, "These cases are all so rare, Detective. That it is hard to say, but when they come, my door is always open for help and spiritual guidance. After all, I am on a mission to save souls."

"Well, I guess that'll be all for tonight." The detective grabbed his coat and hat as he proceeded to leave. "Uh, don't try to be a super-hero, Father. Besides, they're all dead."

Speaking in a low tone of voice behind the detective's back, he said, "Perhaps a dream is all that a man has to hold onto, Detective."

When Detective Rio left the premises, Father Time locked off all the exits. He then heard a noise in the hallway and grabbed the chain connected to his crucifix and kissed it. "The Father, Son, and Holy Ghost, Amen. Anyone here?" There was the sound of the wind smacking against the window shutters. A storm was coming. Father Time walked into his office and looked into his desk drawer. There, a bottle of red wine sat. He retrieved it. He sipped little by little until he finished the whole glass. An eerie noise came from outside. Father Time glanced out the window and saw nothing but rainwater slithering down the glass. He heard the noise again. Only this time, it was coming from the restroom. He slowly paced his way toward the bathroom door and grabbed ahold of the knob. The door creaked open. A message was written in blood on the bathroom mirror. He was amazed at what he'd seen. Father Time knew it meant trouble.

The message read as follows: "We know who you really are, and we'll be back!"

At night while in bed, he had those same reoccurring dreams. Sweat ran down his forehead, a fever broke out, and a rapid heart-beat pounded in his head. Lightning and thunder roared across the heavens. A multitude of condemned angels fell from the clouds. There were many that followed. God had closed his ears from their screams. He could never forget that awful scream in agony. A black hole had opened up and swallowed them for eternity. Their bodies were shamed, and their wings were destroyed. Impaled upon them were huge spikes, casting them into eternal damnation. Father Time had seen himself fall but spared. Waking up on earth, he was alone and naked. Ants crawled across his chest as he brushed them off with his hand. Birds chirped in the vineyard, and the sunlight beamed upon his skin. He knew then that he was given another chance. A soft hand caressed his right cheek. Father Time awoke, and Sister Mary Claire smiled at him.

"You miss me?"

"I didn't know that you were . . ." he said, sitting up on the bed.

"Here? Dead horses couldn't stop me from seeing you, Time."

"I smell coffee."

"Yes. Would you like some?" She proceeded to reach over the coffee table for a cup already made.

"Thank you. What time is it?"

"Don't worry, you'll make it in time for your sermon this morning. I have something to talk to you about."

"Oh, what about?"

"I went to the hospital for an annual exam this morning, and . . ."

"And what?"

"Time, you are going to be a father." She smiled at him again. Only this time, he wasn't smiling back.

"It can't be . . ."

"Oh, yes, and I, for the first time in my life, am going to be a mother."

"Mary, you are a nun, for God's sake!"

She grabbed her tummy. "And now I'm the mother of your child, Time!"

Time put on his boxer shorts. "I'm sorry, Mary, but I am not ready to be a father. I became a priest before the eyes of God."

She glanced down at the floor. "So what are you saying, Time?"

"I think we should—"

"No, no, I won't do it! I won't kill my baby for you or anyone else!"

She ran out of his room sobbing. Tears of sorrow left a trail upon the wooden floor. Wiping her bloodshot eyes toward her car, she got in and sat behind the wheel thinking, *Dear God, how did I get myself in such a holy mess?* Mary sobbed her heart out while Time stood at the window. He glanced out toward her car.

The weather was warm and calm. Time called the bishops and Cardinals at the archdiocese into a meeting at the church. Father Maloney sat before him.

"So why are we here, Father Time?"

"I have some very"—he sighed—"disturbing news to share with you, Bishop Maloney."

"Oh, and what might that be, Father Time?"

"I have broken my vows . . ."

Their eyes glued onto him. This was much more serious than they thought. "Are you telling us that you . . ."

"I'm telling you that I had sexual relations. Sister Mary Claire and I have been seeing each other for some time now. I have feelings for this woman that I cannot comprehend. She, in return, is expecting a child—my child."

Their faces turned flushed red, and their eyes were fixated on the cross around his neck. "Father Time, that cross around your neck represents the death of Christ and the fact that he died for our sins. Didn't that mean anything to you?"

"The fact that Christ died on the cross for our sins means a great deal to me, Monsignor Maloney. I, in return, paid the price for it as well."

"And what is that supposed to mean?"

"You wouldn't understand, but Sister Claire does. I only hope that when you do that you'll forgive me as well."

Cardinal Brown spoke, "Father Time, what you have done was a serious offense. You have broken your ties with God."

"I have done no such thing. I love God with all my heart, and I will die for him. I realize that this was a big mistake, and if you want me to step down, I will."

"What about the child, Father Time? How are you going to find time to raise a child?"

Father Time sat there and thought about his actions. "I'm . . . I'm sure we'll think of something."

"In the meantime, Father Time," he said, grabbing his coat and hat, "I want you to remain a priest here at the cathedral until I find someone to replace you. Is that understood?"

"Yes, Monsignor Maloney."

Father Time just sat in the chair, staring at the walls. He suddenly slumped in his seat and knelt down on his knees. "Dear God, I have failed you, and I am sorry. I wanted so bad to please you, but when temptation got in the way, I failed the test. I thought I was strong, but I was weak. Please forgive me, Father. It isn't the child's fault for my mistake, but it's a mere miracle that I can even have children. Please forgive us, dear God. Amen."

"Tracey, hey."

Tracey was an alluring fifteen-year-old who was popular, bright, and intelligent. Pam was the bookworm in the group; she consistently read a lot. Faye was oh so hip and different; she was into the latest do.

"Hi, Sister Mary Claire, how's it going in sisterhood nowadays?"

"Great. How are you guys?"

"Fine."

"Have any of you seen Jenna? I haven't heard from her in a while."

"You mean you haven't heard?"

"Heard what?"

The girls glanced at one another in amusement.

"Jenna went mental."

"What?"

"Yeah, the rumor is, it was storming one awful night, and everyone was asleep. Except Jenna. She had a hard time resting. The dog was barking in the backyard, so she got up to see what was wrong. She could hear tree limbs falling upon the roof of the house, so she went back to bed. The next thing she knew, something was on top of her, raping her, penetrating her hard under the sheets. She began to scream, but it held her mouth shut. The bed shook for at least five minutes, and before it was all over, Jenna got up and immediately ran into the bathroom. Her undies were blood-soaked red. She even had a deep scratches that surfaced across her chest. She kept asking herself, 'What was that thing there?'"

"Oh my god."

"Yeah, 'What was it?' was the question. She never told her folks in fear of people laughing at her, and every night was a nightmare. The rapings, tearing at the flesh. It got to the point that she quit taking gym. The gym coach called her parents to inquire her missing class. When her mom found out about her cutting class, she became furious and waited for her to get home. By the time Jenna got there, her mother yelled at her and grounded her. Jenna didn't want to alarm her parents about the news for they loved that house so much. There were nights that her parents could hear furniture and things thrown against the walls. That was the breaking point. When Jenna told her parents about what happened to her, they didn't believe her, even when they'd seen the evidence before them. They even wanted her to see a shrink, which caused her to move out. She ended up on the streets for days before she went insane. I still find it hard to believe."

"Oh, Jenna, oh, my poor Jenna. Why . . . why didn't she call me? I would have been there for her."

"You are not well liked in her family. She promised her parents that she wouldn't see you again."

"Where is she? I must find her."

Faye handed her a note. On the note was the following:

Dear Sister Mary Claire,

I know you won't believe me. No one believes me, but it is true. I am a victim of the paranormal. I am the only one who can see or feel this thing. It only comes out at night, attacking me in my sleep whenever it pleases. Sometimes I feel like killing myself. Maybe that would be the only way out. It would be so easy. The pain would go away. You can find me at St. Adam's Psychiatric Hospital for the Mentally Insane. Hurry, I'm not too sure how much of this I can take. Please help me before it is too late. You are my only hope.

Love,

Jenna

"I must go to her."

Sister Mary Claire caught a cab to St. Adam's Psychiatric Hospital. Sister Mary Claire paid the cab driver and stepped out of the cab. She kissed her holy rosary from around her neck before entering the building. Gazing up at the five stories, the building looked prehistoric and rundown. Sister Claire walked up to the information desk. The nurse was watching a comedy sitcom, laughing.

"Yes, I'm here to see a Jenna Meyer."

"Damn, this shit is funny!" She turned up the tube, laughing out loud to herself.

"Excuse me, I'm here to see Jenna Meyer."

"Get the hell out of he—"

"Ma'am, I'm here to see Jenna Meyer!" Sister Claire slammed her hand down on the counter.

"Okay, okay hold your horses, missy." The nurse grabbed a key and escorted her to Jenna's room. Patients walked down the hallway distorted, sick. Some carried meds in one hand and a cup in the other. An old man approached her. "She belongs to the devil now." Another patient grabbed her arms and swung Sister Claire around to face her and stared deep into her eyes. "When you see her, look away, 'cause whatever's inside that girl will get inside you too."

"Excuse me." Sister Claire pulled away from her and proceeded toward Jenna's room. She had finally reached Jenna's room, and the nurse unlocked the door. Jenna was strapped in a straightjacket, sitting in a corner. Her eyes were tired, and her skin looked pale. She wasn't the same little girl she knew anymore. The nurse left Sister Claire alone with her.

"Jenna, Jenna, it's me, Sister Claire."

Saliva dribbled from her cracked lips. Four walls kept staring at her.

"Jenna, Jenna, look at me." Sister Claire grabbed her straightjacket.

Jenna faced her eye to eye.

"I'm here. Do you remember me?"

Jenna tried to speak, but her voice was weak.

"What happened to you?"

"It was evil. The first thing I knew was that I was asleep, and this thing kept attacking me, raping me in my bed." Jenna began to weep. "I tried to tell my folks, but they wouldn't believe me. They refused to believe their own daughter. I-I can still see it."

"Tell me, Jenna, what is it?"

"I-I . . ."

"You can talk to me, Jenna. What's this thing you're seeing?"

"I-I can't . . ."

"What does it look like?"

"No, no, you must leave!"

"Jenna, tell me what it looked like!"

A man's voice spoke out from Jenna's diaphragm. "I know you, Sister Claire. You fucked a priest, didn't you?"

"Pardon me, who are you?" Sister Claire grabbed her by the cheeks and got up in Jenna's face. "You get out! You get out of this child!"

"I'm not going anywhere!"

"In the name of Jesus!"

The demon portrayed Sister Claire's voice during lovemaking. "Oh, Time, oh, Time, don't stop—"

Mary yelled at it, "Stop it!"

"Oh, Time, deeper, faster."

Mary kept yelling at it, "Stop it, I tell you!"

"Tell me, was it good?"

The demon laughed as Sister Claire ran to the door and banged on it, screaming, "Let me out of here. Let me out!"

Father Time tried calling Sister Claire but couldn't get ahold of her. He then called one of the other nuns. Her name was Sister Joyner. "Sister Joyner?"

"Father Time, it's so nice to hear from you. How may I help you?"

"I'm trying to get in touch with Sister Mary Claire. Have you seen her?"

"Sister Claire mentioned something about visiting the cathedral academy."

"Did she mention why?"

"Let me see here," she said, checking her files on troubled youths. Jenna Meyer's file sat on her desk. "Every so often, the sisters visit the academy for troubled youths to inspire our youths to complete their education. Jenna Meyer is our youth for today. You can find her there."

"Thank you, Sister Joyner."

"Father Time?"

"Yes, Sister Joyner?"

"Is . . . is everything all right?"

"Yes, yes, it is."

"I ask, because Sister Claire has been sick a lot lately. She hasn't been able to hold down her food. I'm concerned about her."

"Well, I can reassure you there's nothing to be worried about. I'm sure she'll pull through." A lie was all it took. He hoped Sister Joyner would forget all about it and move on, but it wasn't that easy. It just wasn't that easy. He had a feeling that she was on to them, and that meant trouble. If Sister Joyner found out about her pregnancy, it would ruin them both.

"Thank you for being concerned, Sister Joyner."

Sister Joyner hung up the dial and waited for Sister Claire's return.

It was 9:00 p.m, and Sister Claire came running through the doorways of the dorm. Her eyes were red from weeping. Entering her room, she slammed the door. Her roommate, Lacy Johnson, awoke from the noise. Lacy could see how sad she was and sat up on her bed to tum on the dresser lamp. She was a bright, dimpled, blue-eyed blonde who always wanted to become a nun and became friends with the unknown. Sister Claire ran into the bathroom and threw up into the commode. Sister Johnson stood at the doorway, staring at her.

"Are you all right?"

"Do I look all right?"

"I'm . . . I'm sorry for prying." Sister Johnson attempted to walk away.

"Don't . . . I'm sorry, Lacy. I haven't been myself lately."

"I see." Lacy knelt down beside her and brushed her hair from her face with the palm of her hand. "You're so pretty. What happened, Mary?"

"I went to see a friend today at the academy. Came to find out she wasn't there. A couple of her friends said that she got put out from where she was staying. They told me where I could find her, and when I got there, she was a complete mess. She . . ."—Sister Claire wept—"she was in a straightjacket. Drooling from the lips. Cursing the Almighty in Latin. Her skin was as cold as ice, and her eyes were sunken in. She suddenly started climbing the walls. She was possessed, and I could not help her. I couldn't help her!"

Sister Johnson embraced her as Sister Claire wiped her mouth.

"Thank you for listening."

"How long did you know her?"

"For some time now. I was her only hope, and now I failed. I failed her!"

Lacy grabbed her hand.

Snow globes sat upon the dresser drawers. The Virgin Mary holding Baby Jesus was encased inside. It was engulfed in water and glitter.

Sister Claire stood up on her feet and grabbed a towel. "Thank you. I feel so much better now. I think I'll take a shower."

Lacy stood up. "If you ever feel that you need a friend, I'm there for you, Claire." Lacy held out her hand, and Sister Claire grabbed it and held onto it. Sister Joyner knocked on the door.

"Come in!"

"Sister Claire, may I have a word with you?"

A troubled nun walked into the bedroom and unveiled her beautiful red hair. It draped across her shoulders and her face. Sweat was dripping into her eyes, and she wiped it with the towel.

"I'm sorry to bother you so late at night, but Father Time has been trying to reach you."

"He has?" .

"Yes, he has. Is everything all right, Sister Claire?"

Sister Claire paced over to the door and opened it. "I'm afraid I'll have to ask you to leave, Sister Joyner."

"You never answered my question, Sister Claire."

"That's because it wasn't a question that I wanted to answer."

For the first time, Mary got her confidence back, and this time, she wasn't letting up. Sister Joyner left the room angry, while the two nuns were smiling and laughing the whole time. Lacy walked over to her dresser drawer and pulled out a crucifix. The cross was sterling silver, a beautiful, authentic piece. Sister Claire glared at it in amazement and smiled.

"I want you to have this. My mother gave it to me, and now I'm giving it to you."

"Why . . . why not leave it for your blood relatives?"

"Mary, I'm dying . . ."

Sister Claire glanced at this young, beautiful woman who was obviously very sick and whose future was cut short.

"I'm dying from cancer. The doctor gave me a few months to live. I have always wanted to be a nun before the eyes of God, and now that I am, I have fulfilled my destiny. Every time I look in the mirror, I see a woman with one foot on concrete and the other buried in six feet of earth. I am ready to let go now."

"I don't know what to say." Mary wiped her eyes.

"Mary, I feel like I've known you for some time now, and you have always been an inspiration to me. You gave me the courage to go on. For the first time, I've seen you stand up for yourself, and I'm proud of you." Lacy took the cross and placed it over her head, around her neck.

"Thank you, Sister Johnson, and I shall never forget you!"

"Likewise, Sister Claire, likewise."

They were friends for life, joined by faith, love, and kindness, each searching for hope in their own way. Sister Claire smiled at her. Sister Lacy's heart was good, and God knew it and was calling her home, for she was glad to go.

Sister Mary Claire and Sister Lacy Johnson stood at an open window, staring at the night sky. An owl was hooting on an hallowed old oak tree that stood high next to the church.

The next morning, the sisters met at Holy Communion. Sister Mary Claire grew sicker from her pregnancy. Their heads were bowed while Father Time rubbed ashes on their foreheads. When he got to Sister Claire, he smiled and rubbed ashes on her head twice. Sister Joyner noticed it and knew then that Sister Claire was expecting. After the Passover, she called Sister Mary Claire in for a private meeting. Sister Joyner sat behind a wooden desk as Sister Claire came in.

"You asked to see me, Sister Joyner?"

"Oh, do have a seat, please." Sister Joyner had an open box of delicious chocolates sitting on her desk. "Sister Claire, I'm afraid that you're not being honest not only with yourself but to God as well."

"I'm sorry, but I do not understand—"

"You were late checking in the other night and weren't willing to tell me why. Is there something that I should know?"

"No more than what I've already told you, Sister Joyner."

Sister Joyner glared at her stomach and smiled. "Would you like a box of chocolates, Sister Claire?"

Sister Claire glanced at the box of chocolates sitting on her desk and licked her lips. She was hungrier than ever and slowly reached over to grab one but couldn't. Her mind had quickly focused on why she was there. Sister Joyner smiled at her.

"You think I don't know, Sister Claire?"

"Know about what?"

"Know about the pregnancy. How long have you've been keeping this a secret?"

Sister Claire sat stiffly in her seat and never said a word. She kept her head down.

Sister Joyner stood up and walked around her seat in an authoritative manner. "You didn't think that I would find out, did you?"

"Frankly, I didn't quite care, Sister Joyner."

"You didn't care, hmm. Who is the father, Sister Claire?" she asked, glaring into her eyes. "Who's the father of that little bastard you are carrying?"

"Please don't call my baby that. You have no right!"

"I have no right? I have no right!" Sister Joyner's yellow teeth gleamed with silver refills around each tooth. Her teeth were in bad condition, and she had bad breath. She yelled at the top of her voice, "Sister Claire, as long as I am in charge, you will follow my orders. Do you understand?"

"Yes, Sister."

"Now I will ask you once more, who is the father of this unborn child you are carrying?"

"I can't tell you that!"

"And why not, Sister Claire?"

Tears ran down her cheeks and upon her black shroud. "Because . . . because I love him. I love him, Sister Joyner."

Sister Joyner became very concerned about this and set up a personal meeting with Father Time by mail.

Father Time tried calling Sister Claire but with no luck. He then went into his room and sat down at his desk. He went to get out his pen and pad to write to her.

Mary,

Monsignor Maloney paid me a visit. He knows about the pregnancy. I may have to make plans to leave. You know where to reach me.

Love always,

Time

Lying his head down upon his desk, he slept.

CHAPTER EIGHT

Julie and Oblivion were standing on the porch and kissing. His bags were packed, and Meredith and Ms. Dumplings were glancing out the doorway and smiling. She knew then that her mother was finally happy.

Julie grabbed ahold of his cross and kissed it too. "Bring him back to me, okay?"

Meredith walked out onto the porch to hand him a gift. It was a stuffed, minted teddy bear named Rocky. She would never depart with this but figured he would return it someday. He stooped down to say good-bye.

"What's his name?"

"Sergeant Rocket. I want you to have him."

"Why, thank you, Meredith. That was awfully very nice of you. I'll make sure that I keep Sergeant Rocket with me at all times. Will you do something for me?"

"Sure. What is it?"

He dug into his pocket and pulled out a bright stone, a beautiful green emerald. It wasn't your ordinary stone. It glowed in the dark and had powers among her wildest dreams. "Take care of this for me, okay, pumpkin?"

Meredith's eyes lit up like a Christmas tree. She had never seen anything so beautiful and unique.

"Sure!" she said, stuffing the emerald into her pocket.

Julie and Oblivion walked over to her vehicle and got in. Julie smiled and waved at them both. On their way back to town, her wheel had suddenly rolled over a rusty nail and gotten a flat. She immediately got out of her car to check the damage. "Damn!"

He got out to examine the problem. "What's wrong?"

"A flat. I don't have another spare. I guess we'll have to walk it."

Suddenly, a swarm of giant mutant bees flew out of nowhere.

"Is that . . . is that what I think it is?"

"Get in! Quick!"

They both jumped into the car and immediately rolled up the windows. They stuffed the air vent with old cloth, which was in the glove compartment. The giant bees smacked into the windshield, smearing their guts onto the glass. There was the sound of bees buzzing all around them, working their way into the vehicle. Julie began yelling and screaming. The vehicle was covered. Oblivion placed his hands upon the window shield. He closed his eyes and prayed. The bees gradually left them in peace. The sound of birds chirping filled the air.

"How did you do that?"

Oblivion smiled, got back out, and walked out into the woods.

"Wait a minute, where are you going?"

Suddenly, he stumbled onto a spare tire that matched hers and rolled it out from among the trees. Out of words and shocked, Julie laughed out loud and jumped up and down.

"I don't believe it. I just don't believe it. You are full of surprises."

Oblivion changed the tire for her, and they both got back into the vehicle. Julie had misplaced her keys and glanced around the seats for it.

"What's wrong?"

"Seems like I lost my keys."

Oblivion snapped his fingers, and the keys were in his hand. "Are you looking for these?"

"You are a lifesaver, you know that? Thanks."

They drove off into town, arriving at the shelter. Julie smiled at him. "If you need anything, call me, okay?" She wrote her number on a piece of paper. He reached for it, and she immediately kissed him on the lips. "I'm yours forever."

"Likewise," he said, shutting the door. It was hard to say goodbye. It had to be done.

Oblivion walked into the rehab a clean person and approached the front counter. "Is Vivian still here?"

"Vivian? I'm sorry, but Vivian's dead."

"What happened?"

"I'm sorry, but I'm not at liberty to share that information with you." He began to run up the stairs to her room. "Excuse me, but you need a pass to enter the rooms, mister!"

Her door was ajar, and he slowly pushed it open. The furniture was strewn about. Broken glass were upon the floor, and a bottle of booze was on the kitchen counter. Oblivion walked over to it and opened it. "So they got you too, Viv." He held up the bottle and said, "Here's one for old time's sake."

A reflection of a shadow, seen on the bottle that he was holding, opened the door, came in, and shut it. He dropped the bottle. "Who's there?" A loud hissing sound slithered around the room. "What in hell . . ." A giant anaconda attacked him, biting into his arm and tossing him like a rag doll around the room. The head of the serpent was huge and too strong to loosen its grip, throwing him clean across the room.

The woman at the counter could hear the commotion upstairs and called the police. Oblivion grabbed his cross and changed into an angel. The crucifix had transformed into a sword. He then slashed the creature in two. Its body reconnected back together. It slashed and cut at the wind as it dodged every blow. It then bit into his arm again. It slammed him against the wall, busting holes the size of basketballs into the wall. When it finally loosened its grip, Oblivion quickly slashed its head off, killing it dead. The authorities suddenly burst into the room, and the room was vacant. No one was there, and the creature was gone.

"Hey, I don't understand. He had to have been here. Oh my god, look at the walls. Who's going to pay for this shit?"

"Okay, ma'am, if he was here, look's like he's gone now."

Oblivion was standing outside on the balcony. He then jumped from the balcony onto the hood of a parked vehicle, landing safely on both feet. A drunk saw him jump and dropped his bottle of whiskey, shattering glass upon the pavement.

MELVINA HAWKINS-PATTERSON

"Spiderman is real!"

While walking through the slums of New York, a gang by the name of Genocide approached Oblivion in a rude manner, attempting to rob him. "Give me all your money, punk!" Oblivion smiled and reached into his pocket. "Slowly. Don't make me blow your damn head off, man!"

"You're right. I wouldn't want you to hurt me." He immediately grabbed his crucifix, which transformed into a huge sword. An angel appeared before them. The boys tried jabbing punches at him and swinging bats and knives. Oblivion jumped high into midair and flipped, landing on the ground. He swung his sword in all directions, cutting some in the face and slashing open their clothes, wounding them in return. Others double kicked him into the chest, knocking him into a row of trash cans. Oblivion flew into them with both fists, knocking them out cold. One gang member pulled out a switchblade and swung his knife at Oblivion's face but missed him at all angles. Oblivion spat a white powder into the boy's face. The boy's facial tissue melted off his skull like wax, killing him in return.

At Saint Hosea, Father Time stood at the altar. Two condemned angels walked into the church and sat down at the back pew during Sunday service. Their names were Zantor and Tobias. "Dear God, forgive us for our sins and for those who persecute us day to day."

Zantor stood up and walked up to the pulpit. "You are a hybrid. Do you know what that is?"

Father Time smiled at the church members that were seated. "Please seat yourself, my son."

"Your son?" Zantor said, pacing the floor. "You are not a real priest, Father Time. In fact, you have been deceiving your congregation for a while now. Why don't you tell these helpless souls who you really are?"

The room was so quiet. You could hear a pin drop. "I'm gonna have to ask you to leave. You are disturbing my congregation."

"Am I? Or haven't you've heard the old saying 'Once a condemned man, always a condemned man'?"

Father Time got angry and shook holy water into Zantor's face. The blessed water burned his flesh and cooked his insides. A steam of smoke could be seen. "You are like a wild beast from hell looking for a way out. Get out of my church. Then get out of my life!"

Tobias stood up and smiled at him. "You are in denial, Father. Don't worry, when I open your eyes, I'll do you a favor by cutting them out."

Sister Mary Claire sat among the church members and watched as the men left. She became worried.

After church service, Father Time stood in his room alone. His head was down, and he was staring at the wooden floor, thinking. Sister Mary Claire entered his room.

"I got your letter, Time. What do you mean you're leaving, and who are those evil men?"

"Its over!" Father Time slowly walked around his desk. His eyes were red.

She immediately ran to him, wrapping her arms around his waistline, embracing her head against his chest. "When I wake in the morning, I wake for you. When I breathe, I breathe for you. When I eat, I eat for you. Your baby is inside of me, growing, yearning to meet you Time. I will travel to the ends of the earth to make sure that happens. I realize that you're not of this world, but it doesn't matter to me anymore. I love you. I love you, Time . . ."

He caressed his fingers through her beautiful red hair and held her tight in his arms. "I love you too. Don't ever leave me, Mary. I don't know what I'll do if you ever left."

"I won't, my love. Time, who were those evil men?"

He never answered. He never spoke a word, because he knew.

Oblivion stopped at a hotdog stand and bought one to eat. At a deserted bench in a park across the street, he saw pigeons eating shredded bread and decided to join them. Smog tilled the air, and at a nearby harbor, a ship was sounding its foghorn. Oblivion sat on the bench, eating his hotdog gleefully. A pigeon flew upon his shoulder and pecked his head. Oblivion gently grabbed the bird and rubbed its beak. He fed it part of his bun.

A strong bond over a period of time grew between them. He would visit the park often to see his friend. He gave the bird a name: Sho. Sho would eat from his hand every time he came. Oblivion decided to keep the bird and took the pigeon to his room at a run-down hotel. A bird cage was waiting for him there. Sho was different. He could tell if someone was coming. He would chirp twice before someone knocked on the door. Oblivion tested him more than once by taking him to the park. Two joggers were approaching, and the bird chirped twice again. Oblivion called him the Lookout Man. He then called the church, and a parishioner answered.

"Saint Hosea, how may I help you?"

"Hi, is Father Time in?"

"He just left. Would you like to leave a message?"

"Would you let him know that his friend is in town, and that it's important that we meet as soon as possible?"

"Yes, sir, I will do so."

Sister Claire and Father Time drove up to the mountains to spend some quality time together. They walked across a field of wildflowers, which bloomed every summer. Father Time picked one and placed it gently into her red hair. She laughed and ran, hoping he would chase her. He suddenly grabbed her by the waistline. Her lips locked onto his, and they passionately kissed. Two people, forbidden to see each other, secretly in love. They overheard and noticed two squirrels mating up in a nearby tree.

"This baby is going to be so happy, Time."

"Mary?" He grabbed her by the arms to sit on a tree stump.

"Yes, my love?"

"I'm not too sure having this baby would be a great idea, Mary."

She paused in anger and pressed his cheeks with the palms of her hands. "Wild horses couldn't stop me, Time."

"Think about it. You'll have to give up your profession as a nun. Do you want that?"

"Right now, I don't know what I want, but I do know that I am in love with you, Time, and I can't stop wanting you."

Father Time leaned over upon the grass to pray. "Oh, dear God, what have I've done?"

Sister Claire tried to lift him by his shoulder. "Get up, Time. You've done nothing wrong. We both wanted this."

"What will you do if I die?" Sister Claire just stared at him. "That child will grow up without a father."

"In case you forgot, God is his father, Time, God is . . . two people in love, holding hands and not knowing what tomorrow has in store for them. An unborn child eager to know them both, promised to live and destined to die." Her black robe blew with the wind as her red hair curled around his fingers. Father Time had finally met his soul mate, a nun who helplessly fell in love with a priest, with an unborn child.

CHAPTER NINE

Zantor and Tobias walked into a bar and ordered two beers. They were two studs dressed in black leather. A prostitute by the name of Kiki had caught their eyes. She had cheap perfume, a sleazy mini, and deep-red lipstick that stood out like a sore thumb. A five-dollar lay, attractive, but rather wild at heart. Kiki just didn't care but gained for anything new. She had noticed them too and walked over to their table.

"Mind if I sit?" The men were quiet, drinking their beer. Kiki sat down, opened her purse, and got out a cigarette to smoke. She placed the cigarette into her mouth, hoping one of them would light it. Tobias lifted one foot across his knee and scraped his fingernail across his shoe. His fingernail immediately caught on fire. He lit her cigarette.

"Thanks, handsome. Where you two from?" They just glanced at her adoring figure. "Hey, you look familiar. Oh, I know you, you're from that new TV show. No, don't tell me. I know the name . . ."

Four men shooting pool noticed them too. They didn't like all the attention they were getting and got jealous. One of them approached them and asked, "Where you guys from?" They never spoke and fixated their evil eyes on him. If looks could kill, he would've been dead. "Cat's got your tongue?" Tobias sat there in a cool position.

Kiki got worried and stood up. "Look, why don't you continue with your game. These guys aren't bothering you."

"Stay out of it, bitch!" he said, shoving her against one of the tables. "I'm going to ask you one more time." Tobias and Zantor stood up and grabbed the guy. They tossed him high into the air across the room against the wall. The man's body smacked pieces of concrete off the wall. The three men realized what was happening and began to attack them. Bodies flew over barstools. Beer bottles were smacked against skulls, and blood splattered all over the tables. The furniture was destroyed, and the four men were knocking on death's door. Tobias and Zantor decided to kill them by feasting on their jugular veins, ripping their weak bodies apart, and they left the bar unharmed. Kiki, in shock, slowly picked up her purse. The owner of the bar hid behind the counter and peeked out to see if they left, amazed to see that the place was left in a complete mess and that more than one homicide took place there. The owner immediately called the police. Kiki began to cry.

"Hey, Kiki, where you going? You've got to report this to the authorities."

She paused for a moment. "I don't know about you, but I've seen enough. I'm getting my ass off the streets."

The county coroners arrived, and four bodies were zipped in black bags and rolled out into a crowd of spectators. An investigator by the name of Officer Reed interrogated Kiki in a room. Another investigator by the name of Officer Zapetee was present. Zapetee, with slow steps, paced around the table where she was sitting. Kiki lit a cigarette to smoke. Her nerves were bad, and her hands began shaking.

"Let's start from the beginning. You said two men walked into the bar and bought beer. Do you know what they look like?"

Kiki began to sob, puffing on her cigarette. "They looked like wild beasts. Is that good enough for you? They . . . they sat there, drinking their beer. I walked over to offer them company, and . . ."

"And what Kiki?"

"Some guy came to the table. I believe he was one of the ones playing a game of pool. Started a fight among the two, and before I knew it, they ate them—they literally ate them!" She hysterically sobbed, her tears hitting the table.

"Okay, that'll be all."

Kiki got up, and Officer Zapetee opened the door for her to leave. She strutted herself out of the room. Officer Zapetee shut the door from behind her.

"This is harder than I expected, Reed."

"I know. Seems like we've got two mass murderers on our hands." Officer Reed had wiped the table and sat down.

"If we don't find them, this city is going to have trouble on its hands. We've got to find them." Zapetee checked the info Kiki had mentioned during the interrogation. "Okay, what do we have to go on?"

"Two men walked into a bar, dressed in black leather. They both ordered a beer. A man playing pool approached them, and a fight broke out, leaving four men dead."

"Sounds about right. What about when they left?" Investigator Zapetee pointed at Reed's notepad.

"She said they disappeared right before her very eyes. Spooky shit, huh? That was when she decided to give up her profession."

"Damn, somewhere out there is another massacre waiting to happen. We've got to find those two before they kill again."

At night, the streets brought on crime, prostitution, and drugs. Drive-by shootings were the norm, and New York was never quite the same. Tobias and Zantor walked into a strip joint. Men flocked the stage, watching women tease them. Tight thongs were worn on tight bodies swinging across the railings. Money was thrown at the dancers, and a stripper by the name of Cocoa Puffs saw Zantor watching them dance. She became very intrigued by his muscle-bound arms and immediately approached him, strutting her million-dollar legs toward their table.

"Like the scenery?"

"That all depends on how much the view is."

She blushed and sat at their table. "I don't think I've ever seen your kind around here before. Where you from?"

Gazing into her eyes, Zantor said, "A place dark and dreary, where men become slaves and their souls were snatched from them."

"That sounds a little farfetched, don't you think? Human and all."

"If I prove it to you, you may not want to know me."

"Try me."

He grabbed her hand and led her into the men's room. There they kissed as he leaned her against the wall. She moaned in passion, caressing her fingers through his hair.

He then kissed her neck and yanked on her hair in a rough way. "Don't stop." Suddenly, he bit into her neck and ate her. "Hey, what the fuck are you doing, man?" Blood gushed out of her jugular vein. "This is some weird shit! Get off me!" Cocoa Puffs began to scream out in agony. Tearing her from limb to limb, her body fell to the floor as he licked his chops in satisfaction. Some guy entered the men's room and noticed her body lying in a pool of blood. Zantor waved his hand, mysteriously slamming the door from behind him, locking the guy in the restroom with him.

"Uh, I was just leaving, man." The guy tried to open the door but to no success. Zantor transformed himself from man to beast. "Please don't hurt me," the man pleaded for his life. "I didn't see nothing, man. Honest. You can have that bitch. I had her last week." Zantor immediately moved in for the kill.

There were booty-bouncing girls giving men lap dances as Zantor exited the men's room. He tapped his friend upon the shoulder to leave. A waitress passing out drinks and collecting money gazed down the floor and noticed drips of blood that led from the men's room. She slowly walked over toward the restroom door. Loud music filled the air as she slowly pushed open the door and screamed her head off. Her tray of glasses slammed onto the floor, shattering into a million pieces.

Detectives Zapetee and Reed were there at the scene, investigating. A stripper by the name of Bambi was sitting at a table, smoking, while being interrogated.

"I told you everything I know."

Detective Zapetee glanced into her eyes. "Start from the top."

"Two guys came in here at around eleven thirty p.m. It was a full house, as usual, and tips was good. You couldn't help but to notice them. They were gorgeous—I mean, strong bucks. So anyhow, Cocoa Puffs was apparently interested in one of them and proceeded to enter the men's room for, uh, you know . . ."

Detective Reed glanced over at Officer Zapatee and smirked. "Go on."

"Before I knew it, she was dead."

"That will be all for now, Bambi. Thank you."

"Before I go, can I have Cocoa's hairpiece?"

"What?"

"I would like something to remember her by, and that seems to be the only thing that she wore that I can remember. Even though she checked out in it. Strange, isn't it?"

Detectives Zapetee and Reed thought she was a complete airhead.

"Yeah." Officer Reed shook his head.

"Sure, uh, Bambi?"

"What, fellas?"

"Keep your day job, will you? It suits you just fine."

Bambi winked her eyes at both of them. "Thanks, fellas. Stop by anytime. I'll give you a discount."

Bambi left, and Detective Reed shook his head and laughed. "If she kept on talking, I would have gotten out the popcorn. That woman is a riot."

"When they were passing out brains, why didn't she stand in line? Okay, what do you suppose we do, Reed?"

"It's your call. The only thing that I would suggest is for this not to reach the media. We need more time."

"Too late."

A swarm of reporters were outside the strip joint, interviewing strippers. Bambi struck a pose before the cameras and smiled.

"So what exactly happened here, Bambi?" A microphone was placed up to her lips.

"No comment. Sorry." She walks away from the cameras. A reporter immediately stood in front of her.

DEMONS RISING RETURN OF THE DAMNED

"We got word that a homicide took place here. Is that correct?"

Bambi rubbed her eyes. "I'm sorry, but I was told not to comment on the case. Sorry." Bambi ran down an alleyway, away from the bright lights that blurred her vision. She cried about what had happened to her friend who got killed. Every window she'd passed told her a story about that person. She would hear voices in the night. A baby was crying out loud for his mother to feed him.

"Okay, okay, Mommy is here. Mommy is here, love . . ."

"Francine, where's my beer?"

"You get the hell out of here!"

Yeah, she remembered those days. Abusive relationships were common to her. She never really felt loved or had been in a good relationship with any man, so she found love in the streets. Cars would pull up to her, and tricksters would flash their money in her face. "How much?"

"Sorry, not tonight."

This guy wasn't taking no for an answer. "I said 'How much?'"

"Which part of 'I'm sorry' did you not hear?"

"Bitch!" His vehicle pulled off and left her walking. The night was cold, and Bambi would always visit Al's Diner on the corner of Smith and Lane. She'd sit at the counter and order a hot cup of coffee, crying. At times, Al would comfort her.

"What'll it be, love? The usual?"

"Al, what is wrong with me? Every time I meet a guy that I'm attracted to, he turns out to be psycho."

"Maybe you need to take things slow, Bambi. Give yourself some time to know these bumbs before you get involved," he said, handing her a cup of hot coffee.

"Maybe you're right, Al." Bambi got up from the stool and walked into the ladies' room to wipe her face. Warm tap water flowed from the faucet down into the drain. She gazed into the mirror. She realized how beautiful she really was. Bambi smiled at herself and rinsed her face. She then dried her face and proceeded to exit the ladies' room. Only this time, Al wasn't there.

"Al, Al, where are you?" He wasn't anywhere to be found. The smell of hot coffee brewed in the air. Slowly, she paced her way to get her purse, until a hand grabbed her from behind. It was Zantor with Tobias, soldiers of the Legion of the Damned. Bambi became quite frightened and shivered.

"Who are you, or should I say, what are you?"

"Where we come from, we are many. Tell me, do you believe in heaven or hell?"

"I never gave it a thought. Why?"

"You must believe in something, because if you didn't,"—he grabbed a necklace from around her neck, and she pushed his hand away—"it would be a shame to lose your soul."

"What do you want from me?"

"Oh, what I want, money can't buy."

"What have you've done to my friend Al?"

Tobias caressed her cheek with his right hand. "He's around. I want you to come with us now."

"You don't want me. I'm nothing but a worthless, cheap-for-nothing cunt!"

"And my kind of lady. Don't worry, there's plenty where you came from."

"I don't even know you!"

"In due time. I've got work for you to do." Tobias snatched her by the arm.

Father Time and Sister Claire were cuddling together on the bed in his room and laughing like two teenagers in love. Her rosy cheeks gleamed upon his shoulder as he kissed her forehead. "I'm happy right now, Time."

"I am too, ever since we met. We were like two stars that wandered off its axis into time, drifting off in space, only to collide into each other. And now that we've met, I am not willing to let you go. Even if you are a nun, I love you, Mary. I love—"

She gently placed her finger to his lips. "Sshhhh, we'll have plenty of time for that. Right now, I want to spend eternity right here with you."

Time—a man, a priest, or a beast? A love so strong bonded them together for life. Mary, a soon-to-be mother and a nun, was fortuitous to find love.

She could feel her unborn child inside her kick, and she grabbed his hand to place it on her tummy.

"Our son is kicking."

Time leaned his ear against her stomach. "How do you know it's a boy?"

"Oh, I have my instincts. He's going to be tall, dark hair, and good-looking like his father. With dreamy eyes that a woman can't resist. I shall name him . . . Jarnigan."

The power in the church went out, and the legion sat outside the chapel, waiting for Father Time.

"They're here!"

"Oh, what will we do, Time?"

"Fight!"

Father Time walked into another room that was private and transformed himself into half angel and half beast. The crucifix around his neck snapped and fell to the floor. He picked it up as it evolved into a sword. Drooling from his mouth, he became Time, avenging punishment upon demons who set out to kill him. Sister Claire unveiled herself as Marissa the Remover, a nun able to zap objects with her hands into destruction. Two urban heroes teamed up to fight injustice in America. Her white robe wrapped around her legs and arms like a skintight jumpsuit. A black cape draped behind her. She snatched the cross away from her neck as it transformed itself into a sharp sword. Father Time flew upon the windowsill and heard the howling of the wolves, only to realize that it came from the Legion of the Damned.

"They will never leave us alone, Time! Never!"

"I wish my friend Oblivion was here to join us."

"Either way, we'll have to fight without him."

"I do agree, Mary, I do agree."

Together they flew high into the air and landed onto the roofs of two vehicles. A demon came at Mary full force, gripping her from around her neck. Gasping for air, she elbowed the creature into the abdomen and knocked it off her. Another creature came at her and tried to rip her apart with its fangs. Swinging her sword, she was able to cut deep gashes across its face. Blood trickled down its jaws as she swung again and decapitated its head off. Time decapitated arms, legs, and hands into the air while the demons jumped at him. Some were kicked off, and others punched, sending them flying into parked vehicles. Others were kicked through windows. Cracked glass flew onto the seats. Father Time used martial arts, cracking ribs while punching. Sister Claire placed her hands upon their shoulders. One by one they disappeared into thin air. The few that were left flew away to warn the others.

"There will be more. What do you suppose we should do, Time? We can't kill them all."

Time slowly stepped off a parked vehicle. He had a slight limp. "I must get in touch with my friend before it is too late." Father Time's body was weak and frail. "There are too many of them to defeat. I need help to cut down the numbers."

"There is no way that you can win this fight alone, Time. You'll need my help even though I am pregnant."

"That is too much to ask of you, Mary. You'll be putting our unborn child in danger."

"God will protect him. Where's your faith, Time?"

"You're right, Mary."

She smiled. "When I'm dressed like this, I'm Marissa the Remover." Waving her hand in circles across her face, Sister Claire changed back.

"Welcome to the team, dear."

Yes, a team—a team of three marked for life. Sister Claire helped Father Time into a parked vehicle and drove him to a nearby hospital. There, the doctor's name was Dr. Boortz. Time sat up on the table, being examined. Dr. Boortz examined his breathing with a stethoscope. Time's breathing was abnormal, and he got nervous and shoved the physician away.

"Something wrong?" Dr. Boortz glanced at him.

"No. I'm sorry, Doctor, it's just that I haven't had a physical in a while. Till this day, it still makes me sort of jittery."

Dr. Boortz put away his stethoscope. "I understand. I would, however, like you to come back to my office tomorrow for further observations."

"Why? Is there something wrong?"

"Your breathing is abnormal, Time, and out of all my thirty-five years of practice, I have never encountered that type of respiratory condition before. I would like to run more tests, if you don't mind."

"There won't be a tomorrow, Doctor."

Time attempted to put on his shirt. Sister Claire assisted him from behind and smiled. They left together, holding hands under the moonlight. Their clothes were ripped in shreds, but that didn't stop them from loving each other. Slowly walking through a city park, Sister Claire immediately threw her arms around him.

"I love you to the moon and back."

"Same here. How do you feel so far?"

"Tired, I guess. Oh!"

"What's wrong?"

"I don't . . . I don't know. I felt a sharp pain in my stomach." Sister Claire leaned over, grabbing her tummy, panting. Father Time helped her over toward a nearby bench.

"Maybe we should go back to the hospital . . ."

"No, I'll be fine. Oh!" She coughed up blood. He immediately grabbed her from underneath and carried her to the emergency room.

By the time they got there, the room was crowded, and Time approached the front counter.

"Excuse me, but she's expecting, and it's an emergency. She needs to see a doctor quick."

The nurse realized that it was a nun and grinned in shame.

"Is there something funny, ma'am?"

"No. It's just . . . she's a nun, Father."

"She's also the woman I love. Please help her."

The next day, Sister Claire lay in bed, sleeping, while Father Time stayed at her side, holding her hand. The sun rose and gleamed upon her face, waking her from a very deep sleep.

"Time, I didn't know you were here."

"Did you ever think I wouldn't . . ."

"I never doubted, but it sure feels good to see you again."

"How do you feel?"

"A little weak. Did they say anything about the baby?"

"You almost lost it. You'll need to rest, Mary, and leave the fight up to us."

"I understand."

The nurse came in to take her vital signs, inserting a thermometer into her mouth. She then checked it and left the room. Sister Claire smiled at him and clutched her tummy. A legacy she carried, a legacy was due. She could feel a sudden kick inside her womb. Her unborn child was soon to be born. Father Time gazed into her eyes and smiled back at her.

CHAPTER TEN

Meredith was in class, reading, when two boys, named Reece and Sweat, ran up from behind her and yanked on her hair. They began to laugh, but she found no humor in their tactics. She immediately stood up before them.

"That wasn't funny!"

"Oh yeah? Well, what are you gonna do about it?" They began shoving her around.

"I'm . . . I'm not afraid of you."

"Sure you're not." Sweat shoved her down onto the floor. She skidded her knee as she stood up. The green emerald that Oblivion had given her was in her pocket. She never forgot the secret behind it and smiled to herself.

"What are you smiling about?"

"Yeah, what's so funny, Meredith?"

"Wouldn't you like to know?" Meredith held the precious stone behind her back.

"What is that you've got behind your back?" Reece and Sweat ran after her. Every step they took seemed like a mile.

"When I get my hands on you, Meredith, I'll kill you!"

Meredith ran into a dead end and was cornered by them. Anger was on their faces, and she tried to find a way out. The green emerald, clutched tightly in the palm of her hand, began to glow and gave her incredible strength. She had suddenly lost the fear she'd always felt inside and fought the two boys, punching and kicking them high into garbage cans and boxes that were set outside at dumpsters. The fight only lasted a few seconds, knocking both boys out unconscious. Meredith couldn't believe her eyes and smiled.

Father Time had returned at Saint Hosea, and one of his parishioners entered.

"May I have a word with you, Father?"

"Yes, how can I help you?"

A note was placed in his hand. Father Time slowly read it. "He's here."

"Who's here, Father?"

"If anyone asks for me, tell them that I will get back with them soon." Time left, getting into his vehicle, and drove off to a hotel in the heart of New York.

Rooms were booked at the Le Casa Inn. One who was once a homeless man awaited for the return of an old friend. He was standing on the patio, drinking white wine. A full moon reflected upon his skin as he paced the floor. Oblivion could suddenly sense his presence behind him.

"I knew you would return!" Oblivion turned around to face his longtime friend.

"Did you ever doubt that I would?" Father Time smiled at him.

"Now that I think of it, no."

"The legion is getting stronger. We'll need your help."

"'We?' I'm sorry, did you say 'we'?"

"The woman I love is teaming up with us, Oblivion."

"A woman . . . is she fallen, like we are?" he asked, pacing the floor. "Was she considered a condemned soul? No, I think not. We were chosen."

"Two were chosen, yes, I understood that very well, but she's different. I don't know. She's . . ."

"She's what, Time? Does she realize what you are?"

"We have a child on the way."

Oblivion found a sense of humor and laughed out loud to himself. "You are a hybrid. That child will be one too. Why would you take the time to create another? The curse has not been lifted."

"I know that, but we're in love. She's a nun."

"Before the eyes of God, you—"

"And I regret the day I laid eyes on her body, but I couldn't resist."

"You were weak. You couldn't resist the flesh, that is. How far along is she?"

"The baby is still in its early stages."

"Good, then she'll have to terminate the pregnancy."

"I won't do that. She's the mother of our child!"

"Yes, and that child is cursed! That child shall someday grow up and kill you."

"How would you know that'? You don't know her like I do." A tear came to his eye. "When the sun rose, her eyes gave me the sense of hope of wanting to go on. I felt like giving up, until she came into my life."

They came with a vengeance. Their blood ran cold as ice, tasting the hate that yearned from within. Saliva drooled from their lips. Their third eye could pierce a man's soul and cut him in half. Their screeching voices echoing, they were a legacy never to be forgotten.

Hell's angels surrounded Saint Hosea while Father Time, Oblivion, and Sister Claire were kneeling on the pew, praying. An angry crowd of demons holding swords growled. Sister Claire cried out for peace on earth as Father Time got up to embrace her in his arms. "Mary, this war is against the legion and myself. You should have stayed at the hospital."

"But I don't want to lose you, Time. I love you."

"Don't worry, you won't. We'll have to do everything we can to save the unborn child that's inside you, Mary. It's just a matter of time before they'll attack us." He gazed out of the stained glass windows of the church. The enemy sat on top of the statues. Sister Claire got up to prepare to fight, transforming her cross into a sword. She became the Remover.

Oblivion levitated off the floor. His angelic purple wings flapped in midair. Father Time entered his office and kissed his holy rosary. Time was all they had.

Millions of unsaved souls slithered through the cracks of the quake, and thousands of humans were slaughtered by the hands of the fallen. The earth shook open and released the legion. They came by numbers and never forgot the two that were chosen.

The earth was consumed by fire, and buildings crumbled, tumbling down, killing millions by the wayside. Good against evil graffiti were on the walls and churches. Tobias and his army of demons sought after the chosen, raping and pillaging the innocent that stood in their way.

Father Time and Oblivion ripped into battle and fought off their adversaries. A gut-wrenching sword fight took place, cutting them from limb to limb. The world was different. The legion had taken over and changed our lives forever. More blood was shed, and those who were sacrificed were killed for nothing. Some were taken as slaves. Others were thrown into the river to drown.

Two worlds collided against each other in search of the chosen two, who were to save mankind. A new government came as the Antichrist gave his announcement over the air waves, smiling from ear to ear.

"Who is this man?" uttered the words of a homeless man. Wars had ceased to happen as he delivered his doomed speech.

"This is a new time. This is a new day. This is a new beginning." The ignorant followed him and cheered.

The sky had suddenly cast dark clouds, causing serious winds that blew homes into the ocean. There were twisters carrying truckloads of tractor trailers, vehicles, and debris. Humans were buried alive, swallowed into the storm. Small specks of gargoyles flew from the crack of the quake. The magnificent three stood on top of the roof of the chapel, waiting—waiting for the fight to begin. When good shall reign over evil and all men shall bow before the coming of the kingdom of God.

Two gargoyles leaped and pounced on Father Time, gripping their nails into his clothing. Father Time grabbed one by the throat and crushed its bones with his bare hands. There were hundreds, thousands of them. Some with swords, knives, battle axes, and arrows. Others wore metal jousting armor with shields. Father Time impaled those with broken wings. Oblivion began punch-kicking, caving their chest cavities inward. Each force that was inflicted upon them sent them careening into the street.

The glass windshields shattered as Sister Claire began punch-kicking them into parked vehicles. The fearsome three drew blood by many. The war was on as the savaged creatures deserted the premises, leaving the wounded limping. Oblivion's wings dragged across the concrete floor. Droplets of blood oozed from his chest. Each wound engraved a shadow, a shadow of a beast whose claws scraped away his flesh. A crowd had suddenly immersed around the fearsome three while paramedics immediately rushed to their aid. A very concerned medical worker by the name of Lisa Simms checked Father Time's blood pressure.

"We just got a call that you were in some kind of trouble. What happened here, sir?" Sirens of police cars could be heard approaching from miles away.

"You wouldn't believe me if I told you," he said, limping over toward the van.

"Try me." Lisa tried taking his blood pressure.

"It's rather complicated."

Lisa smiled at him and checked his pulse. She gazed around and noticed dead corpses that weren't quite human lying on parked vehicles and destroyed in battle. She slowly paced toward one of them. Lisa bent down to touch it.

"Don't touch it!"

Its third eye made her nervous and shiver. It would just stare straight at you as though it could see you, read you. She began to stutter in disbelief.

"What . . . what . . . what exactly are they?"

Father Time limped over to her. "They're something that time forgot. What used to be an angelic angel shot down from heaven is now considered a condemned soul sent to Gehenna and never to return. So this is what it is like to sin against the Most High and to be cast out of the kingdom of heaven. That's what they are—a curse. Sounds like a myth, but it's true. I have long waited for this day to come, and now that it's here, I must finish my mission."

The juvenile detention center had bred a new breed: a rebellious child on a crusade to regain her own soul. Her street name was Cutter. She was a child known for slashing her own wrists. She was rushed into the emergency clinic on several occasions and came close to death. Cutter was released on good behavior. She'd heard about Saint Hosea and decided to pay the cathedral a visit. She was a pathetic child overshadowed by grief and destruction, whose eyes were empty and as glassy as icicles. She had a runny nose that wouldn't stop, and her skin was dry and pale. She was an unpopular kid, and anyone who knew her dreaded the sight of her.

A lonely drifter carrying a backpack walked into trouble standing on a street corner. A group of girls approached her in a rude kind of manner. "Bitch, don't you owe me some money?"

Cutter got nervous and scratched her head. She set her bag down.

"Yeah, I know you. You owe me money all right, and it's time to pay up. You know what I mean?" The other girls laughed out loud. Cutter was quiet, timid, and never spoke a word.

"Cat got your tongue, bitch?"

Cutter immediately punched the girl in her mouth, seriously chipping her front tooth. The girl yelled out loud in agony as Cutter reached into her mouth and pulled her tongue. She cut her tongue off with a sharp razor. Once the others got the message, they ran away in a hurry. The young lady fell over upon the pavement and cried. Blood ran over her bottom lip and drenched her hair.

"I am the cat." Cutter held her tongue and tossed it into a can. She reached into her pocket for a stick of gum. Cutter chewed on it and quietly grabbed her bag and walked away, whistling "Dixie." Cutter never fought fair. That was just the way she was.

The sky grew dark as the lonely child walked upon the cathedral. She had walked for miles until she got there. A dangerous mind had arrived. A menace to society, she smiled gleefully, chewing a cherry liquish candy. After entering the chapel, Cutter slowly paced her way up to the pulpit and knelt down on one knee. Her eyes were red, and she cried.

"I've been a naughty gal, and . . ." Mucus ran from her nose and saliva came from her lips as she spoke each word. "I'm sorry, but that gal had it coming."

Father Time stood behind her unnoticed. "Who are you, and who had it coming?"

"Oh, hi. Father Time? I've heard all about you," she said, standing up. "They call me Cutter. I was recently released from the detention center." She extending her hand out in friendship.

There were small traces of blood on her hand. "Cutter, that is an unusual name for a girl, don't you think?"

"Oh, believe me, Father, I've earned the reputation."

"Why are you here, and how can I help you?" He'd noticed that she wasn't your average teen. Everything she'd laid her hands on would burn. A slight smell of burned flesh engulfed the air. Father Time knew something was wrong with her, but to what degree?

"Who are you, or might I ask, what are you?" he said, clutching his crucifix in his hand.

"I've lost something very, very dear to me, and I'm hoping you can help me get it back."

"And what would that be?"

"My soul. You see, it all started five years ago. I had a real bad drug addiction. It was hard for me to kick. I was strung out on heroin, cocaine so bad that I'd find any kind of dirty needle on the streets and use it. An unclean traveler, you might say. Eating out of dumpsters, garbage cans. Stealing in order to survive. I even had sex with men to get my next fix that women would puke over. Yeah, I hated myself that much. A *monster* was too much of a word to describe it. The next step was murder. I killed a cop and almost got away with it until something or someone paid me a visit. It gave me a choice. Unfortunately, my soul was used as collateral, and I was deceived."

Father Time placed his hand on her left shoulder. "I don't think I'll be able to help you."

"Please, you must. You are my only hope."

"Do you know what you've done? Once you've lost your soul, you have lost salvation. I don't think it's possible, Cutter."

"Please, call me Janice." Janice began to sob and leaned on the edge of the seat. "I don't want to continue burning in eternal damnation. You must help me, Father, please."

"There's only one way that I know of, Janice. You want your soul back? You must fight for it and win."

"I'll do whatever it takes, Father, whatever it takes."

An aberrational child entered the house of God and found hope for tomorrow. She trembled with fear, not knowing what tomorrow will bring. Father Time allowed her stay at the church until she got on her feet. Janice entered a room behind the chapel and laid her head upon a pillow to rest. Father Time watched her as she fell to sleep, wondering how on earth this could happen to such a young child. A tear surfaced on his cheek as he left.

"We've got a long road ahead of us, Janice. A long road."

In the middle of the night, Cutter sat up and went through her pockets for a razor. She found one and started slicing her wrist open. Each time she cut herself, she felt no pain, as if her body didn't have any feelings at all. Her wrist bled slowly, but the pain wasn't there. She just wanted to feel something, but her body went numb. Her arms had shown years and years of abuse. Scars shaped like steps into her flesh.

Father Time checked in on her to see if she was okay. "Janice, are you—"

He couldn't believe his eyes. All that blood, and she was lying on it, unconscious. Father Time immediately held her in his arms and applied pressure to both her wrists by tearing a piece of cloth in half and wrapping it tight around her wrists. The blood stopped, and he prayed for her. The next morning, Janice awoke on the sofa. The sun was bright, and the hummingbirds chirped. The aroma of hot coffee was in the air. Bacon and eggs were cooking on the stove, while sweet blueberry muffins were baking in the oven.

Sister Claire carried a breakfast tray of food to her while Janice lay there. She was too weak to speak.

"Hi. Oh, no need to say anything, my dear." Sister Claire smiled at her. "You can call me Sissy, and you're?"

"Janice. Janice Starling," she said, crying over her food.

"Now, now, your eggs are fried already." They both laughed.

"You all are so nice to me, Sissy. I'm not quite use to it, that's all."

"We are good people around here, Janice. Tell me, what really brought you here?" Sister Claire sipped on a hot cup of coffee.

"All my life, there's been emptiness," she said, eating a blueberry muffin.

"What happened to you back then?"

Janice began tapping her cup with her fingers while holding it in the palm of her hands. "My daddy repeatedly raped me when I was six. He took me, and he . . . I bled for days, and my mother thought I started on my cycle. I ended up in the hospital with internal bleeding. She would call to see if I was okay and wouldn't even see me . . . They had me hooked up to IVs, and she wouldn't even take the time to visit her own daughter." Janice leaned her head over. "She didn't care!"

"I'm sorry. It must have been hard for you. Have you been back since?"

"No." Janice got up and walked toward the window. Gazing out, she saw a couple and their children eating on the patio. The two seemed happy, and their children were playing. "I know that I can never be happy like that again."

Sister Claire approached the window and placed her hand upon her shoulder.

"You mind if I ask you a question, Sissy?"

"Sure."

"You're a nun. Why are you pregnant?"

Sister Claire got nervous as Janice gently placed her hand upon her tummy. "It's a long story. You wouldn't understand if I told you."

"Nuns don't get pregnant, unless . . ." Janice glanced at her and smiled. "Do you love him?"

"More than life itself. I wouldn't have it any other way."

Janice politely set her tray upon the coffee table and went into her bag for her diary. She handed it over to Sister Claire to read. "Whenever I am down, I write about that moment. The time I felt so lonely one night or just anxious to do something that day, I'll jot it all down here."

"That's strange. Why are there blank pages here?"

"That was the night I'd lost my soul."

Sister Claire glanced at her. "I'm . . . I'm sorry to hear that. What happened, or what exactly are you going to do?"

"I'm going to get it back." Janice just sat there, sipping her coffee, while Sister Claire was in disbelief.

"What if you can't? What would you do then?"

"Then I will personally send myself to hell by taking my own life, and I won't do that unless I can save myself."

"You can't save yourself, Janice. Only God can do that. I'm shocked. When did this happen?"

"Long, long ago. I have to get it back, you know. I just have to. I can't go on like this, wondering if I'm coming or going. I just hope God will give me another chance at salvation. I heard about this man called Christ. Is he coming back someday?"

"Yes, yes he is." Sister Claire embraced her in her arms and cried. She whispered softly in her ear, "And he's coming to get his children."

CHAPTER ELEVEN

Word had got out about Cutter. The girls who were present when their leader got butchered sat around in an abandoned building, smoking weed. Geneva laughed out loud to herself, thinking—thinking about how she's going to get even when she'd catch up with Cutter. She was a roughneck born in the Bronx.

"When I see her, her ass belongs to me! Did you see what she did? And you, you all just ran like pussies. She killed a member of our family. She killed one of us, and therefore, she must die!" They cheered in anger for Janice. They cheered in hatred of the dead girl's honor. They cheered for blood. Janice was not only marked for eternity. She was marked for good, because any and everything was coming at her. The girls stood up together and slit their arms. Blood dripped upon the pavement as they pressed wound against wound. They were blood sisters at last.

They plotted a killing. Their feet stomped hard against the concrete floor. Anger pushed from their lungs. "I got this! Do you hear me? I got this!" Geneva had made her top priority on their hit list, as far as she was concerned. Cutter was dead meat.

Janice was out the next day, searching for employment. She had no skills but was a fast learner. Each joint she visited rejected her application. Time wasn't quite on her side. Finally, she had gotten her break. A sign was displayed on the trout of Joe's Diner: "Dishwasher needed. No experience required. Flexible hours. Great pay. Inquire inside."

"Hi, are you hiring?"

The owner was a sloppy, oversized man in his early forties and didn't seem to care much, by his facial expression.

"Yeah, we need a dishwasher. You wash dishes?"

"I'll wash anything you put in front of me, mister."

"You're hired! When can you start?"

Janice smiled at him. "How does tomorrow sound?"

Janice ran to the church in a hurry to inform Father Time and Sister Claire about the good news. The owner had given her a uniform and a work ID. Janice had gotten her fresh start in life, and she wasn't about to screw it up. On her way to the chapel, one of the gang members had spotted her in the area and informed the others. Instead of buzzing for someone to allow her through the gate, Janice climbed over it carefully. She ran toward the back and knocked on the door. Sister Claire answered it.

"Any luck?"

Janice smiled and laid her uniform across the table. "All right!" They both high-fived. "What's the name of the place?"

"Joe's. Joe's Diner." Janice smiled, and Sister Claire glanced over at her.

"You're happy. That's a good sign."

"I hope so, I really do. I want so bad to get it right, you know?"

Sister Claire gently rubbed her hand across Janice's hair. "I will do whatever I can to help you, Janice."

"Thank you." Janice smiled at her and proceeded toward the bathroom to take a shower. Sister Claire could hear running water. "I can't wait to tell Father Time!"

Tonight was unlike any other night. Dark forces had invaded the earth, with the motive of extermination. Only one man could help save the planet, and his name was Time, who was alone in his room, sleeping. Premonitions of a multitude of the fallen came flying down from the heavens. Father Time lay in his bed dreaming. Sweat slithered from his forehead. His head shook feverishly upon his pillow. The world had encountered a grim reality as the gargoyles taunted his mind and soul. The sound of flesh smacked into rusted nails, which stood high above rough soil. Blood trickled down from bare bodies that were considered condemned. There were loud cries from the damned who were walking, carrying burning, charred remains of the deceased. They were burying them deep into a huge pit—a never-ending nightmare with a return address. Father Time had suddenly awoken. The time was 2:00 a.m. He was restless and discouraged by that same reoccurring dream. Shaking it off wasn't easy. It was a thought that could not be forgotten.

A broken glass window was exposed. Chipped pieces of stained glass crystals reflected the color of the moon. The room was invaded by demons, and Father Time immediately jumped up and pulled on his trousers. He snatched off the crucifix from around his neck, which transformed into a caliber sword. A black cape draped across his legs as he became Time the Demon Slasher. His eyes glowed in the night, fixated on the inevitable. He was a chivalrous priest on a mission to save mankind from destruction.

"Time! Time!" The dragon beast called out his name, approached him, and laughed out loud. "You think you have time on your hands, but I will cut that short here and now!" The wind began to rapidly circulate around the room, forcing Father Time against the concrete wall, knocking the wind out of him. Lit candles tumbled onto the floor, causing a small fire.

"I won't be defeated!" Father Time was slammed against his desk, splitting it in half. The wood shed into the air. The heroic priest spat blood and held out his sword.

"God shall prevail!" The two engaged into battle. Father Time waved his armor at the creature, repeatedly slashing into its lizard flesh. The demon then lashed out at him, sending Father Time careening into the ceiling. Boldness was he who dared to die for what he believed in. The beast spat out hot, burning acid. Bolts of acid struck the priest on the chest. Father Time tried decapitating the creature's skull off. An unforeseen curse was lifted from a man once forbidden, while danger came knocking at his door. Time punch-kicked the creature, forcing it toward the open window, and finally punch-kicking it over the ledge of the windowsill.

A dozen more of the unforgiven landed on the ledge. Father Time grabbed a vial of holy water and threw it into their faces. The demons went up in flames.

"The power is in the water." He knew the secret to the umbrageous.

Father Time marked the closet door with his holy water and slept on the floor. He remembered—yes, he remembered how they laughed. That hideous laugh and how they defied God. The demons were cast out of the kingdom of heaven. They wanted to get even because our lives were spared. They won't stop until they do. The magnificent three continued to fight and stay alive—alive long enough to conquer those who were against them. There was an evil dynasty that had perished forever into the storm and God's raft to deal with. Father Time and his friends joined together in forces in hopes of destroying the demons of the damned. He exercised and practiced using his sword to cut hung cantaloupes and watermelon. Sister Claire touched objects and made them gradually disappear. Oblivion levitated off the pavement floor and used his powers to zap objects into inferno of flames.

Cutter wasn't sure what she was but soon realized that she was something—something that threw spinning razor blades into midair, slicing open pieces of raw meat. She was sharp and right on target. Injuring her target was her mission. Killing them was a game. Business at Joe's Diner began to pick up, and Joe was impressed of how fast Janice worked. He eventually gave her a raise as she became able to do more for herself.

The neighborhood punks kept an eye on her and followed her to her job. A young and troubled child was washing dishes until another entered Joe's Diner. Acne was her makeup. Cold sores were seen on her dry lips as she grinned. She was missing several teeth in her mouth. A waitress approached her.

"Hi. Cutter here?"

"Who?" the waitress said, waiting to take her order.

"Her name is Cutter."

"Never heard of her, sorry." The waitress walked away, tucking her receipts into her apron.

The youth slammed her hand down hard upon the table, got up, and rudely approached the waitress. "Look, I know she's here, and I came to deliver a message."

"Oh, and what might that be?"

"She's a dead bitch!" The girl stormed out of the diner.

The waitress got worried and hurried toward the back to speak to Janice. "Janice, when you have time, I need to have a word with you."

"Sure." Janice smiled and took off her apron. "What's up, Alice?"

"I don't mean to dip into your personal life or anything, but are you in some type of trouble or something?"

"I don't believe so. Why?" she asked, nervously biting her nails.

"Someone, or should I say something, paid you a little visit today. What she had to say was quite disturbing."

"Well, what did she say, Alice?"

"It's probably nothing. Look, whatever you do, watch your back, okay? Would you like for me to give you a lift home?"

"You don't—"

"Look, kid, you know I don't mind."

Janice exited out of the diner while they watched. Evil stood outside Joe's Diner and waited for the diner to close. Alice locked the doors and drove Janice home. There was the sound of graffiti cans spraying onto the store's windows. The juveniles broke into the diner. Glass jars, dishes, and plates shattered against the marble floor. Some girls even defecated on tables and spat on the floor.

A blue sedan pulled up in from of Saint Hosea, and Janice got out of the vehicle.

"Thanks, Alice."

"No problem, kid. You be careful, you hear? And stay out of trouble!" Alice sensed that she was in danger.

Janice smiled and walked toward the front door. She heard footsteps behind her and immediately turned around. It was Sister Claire.

"Don't worry, it's me." They entered Janice's apartment. "How was your day at work?"

"They found me," she said, packing a small bag of clothes that were hung in her closet.

"Who found you, Janice? I'm afraid I don't understand."

"I must leave before another one dies."

Sister Claire snatched her bag away. "You . . . you can't. Besides, you just got here."

"Don't you understand? If they catch me here with you, blood will be on your hands. I may not be able to control myself!" Janice's face had suddenly changed as the room got dark. A silhouette of her shadow reflected on the wall. "I will devour all their lost souls and spit them out. I am not human, neither normal. Many have crossed me in the past and felt my fury, for I am a warrior by heart. I am the Lost Soul."

Sister Mary Claire walked up to her slowly as the darkness went away and embraced her. "I will do whatever I can to help you, Janice. For you are my friend, and friends don't watch friends die."

The child inside Mary kicked, and Janice could feel it. Janice knew then that it was a very special child.

While the moon beamed upon the stars, she awoke. She was cutting and slitting her wrist with another razor. Her eyes rolled back into her head, and blood spurted out onto the sheets and pillow. Gritting her teeth so hard, it made her lips bleed. An evil grunt came from deep within her frail body. She was a child lost, trying to regain her lost soul. The bed began to shake as a cool breeze pushed strands of her hair from the side of her face. An evil force had entered her room, and the room got darker and gloomy. A chill was present in the air. She suddenly found herself talking to it.

"I hate . . . I hate you. You tricked me and took my soul. I'm going to get it back. I will. You can't have it, you bastard!"

Suddenly, books flew at the speed of light in midair, crashing into the wall. Dishes and silverware came smashing to the kitchen floor. The sofa and recliner tipped over. Something evil was approaching her bed and lifted her sheets. Her panties were ripped off, and she had found herself pinned down on her back. She began to scream and kick, but nothing was there, until she felt herself being brutally raped. Something began tearing at her flesh. The bed shook and shook until everything came to a standstill.

Her eyes were heavy with burden, and her heart was empty. Janice had gone through this before. Night after night was a different party to encounter. Trembling with fear, Janice crawled out of bed to get to the phone. Blood ran down her legs. Her lips were dry and chapped. She managed to dial Sister Claire.

"Janice, is everything all right?"

"No, I was raped—"

"What happened? Never mind that. We'll be right over."

Father Time was notified, and he immediately rushed over to her rescue. Kicking the door open, he was amazed to see what he saw.

The place was in total shambles. Janice was found lying on her back upon the rug. A bloody, pale, and frail frame stood stiff as a board. He gently raised her from the wooden floor and carried her back to the bed. Dialing 911, it wasn't long before the paramedics arrived. Then she had a slight seizure. The paramedics managed to stabilize her vital signs and get her safely to the hospital.

Hours went by, and Janice was sent to room 105. There was the sound of wheels rolling in the gurney, and Janice was still unconscious. Visions of dark forces came over her, and she couldn't move. She was trapped in a body with no chance of recovery. She thought her life was over, but she thought wrong. Sister Mary smiled upon her.

"Where . . . where am I?"

"You are in a safe place. Janice, why do you keep hurting yourself?"

"Hurting myself?"

"Yes. See." Sister Claire lifted her arms. "You are butchering your arms, why?"

"I'm headed for damnation, and there isn't a damn thing that I can do about it."

"Yes, there is. Yes, there is. You can repent."

"What?"

"Ask Jehovah God for forgiveness, and maybe, maybe he will forgive you. It may not be too late for you, Janice."

"I hate hi—"

"Jehovah God didn't do this to you, Janice. You did. Love him, as I do, and he may forgive you. You are still alive and on earth not by chance but for *a* reason."

Janice slowly raised up from the bed and started snatching needles inserted into her veins. She sat up on the edge of the bed.

"Is this my reason?" Two packs of razor blades that sat in a drawer suddenly came flying at full speed into the ceiling. "See, I'm condemned." Her eyes were flush red while her body shivered.

Sister Claire held on to her and whispered into her left ear, "And there's still a chance that you may be granted everlasting life."

"Oh, Mary." Janice sobbed, for that was the beginning of a new revolution. Janice felt abased and ashamed to talk about it.

"I want you to get well, you hear me?" Janice nodded, and Sister Claire left.

The next day at Joe's Diner, Joe and Alice sat on barstools in shock, wondering what had happened to their diner. A detective by the name of Detective Gaines questioned them at the counter, while cops took fingerprints.

"So what do you think happened?"

In a fit of rage, Joe had taken the salt shaker and threw it over the counter onto the floor. "I'll tell you what happened. It's these rug rats we're raising. You feed 'em, clothe them, and how do they repay you? This!"

Alice approached the detective and grabbed his arm. "We'll call our insurance company. Thank you, Detective Gaines."

"If you need me for anything, here's my card."

"Thank you, Detective." He left drinking a hot cup of coffee.

"We'll need to install an alarm system, Joe."

"Yeah, I know, I know. Eh, you think this had something to do with that kid we hired?"

"No, I don't think so." Alice knew that Joe was on to her.

An abused child had walked into the diner, limping. It was Janice.

"Jeez, what happened to you, kid?"

"Nothing." It was more than nothing, and Joe knew it. Alice ran over to her and helped her into the back kitchen. Stepping over broken glass, canned goods, and porcelain plates. Janice was in a daze as Alice whispered into her ear.

"We need to talk. Joe is on to you, sweetheart. You know who did this, don't you?"

"No, not exactly."

"Janice, this is serious. A cop by the name of Detective Gaines was here today, in regard of this mess here. If you know anything about this, you could be prosecuted. Anyway, what in the hell happened to you?"

"It's a long story, Alice."

"Well, in a situation like this, a long story would probably get rid of this bad headache I have."

Janice gazed around the diner and noticed the damage done to it. The gang she had encountered in the past came to mind. "I'll help you clean up this mess."

"Great. There's a broom and dustpan in the pantry. We don't want to get it too clean. Our insurance company is coming, and the least we could do is keep it halfway decent for them."

Hours had gone by before the insurance people had came and left. Janice and Alice sat down at a table to eat a bologna sandwich with chips. Joe stood behind the counter staring at Janice, wondering if he had made the right decision in hiring her. In the back of his mind, he felt that it was time to let her go. Taking off his robe, he approached them at the table.

"Look, kid, you can pick up your last check tomorrow."

"You letting me go, Joe?"

"I have no other choice, hon. I need time to think about what happened here."

"Oh, yeah, well, I had nothing to do with it." Her eyes got watery. She had finally found a job that she belonged to. "Can't you at least think about it, Joe?"

Alice liked her and smiled at her. Janice felt the same about both of them. She didn't want to lose her job.

"I'll think about it, kid, and let you know tomorrow, okay?"

"Sure." Janice politely got up from the table and wiped her mouth. Anger surfaced up from within, and getting even was her next option.

"Do you need a ride home, kid?"

"No thanks, Alice. Where I'm going, it's a scorching hot day for getting even." She left and walked out of the back of the diner.

"Now I wonder what she meant by that, Joe?"

"Beats me. I hate to be the one she's getting even with. That child looks stark crazed out of her mind."

Hell had a name, and its name was the Lost Soul. Janice slowly stumbled home on foot. She felt that she was being followed. Two of the gang members had followed her.

"Going somewhere, bitch?"

"As a matter of fact, I was." Her eyes rolled up into her head, her dry skin cracked open, and a dark shadow engulfed her presence. A deep, evil voice belched from her lungs. "You belong to me now!" Janice's thin figure levitated in thin air. Her skin was deathly pale. Sharp razor blades ejected from her jacket, slitting their face, eyes, and flesh. Janice's piercing eyes fixated on the sky above her as she spun around in circles. Blood gushed from their jugular veins as the girls screamed out in agony, dying horridly on the streets of New York.

The county coroner's had soon arrived and bagged up their severed corpses. Detective Gaines interviewed several eyewitnesses that were there.

"What exactly did you see, miss?"

"Ms. Wright." He'd written down her name in his pad.

"Yes, Ms. Wright."

"I heard a screeching noise coming from outside. So that's when I looked out to see what had happened. I'd seen this thing, or should I say person, floating in midair." Her body began to shudder from talking about the incident. "Pieces of sharp objects came flying at them."

"At who, Ms. Wright?"

"The girls that were there," an Old Woman spoke out.

"I had never seen such a sight ever!" The woman began to sob.

"That will be all, Ms. Wright. Thank you." As Detective Gaines proceeded to walk away, the old woman grabbed his shoulder. "Pardon me?"

"If I were you, I'd forget this all ever happened."

"I'm sorry, and you are?"

"Just bag up the bodies and call it day. You don't want to run into her. Besides, I know what she is, and I know what she's capable of, Detective. I saw it all."

"You saw what?" The old decrepit woman proceeded to walk away. Detective Gaines walked up to her again and grabbed her shoulder. "I'm sorry, but I never got your name."

"You never saw me. You never heard from me. We never met. Do you understand?" A strange feeling came over him as she left. It was almost as though she were afraid of something and knew more than what she was telling him. He had to speak to her, and so he followed. The old woman lived in a boarded-up, abandoned building.

A sign was posted on the building, stating that it was to be torn down. She lived in the basement. Detective Gaines peeped through a boarded-up window of a place she once called home. A hot kettle of tea was boiling on the stove, and the table was neat and clean. A cot was located in a corner, whereas what looked like a journal sat on the table.

Detective Gaines had to speak with her, and he knocked on the door. The woman folded her arms. She had a keen sense of knowing when she's being watched.

"Yes, Detective, you may come in."

"How did you know I was here?"

"When you get to be as old as I, Detective, nothing crosses your mind anymore. Would you like a cup of tea, Detective?"

"You can call me Gaines, and your name may be?"

"You call me Addie. Addie Shire."

"Well, Ms. Shire, if I'm not intruding, yes."

"Well, you've given the word intruding a whole new meaning, Detective," she said, pouring the tea into his cup.

"How long have you lived here?"

"Oh, I would say most of my adult life," she said, sipping her cup of tea. "I moved here in 1935. I got a job at Saint Hosea Presbyterian Hospital. I worked in the maternity ward. I was eager to move up in the medical field then, until I met Janice."

"You met who?"

"Janice, the young lady that you are looking for, Detective. Every time that child came in with her mother, it was the same excuses: she fell down a flight of steps or she burned herself with a pack of matches. Just one excuse after another. No one would take my word for it. I looked into the woman's eyes and saw the face of a beast. I knew she was lying. That little girl must have gone through hell. One fracture after another, I couldn't bring myself to understand why she would do a thing. That poor, defenseless, beautiful child. I cried many nights, Detective, over that, hoping that justice would be done."

"How long did you know her—the young lady that committed these crimes, of course?"

"Oh, for a long, long time, I guess. Her mother was pure evil. I cannot begin to tell you about this woman but that her mother acquired powers beyond belief. I knew then she was different."

"How different?"

"So different that she passed whatever she had onto her daughter."

Detective Gaines went up the stairway and dislodged the emergency exit door on the seventh floor. Gazing down the stairway, a number of steep steps cascaded down to the first floor. Walking down the dark hallway, a stench was in the air. He got sick to his stomach. Apartment 702 was on his left. Detective Gaines began to shiver with fear as he pushed open the squeaky door.

Inside, cobwebs covered an antique chandelier that hung from the ceiling. A small sofa sat in the middle of the floor. Holes and stains covered it. Dirty Pampers, glass, and *Reader's Digest* books were scattered upon the wooden floor. The curtains aligned against the windowsill were torn and ripped into shreds. Entering the child's bedroom, he saw a very old crib sitting in the middle of the bedroom floor. Along the walls were graffiti markings, swastikas, and biblical messages foretelling the end of time, the Antichrist, and the Revelations. A huge painting of Christ was painted on the wall. The head of thorns he'd worn had blood pouring from his flesh.

What looked like the act of a nail gun had nails impaled into an eighteenth-century doll, which sat in the corner of the crib—the crib where the accused assailant slept as an infant. The kitchen sink had broken pieces of porcelain plates. Cockroaches and rats crawled on it and the stove as Detective Gaines got further into the apartment. He stepped onto a hollow pan of the wooden floor.

Deep within the crevice of the floor was an old diary that supposedly belonged to Janice's mom. Turning the pages, he read about how it all started.

Day 1

It was the four of us, and we were all holding a séance. We sat around in a circle holding hands, smoking weed. A pentagram drawn in white chalk encircled the floor, and a lit candle. Once the party got started, strange things happened that I could not comprehend, and the lights went out.

Day 2

I chanted, and Samantha broke the circle. Something came in through the portal, something evil had entered our world, and that was when it all started.

Day 3

I'd see her at school sometimes, and it was like she was in daze. A zombielike state, she was sent home from school, and her mother had taken her to a doctor. They couldn't find a diagnosis for it. I didn't have time to see her because of my baby, Janice.

Day 4

Whatever it was made her worse. We had never seen her sick like that before. Open sores had surfaced on her skin. Her eyes were sunken in. She was drooling all the time, spitting, and blasphemy.

Day 5

Her symptoms got worse, and doctors had given Samantha less than a week to live. I went to see her one last time and asked her in private if she remembered anything about that night. Whatever entered her entered me. Samantha died that fateful night. A part of me went with her. I lived with it, grew with it, and became whatever it was.

Detective Gaines closed the diary. "Her mother was possessed."

Father Time had set up a meeting with his close friends. Oblivion, Sister Claire, and Cutter got together at the chapel. Slides were shown of their adversaries from a projector. Father Time gave the presentation.

"This here is Tiberious. He has put the hit out, while the legion has stood by awaiting the slaughter. Zantor and Tobias had left a sea of carcasses. Others missing and never found. The war has started, and we have a tough fight ahead of us. We must turn to our Father for protection and strength. We must stick together and await judgment. Christ will return soon and take his children with him. I only pray that our souls are spared when this time comes."

"When do we fight, Father Time?"

"When the earth opens and unleashes the extreme abominating plague upon us. When innocent human lives are wasted and man lies in total desperation. Only then, only then we will fight."

An unpleasant sound stemmed from the legion approaching Saint Hosea.

"They're coming! Close all the windows!"

The sound of a million bats could be heard miles away from the cathedral, their wings flapping rapidly in the cold wind. Father Time and Sister Claire gazed out of the storm window and saw people run-

ning, scurrying across the street in sheer terror. They were screaming for their lives as the condemned snatched them up by numbers,
leaving a land of carnage. Rats were squeezing themselves under the
chapel door to hide.

Sister Claire screamed, "Where are all of these rats coming
from?"

"The legion . . . the legion is here!"

Sister Claire embraced her head upon his shoulder. "I don't
want to lose you, Time."

"You won't, Mary. I want you to stay here and take care of our
unborn child."

"No, I won't. I'll do whatever it takes to keep you here with us."

"I know, my love, I know. But right now, I need . . . you're
needed here. Do you understand?"

"I understand."

The Magnificent Four sat around at the conference table, deciding on their next move.

CHAPTER TWELVE

Father Time walked toward the pulpit to pray, kneeling down on the pew before God. A statue of the crucifixion of Christ nailed to the cross hung from the ceiling. Father Time gazed at it and cried.

"I know that I haven't honored you the best that I could have, Father. Forgive me, dear God, forgive me. Praise be to you Jehovah God, and you only."

The four of them had changed into their armors and prepared for battle. Oblivion approached Father Time and knelt down beside him.

"Let's pray before we fight, my friend."

"Time, I had a dream that I would like to share with you."

"We don't have time, Oblivion. Armageddon is here."

"There wasn't any water to quench their thirst from the intense heat. Demons had scourged unsaved souls that came. The lake of fire had swallowed the cries of those who couldn't escape, and the wicked never repented."

"Sounds like hell."

"I know, and I hope to never visit that forsaken place again."

Hail the size of golf balls came crashing down upon the cathedral.

An African American president of the United States was sworn in, and the world had stopped to acknowledge his inauguration speech and to proudly welcome him. He had prepared an important message in regard of the great catastrophe to come.

"My fellow Americans, we can get through this critical ordeal together."

That was hard to believe due to the fact that soon after, there was an earthquake, which scaled 6.7 in the Richter scale. Thousands were killed and sucked up into dozens of tornadoes that hit the Northern Hemispheres, causing a mass of hurricanes, skyscrapers to collapse, and riverbanks to flood.

Gargoyles waited outside the cathedral for the Magnificent Four to return. Cutter, in the meantime, loaded up on ammunition, inserting rags into empty jars and pouring kerosene or any kind of explosive liquid into them. She had invented a plastic wristband that ejects sharp objects in midair. Sharp razor blades were inserted into it. Sister Claire rubbed her hands into warm wax in a bowl. Cutter got curious and wondered why the beast-like creatures were after them. She grabbed Sister Claire's arm and led her to a secluded area of the church.

"Sister Claire, why are those things after us? What did we do to deserve this?"

"I'm not exactly sure, but we'll get through this together. Believe me, we'll be fine."

"You say that as though we were having a cup of coffee. How could you say that? They don't look like anything of this world. Where did they come from?"

Sister Claire gazed at her in horror. "Hell, they came from hell."

"You mean to say . . ."

"Yes, Janice, that's what they are—flying demons."

Janice glanced at the floor. "Is that what I'll look like if—"

"No, don't say such words. God can forgive you."

"Those creatures are spooky looking. How do you suppose we'll fight them? They have wings."

"And we have power. Right now, I'm not even sure we can, but by the grace of God, we will win. Let's pray. Let's pray for deliverance. We wait it out. Maybe they'll leave."

Hours had gone by, and the demons never left. Some had wings, and others were dressed in brass armor, ready for combat. Father Time stood up and snatched the rosary from around his neck. Beads rolled across the floor as he transformed into Time the Demon Slayer.

A black cape draped to his ankles, and a crucifix transformed into a caliber sword.

Oblivion's skin got flush purple, and he rose up from the floor. A glare of intense light beamed upon him. Sister Claire and Cutter glanced at him and smiled. Their swords were drawn as the Magnificent Four stepped out of the church chapel. The condemned angels lashed out at them with their bare claws. Father Time impaled some. Blood gushed from their veins as he struck them with hard blows.

The lost souls continued attacking them. Sister Claire jabbed them in their faces until they disappeared. Oblivion blew fire into their eyes until they went up into an inferno. Cutter levitated in midair and spun around in circles, ejecting razor blades at them. The impact of the blades cut the creatures in pieces, which left a few demons standing.

Father Time stood before them. "I'm not stopping you." The gargoyles immediately flew away.

They never left and invaded New York City, terrorizing the citizens there. Pedestrians ran across streets and alleyways to evade them. Others were captured and devoured alive. The moon reflected the color of blood that was shed from the fallen victims. The sound of gunfire rang out loud, and the military soon rolled in their machine guns. Reporters cluttered the streets, as well as law enforcement officers. The Magnificent Four glided in the air. Their bodies levitated in a standing position. Their mission, to save the world.

The public viewed them as different. The media viewed them as heroic.

Father Time punch-kicked them into buildings and amputated their skulls. Sister Claire grabbed their horns, and they disintegrated into thin air. Oblivion blew hot flames into their eyes. Cutter sliced and diced them. A reporter by the name of Harry Reid was broadcasted on the *Hot News* station.

"Hi, I'm Harry Reid, and this is *Hot News*, coming to you live from New York. Some call them magnificent, others call them a blessing in disguise, but do we really know who they are?"

The Magnificent Four made headlines from all around the globe. The military was able to kill off the remaining gargoyles. Awaiting the contingency return of thousands, the tabloids all across America picked up on the Magnificent Four. Father Time and his friends were in hiding, avoiding the media frenzy as much as possible.

Sister Claire and the others were eating breakfast that morning. Cutter sat in her room alone, watching the tube. A reporter interviewed passersby in town.

"It was amazing. All of a sudden, there they were. The four of them fighting these unearthly creatures that came out of nowhere!"

"Oh, man, it was awesome. These demon-like monsters came down from the sky and started attacking the people on the streets. That shit was awesome, man, it was," a passerby said, laughing.

"My boy . . . my boy is missing. Have you've seen my little boy?"

One of the female gang members was interviewed, and she relayed a message to Janice over the televised news channel. "I saw you, and when we get our hands on you, it's on!"

Janice turned off the tube and thought about what she said. It was that evening that she sought out her enemies.

An initiation took place in an old school yard. A young girl named Sara Wimsley wanted to join the female gang, but putting her under the test was risky. The juveniles weren't sure about her and covered her eyes with a handkerchief. Janice ran out of the apartment, and while walking, her image had immediately changed into one of the Magnificent Four, the Lost Soul.

Back at the school yard, Sara Wimsley was led into the basement of the school, and the handkerchief was taken off. The leader paced around her.

"Are you ready?"

"Ready for what?"

"The initiation. You must take thirty licks standing. If you are left standing, you're in. If not, we have another alternative in mind."

"Bring it on!"

Five of the juveniles brutally beat her. Sara kept on fighting, but the teens never gave up. Sara kept on throwing punches at them and got restless. The girls had finally punched her down to the floor. Sara wasn't left standing, and she had a slight vision of them standing over her. Sara slowly dragged herself away from them on her elbows. The crowd got wild, banging sticks upon metal garbage cans. The girls began to kick her as she kept on sliding away from them. Suddenly, the glass windows of the school burst through on the inside. Shattered glass came flying at the teens at the speed of light, cutting into their eyes, nose, and ears.

The teens ran in all directions, leaving behind pieces of carnage. Some were amazed at what happened. Others glanced around to see what was coming. The leader got up from the concrete floor and brushed the glass out of her hair. She could see someone or something standing before her. It was the arrival of the Lost Soul. Cutter grabbed her by the throat and threw her three feet into the air, landing her into a pile of empty boxes.

"Remember me?"

The leader got up and pulled out a switchblade. The teens began to yell for her to slash Cutter. Cutter backed off and ducked every move she made. She was swinging punches at her, knocking her into the crowd. The leader got angry and slashed at her again, lacerating Cutter in the arm. Cutter got furious and ejected every razor blade from her wristband into her flesh. Blood gushed from her veins into the air. The girls got frightened and immediately ran.

The leader, left behind, was begging for her life to be spared. Cutter had decided to let her live and helped Sara up onto her feet. Sara Wimsley was thankful and smiled at her. Cutter had made a new friend.

"You okay?"

"I think so. Who or what are you anyway?"

"It doesn't matter. All that matters is that you are safe."

"How . . . how did you ever know I was here? I don't remember screaming or anything."

"Sara, you don't have to join a gang to feel special or popular in any way. All you have to do is find yourself and build on your self-esteem. Life is full of obstacles to overcome, but once you've found your niche, you'll be surprised at how many opportunities it will offer."

"Hey, just how did you know my name?"

Cutter levitated off the floor and began to fly away. "Easy. I'm the Magnificent!"

A gust of wind blew a strand of Sara's hair to the side. Sara walked away alive—alive to start a new lease on life.

The night was different this time. A hot spot named Sir Lance a' Lot drew publicity in the city of New York. A line led out the entrance of the building as the bouncer collected VIP passes at the door. The media interviewed those who were entering from outside.

"So how do you feel?"

"Fantastic!"

"Can't wait to get inside, of course."

"You bet!"

Women danced in line, prepping their hair while waiting. Men collected numbers for possible dates. Celebrities pulled up in limousines, and their chauffeurs got out to open their doors. Women dressed in sequenced gowns, and their men were in tuxedos. It was a night out on the town in glamour.

The aroma of sweet perfume was in the air, until one of the girls gazed up at the stars, pointing. The stars lit up like candles, and the moon sent specks of dark objects flying into the city: gargoyles. The people were immediately on their feet, screaming. Humans were snatched up, disappearing into the clouds. The remains of the slaughter were cast down to earth. A crowd of people stampeded on those who fell from escaping. Some landed on top of vehicles parked in the streets. Gargoyles crushed in hoods with their bare claws.

The lights flickered on and off inside the club as shadows were seen attacking those who tried to escape the massacre at the hands of the enemy. Cries of help followed bloodstained hands that reached for doorknobs. The demons devoured deceased bodies left in the streets, and word got back to Father Time and his colleagues.

"They're back," he said, checking the news clipping on the Internet.

Sister Mary Claire approached him and stood at his side. "What do you suppose we should do, Time?"

"We can't just stand by and let those people die, Mary. We have to do something. Attack mode in mission!"

Hands grabbed a hold of rosaries around their necks as the Magnificent Four transformed themselves into heroes. They levitated and flew away into the city to help those in need. When they got there, it was too late. Those who lived squalled and crawled in waste. Father Time and his friends walked over dead bodies, whose eyes were filled with sheer terror. Their insides were missing, along with their souls.

"There's nothing we can do for them now. Let's enter the building to see if there's any survivors."

Ghastly scenes were scattered upon the dance room floor, and moaning and cries filled the air. Flesh hung from their bones, and their eye sockets were exposed. Sister Mary Claire stooped down to caress the face of a young girl lying on the floor. Her guts were ripped apart, and her internal organs were missing.

Her eyes were fixated on the psychedelic ballroom light upon the ceiling as though she were looking for someone to save her. The worst was yet to come. Sister Claire placed her fingertips over her eyelids to shut them. Praying over her dead corpse, Father Time had his sword drawn for whatever may occur. Dark shadows darted across the hallway, and the four of them bravely walked toward it.

An eerie feeling came over them. Dripping sounds of water came from a room as they approached it. Hordes of deceased bodies piled on top of one another down the steps leading into a basement. Blood dripped onto a stairway leading into hell.

Father Time and the others stepped quietly over them and walked down the stairway. Oblivion began to sweat profusely from the intense heat they had encountered. Cutter extended out her wristband, ready for combat.

Once they had reached the bottom of the stairway, a loud, horrible laughter came from everywhere, the same laughter the chosen two had heard in the Garden of Eden. Pain gripped their stomachs, and the stench of odor was more than anyone could fathom. Burning, decayed flesh engulfed their nostrils. An immense object was approaching them, but they couldn't see it. Heavy footsteps shook the earth.

Cells entrapped what were once humans who were lost due to their sins. Chambers of torment were everywhere. Rats walked in filth, and trash covered the dirt. The prisoners' bony fingers reached out to grip Father Time's cape, but it wasn't in reach. The Magnificent Four was in the center of hell, and they could hear wings flapping, surrounding them. It was a trap, and the hot flames flickered. Demons.

Father Time and the others stopped walking and drew their swords in battle against the beastly creatures. The demon bat creatures flew at them at full force with their jaws open, their sharp fangs hungry for vengeance. The Magnificent Four fiercely slashed at them, ripping into their scales. Sister Claire ran and hid behind a huge boulder that stood out among the hot burning coals, protecting their unborn child from harm's way.

The beastly creatures' clipped wings slapped dirt into their faces. Father Time, Oblivion, and Cutter's flesh began to slightly burn. Oblivion pounded into them with his fist as Cutter flicked razor blades from her wristband, slitting their flesh open, wounding the demons. Father Time swung his sword viciously, instantly decapitating their skulls.

The fiery serpents clawed at his cloak, trying to tear into his flesh. Unseen forces tried to enter their bodies during the battle, but their faith kept it away. Sister Mary Claire came out, punch-kicking them, disintegrating them into dust. Thousands of unsaved souls came running at them, and the fearsome four fought them off.

The sign of the beast was stamped on their foreheads and hands. Each and every time they had killed off an evil spirit, that particular soul changed into a number of ferocious beasts. It was harder to destroy them. Soon they were outnumbered, and the Magnificent Four ran back toward the staircase steps and proceeded to run upward, escaping the madness.

Sister Claire got dizzy and suddenly passed out. Father Time caught her before she fell and carried her up the steps. They soon had made it out safely and sealed the doorway to hell, keeping the forces of evil from being released into the earth. The sound of emergency vehicles had arrived. The Magnificent Four arrived at the hospital. Sister Claire immediately went into labor.

She smiled, squeezing Father Time's hand. It was time. The baby was born. It was a beautiful, bouncing baby boy. Oblivion and Cutter sat in the waiting room, while Father Time waited in the hallway. He could hear his son crying and sobbed. Cutter and Oblivion received the good news and embraced him. The doctor came out, but he wasn't happy. He noticed the priest sitting there with his friends.

"Are you the baby's father?"

"Yes, yes I am. Is there something wrong, Doctor?"

"I'm afraid so. The good news is that you have a son. The bad news is that she went into a coma. We'll do everything we can to help her. I'm sorry."

"No!" It was a bad dream. Cutter cried and covered her face in shame. Oblivion was sad and became himself again. Father Time got angry, while Oblivion consoled him.

"Time, what she needs right now is for you to be strong. Your son needs you, and so do we."

"I tried to tell her not to—"

"I know, but that's behind you now. We can still win this. You must overcome this. Please."

"She's gone. She's—"

"She's just asleep, Time."

Janice slowly approached them. Both her wrists were slashed open. Gaping holes were exposed. Blood came from her veins.

"Oh my god!"

Father Time and Oblivion held her up. "Help! We need a doctor in here. Here!"

Morning came, and Janice had awoken to the sound of chirping birds outside her window. Oblivion was present, holding her hand.

"You okay, kid?"

"I . . . I think so. Is she okay?"

"We won't know for sure."

"I had repented, and I had a dream that she was here in this room with me, and she smiled at me, telling me that God had forgiven me, and that it was okay."

"How did she look?"

"Like . . . like an angel. She was so beautiful. I wanted so bad to thank her, but she disappeared."

"There's a whole new world out there for you, Janice. All you have to do is go out there and grab it. You're still young and beautiful. Why hurt yourself like that? Love what God has made, and before you know it, you'll love yourself."

"I want so bad to believe that."

"All you have to do is accept Christ as your Lord and Savior, and he'll accept you into the kingdom of heaven. Ask for forgiveness, and he will wipe your slate clean. I'm going to check on Father Time. I'll be back as soon as I can, okay?"

"Sure."

The prenatal care unit was full. Babies encased in tiny incubators cried, waiting to be with their mothers. Father Time went to visit his son and placed his hand upon the glass window. Nurses were gathered around his son inside the incubator. A bright light surrounded the infant child.

"Jarnigan."

The nurses smiled at him. Father Time tried to get a glimpse of him and tapped on the glass window. A nurse held him up, cuddled in her arms. Father Time smiled and went to visit Sister Claire.

She seemed peaceful lying there, like a princess waiting for her prince charming to come along and kiss her. She would then awake, but this sleep was different this time. She may never awake again. He sat beside her, holding onto her hand, praying.

"Oh, dear Jehovah God, please watch over her and my son, please." Father Time knelt on his knees and laid his head upon the sheets next to her right arm.

Cutter glanced at Oblivion and held onto his hand tighter. She suddenly became infatuated with him.

"I must go."

"So soon? Why? It's rather nice having you here. You're good company," she said, caressing his hand.

"Janice?"

"Yes?"

"Where is this leading?"

"Well, I don't know. Wherever you want it to," she said, winking her eye at him.

"Don't you think that I'm too old for you, hon?"

"I certainly hope not."

"Janice, you're a nice girl, and sexy too, but my heart is with someone else. I think about her a lot."

"She must be a lucky girl."

"As a matter of fact, when this is all over, I plan on taking her hand in marriage."

Janice looked rather disappointed and glanced over at the window. "Can I ask you a question?"

"Sure."

"Why are all the good ones taken? It seems like every guy I meet that I like likes someone else."

"You have to give yourself some time to grow up, young lady. Don't be in such a hurry to get involved so soon in life."

"Where did you get the fancy crucifix?" Emeralds and diamonds installed within the crucifix around his neck sparkled.

"I'm . . . I'm not at liberty to say. Sorry."

"It's beautiful. Looks unique too. Buy it anywhere around here?"

"Sure, if you are willing to go back in time." He left to see his friends.

The power throughout the hospital went out, and Father Time and Oblivion transformed themselves into the magnificent demon slayers. Janice got frightened and snatched the needles from her wrists and walked into the restroom. A dark cloud came from beneath the door, and she stepped out as the avenging Lost Soul. Father Time glanced over once more at Mary, and Oblivion joined him.

"How is she?"

"Fine, I guess. The doctor says she went into shock giving birth due to the loss of blood."

Mary began to come through. She was weak and drowsy. "Time, where are you, Time? I can't see you."

"I'm right here, my love."

She paused and waited for the sound of their newborn. "Where is our baby, Time?"

"Mary, I have good news. We have a son." She smiled. "He's in the prenatal care unit. He's safe. Right now, you need to keep your door locked. They're back."

"Oh my god, here in this hospital? But what about our son?"

"I need you to rest right now. Oblivion and I have this under control."

"What about me?" Cutter walked out from her room.

"Cutter!"

"What? You didn't think that I would have you kick all that ass without me, did you?"

"Good to have you back."

Loud noises came from the hallway. Doctors, nurses, and patients ran and hid. Others were slaughtered on sight. Oblivion and Cutter stayed with Sister Claire while Father Time ran to see his son. Glancing through the glass window, he didn't see his son, Jarnigan, but the other babies were visible. Fear of his son missing had kicked in. He suddenly heard a baby crying over the PA system.

"Jarnigan!"

Following the baby's cries to the front desk, his child wasn't there. He could still hear his son crying, and this time, a horrible laugh came from the PA system. Jarnigan was in the hands of the enemy. Father Time ran up the fire escape steps that led to the roof of the building. When he stepped out, thousands of demons and gargoyles sat on the ledge of the roof, glaring at him.

The leader, Tiberious, held his son in his arms, caressing his fine black hair with his claws. "Such a beautiful child. Too bad he has to die!"

"Tiberious!"

"Yes, fallen angel? You are a fallen angel, aren't you?"

"Not anymore!"

"Take your rightful place, demon!"

"Sorry, but I'm not one of you."

"I wonder what you bargained for to save your precious soul. You laughed too, Time."

"Oh, how I wish I didn't."

"You know you are one of us!"

"I wouldn't be the likes of you, Tiberious. Your kind will soon be in the past. Jehovah God is running this show now."

A battle pursued. Oblivion and Cutter joined Time in a bloody fight. Their swords amputated arms, legs, and wings. Father Time punch-kicked them off the building. The impact sent them smacking into other buildings. Their swords glowed in pitch-darkness. Capturing the movement and shadows of their enemies, danger came at full force.

Cutter casted out razor blades from her wristband into the eyes of the creatures, blinding them instantly. Father Time and his friends fought until their adversaries were cut down by numbers. Cutter grabbed Jarnigan and reentered the hospital and ran down a flight of steps. Jarnigan cried while Cutter hid inside the laundry room, locking the door. She gently placed her finger across Jarnigan's lips to quiet him. The baby eventually stopped sobbing, and Cutter laid the infant child inside a laundry basket upon clean white sheets.

Suddenly, something was forcing its way into the laundry room. The door was being kicked off its hinges.

"Leave us alone!" The baby began to cry again, and Cutter grabbed him and found an escape route. A huge air vent connected to the wall was big enough for the two. Crawling into it was easy. The door was forced open, flying into the air vent, kicking dust particles into the air. Cutter and Jarnigan were trapped inside. Sweat slithered down her forehead onto Jarnigan's face. Cutter whispered, "Don't worry, little one. I'll take care of you."

Loud footsteps thumped upon the floor. The object got closer and closer. The stench in the air made her sick, and she moved away from it. Suddenly, beastly huge eyes were staring at them. The room was dark, and Cutter wasn't sure if it could smell them out. She began to pray that it wouldn't, and the demon left.

"Cutter, where are you?" It was Oblivion, and she was happy to hear his voice.

"We're in here!"

"Are you two okay?"

"I think so. Looks like the little tike is fast asleep."

"Good. I'm going to see if I can get you two out." Oblivion grabbed the metal with his bare hands and forced the metal vent away from the wall.

"My hero."

"Yeah, something like that."

They left the room safely and went to find the child's mother. Patients were brutally attacked and killed in the hallways of the hospital, and Sister Claire crawled from underneath the bed to confront her attacker. She had transformed into the Remover, power-kicking the gargoyle off the bed and onto the floor. The beast flew into the heater. "Off the bed, creep!"

The beast got up, and its tail slapped her into the vanity mirror, shattering glass all over the floor. Sister Claire wiped the glass from her face with the back of her hand and proceeded to fight again. She immediately spun in the air like a tornado, kicking the creature into the mouth, knocking out several teeth. The evil serpent jabbed her in the jaw, sending her flying across the bed into the wall, leaving an imprint of her body. Sister Claire got up and stood her ground.

"Okay, you've had it your way. Now try it mine!"

She expressed her martial arts skills in a superb way, kickboxing it toward the window. The serpent blew fiery acid at her, missing her within inches. Sister Claire dove in midair, flipping across the bed to grab her crucifix. By the time her feet touched the floor, her crucifix had already transformed into a caliber sword.

"Come get this, you creature from hell!"

Syringes, books, and papers flew in full force at her. The demon beast used its powers to destroy her. It began to laugh so loud it shook the room. The magnificent nun swung her sword at it, trying to amputate its skull, but the ghastly beast sent even more sharp objects at her. Sister Claire got on her knees and prayed for it to disappear. "Dear Jehovah God, if you hear me now, please deliver me from this evil, please."

The room got quiet, and she slowly opened her eyes. It was gone, and she stood on her feet to leave. Oblivion and Cutter arrived. Jarnigan was still asleep while Cutter held him.

"I'll take him. Thank you, Janice." Sister Claire gently grabbed her son to hold him.

"We must go back to help Father Time."

"What's happened to him, Oblivion?"

"That's just it, I don't know. We left him up on that roof, fighting the legion."

"Oh my, we must return to help his father."

The fearsome three ran up the stairway to help Time. By the time they arrived, he was gone. The wind blew hard, and the leaves broke off its branches easily. The moon reflected the Legion of the Damned flying away, holding in captivity Time.

Father Time was under a spell and awoke from a deep sleep handcuffed to a cell. His vision was hazy, but wherever he was, it was too noisy for anyone to bear. Loud, heavy footsteps approached him, and the Leechies unlocked his handcuffs. They began beating and torturing him for an hour before taking him to their leader, shoving and pushing him in shackles. A voice spoke out in the background.

"Our superiors await you."

Time was in great pain. The cuts on his arm got infected, and the bruises on his face swelled. The Leechies put him in another cell. Bambi, the prostitute, sat in the cell next to him.

"Hi. I'm Bambi. Are you all right?"

"I think so." His lips were too swollen to speak.

"I heard them beating you. Those dogs! Hey, what are you anyway?"

"They call me Time."

"Time? Wow, you're the one I'd read about in the paper. Heavy. Why did they bring you here?"

"I'm . . . I'm a priest, and they plan on killing me. I have to find a way out of here."

"You've got that right. Who would want to spend eternity here anyway?"

"Young lady, do you realize where you are at?"

"Las Vegas?"

Time smiled. "Far from it. What did you do to get here?"

"Wow, this is one of those true confessions, right?"

"It's kinda late for it, but okay."

"I was a prostitute. I sold my body for money and eventually became an exotic dancer." One of the Leechies came into Time's cell to take him to their leaders. Bambi immediately grabbed his arm.

"Will God give me another chance, Time? I never meant for it to be this way!"

The corridors were dark and dank. Time was taken before a panel of corrupt judges dressed in dark robes that covered their faces.

"State your name, Priest."

"My name is Time, and yours?"

One of the Leechies knocked him to the floor. His lips began to bleed.

"We'll ask the questions, Priest. You just answer them."

"Where am I, and why did you bring me here?"

"I think you know why. We want you to serve Lucifer."

"I will never serve Lucifer. Do you understand me? Never!"

"Then your sentence will be death!"

Time sat in his cell for weeks before anyone came to his rescue. The Leechies came into his cell and beat him more. "Praise our god or die, Priest!"

"Then I choose death."

The Leechies left as two female witches came in behind them. They were butt naked and approached Time for an evening of sex. Time shoved them away from him as they grabbed his genitals. One tasted him, and the other kissed his chest. They pulled at his suit, and both girls caressed him all over. The resistance was harder than ever as it was two young women engaging in forbidden sex with a priest. Time got upset and immediately shoved them to the floor. He grabbed his crucifix, and it transformed itself into a sword. The girls hissed at him and tried to scratch his face with their sharp long nails. They evolved into cobras. Their tongues slithered around Time, trying to swallow him whole. Time slashed at them while the serpents snapped at him.

Trapped in a small cubicle cell with the most dangerous snakes on earth, Time swung his sword. Dicing them in small areas, blood splattered on the walls. The shackles on his feet broke as he fought off the two bitches.

CHAPTER THIRTEEN

The two witches had changed back into their normal state during death. Time could hear those who were condemned dying in the lake of fire. He waited for the Leechies to return. The dungeon door creaked open, and he slid a sharp blade beneath its throat.

"Give me your keys, demon."

The Leechie gave him his keys, and Time locked him in the cell with the other dead witches.

Sister Claire, Oblivion, and Cutter went to help those who were in need of help.

There were very few survivors. Sister Claire held the head of a dying soldier. His army jacket caught the blood oozing from his head. She prayed over his soul to be released to God, rubbing holy water onto his forehead. "The Lord is my shepherd. I shall not want. He maketh me to lie down in green pastures. He leadeth me beside the still waters." She began sobbing. "He restoreth my soul. He leadeth me in the paths of righteousness. For his name's sake." The soldier coughed up blood.

"Yeah, though I walk through the valley of the shadow of death, I will fear no evil. For thou art with me. Thy rod and thy staff. They comfort me."

He reached up to touch her face. "So beautiful," he said, choking on his own blood.

"Thou preparest a table before me in the presence of mine enemies. Thou anointest my head with oil. My cup runneth over. Surely goodness and mercy shall follow me all the days of my life, and I will dwell in the house of the Lord forever." She ran her hand through his hair. "Do you see the light?"

"Yes," he coughed.

"Go toward it. Don't be afraid."

"Thank you."

"Do you accept Jesus Christ as your savior?"

"Yes, yes I do."

She smiled at him. "God is waiting for you, Soldier. The Lord is our light and our salvation."

Cutter approached them. "Did he live?"

"No, but his soul was spared. What about the little girl you were with, is she okay?" Sister Claire got up and walked over to see her. She pressed her fingertips against her carotid artery. She was dead. Her face was pale and blue. She had taken her last breath from the hands of a monster. So young and fragile. A life cut short.

Cutter began to cry. "Her insides were sitting out. I'm sorry."

"You've done all you could, but we have to find Time before it is too late." Sister Claire gazed up at the stars. A tear fell from her eye. Fear had kicked in, and her heart felt heavy. She was worried about the possibility of losing the only love she's ever felt. Oblivion held Jarnigan in his arms. The baby was sound asleep. He smiled at the child, rubbing his back.

"Don't worry, blue eyes. We'll find your father. I have an idea where he's at. We can find him there."

Before them, Sister Claire transformed into the Remover. "Load up on all you've got. They want a fight, we'll give them a fight."

Bats flapped their wings in pitch-darkness. The magnificent three had entered the church chapel for weapons: holy water encased in water jugs, wooden crosses, and Bibles wrapped in cloth.

Time escaped the cell and found himself outside a pit. The smell of burning flesh in pits made him sick. Too weak to run from the beatings, he walked quickly to hide. The Leechies came looking for him. Huge footprints were left embedded in dirt. A predator stalked the hot, burning coals in hell. Its sound screeched the air—dinosaur.

Its name was zikisaurus, which was part human, part dinosaur. It had a domed skull. Its size in length was 115 feet, it weighed up to 100 tons, and its intelligence was average. It had an impenetrable armor that was sharp like a razor. Flesh-shredding fins ran on either side of its body. It had slashing dagger teeth capable of ripping its predator in half. It was a battle tank crushing everything in its way. The human side was a prehistoric caveman. It's target, Time.

"Where in hell did that come from?" was the question. Time knew he had so much time left. He was stranded in a world of lost hope. He ran as fast as he could, hurdling over large rocks. As he gazed up toward the black cloud, a glimmer of light gleamed upon his face. The Magnificent Four came to his rescue. The heroes levitated above him and landed safely. Sister Claire warmly walked over to him and embraced him and kissed him gently on the lips. His lips were sweet and warm. She was happy to know that he was all right but still in the presence of harm's way.

"We have to leave as soon as possible."

"What's wrong, Time?"

"That!" he said, pointing up at the zikisaurus. Cutter, Oblivion, and Sister Claire's jaws dropped, amazed to see something like that even existed. The dinosaur viciously snapped at them, while the four of them bravely fought it off, swinging their swords and splashing holy water upon it. Its eyes glowed, and its breath blew fire. The smell was enough to gag. Oblivion punch-kicked its skull, Sister Claire tried swinging her sword at its tail, Cutter ejected razor blades at its eyes, and Father Time tried sword fighting it toward an open pit of lava. Its screeching noise echoed miles away. The druids sought out the escapee and lit torches. The sign of the beast on their foreheads, their pupils were jet white, and their cracked scalps were shaved.

Time and his friends continued their holy crusade. The half-human, half-beast creature clawed at them, its flesh-eating jaws capable of devouring a boat.

"The heart! Pierce the heart!"

Time jumped, flipped, and evaded from being stepped on by the monster. The noise attracted other lost souls to attack them. The flesh on their bones was peeling, exposing their insides underneath.

Hands stretched out to apprehend them, but the Magnificent Four evaded their touch. Burned flesh walked into the fiery furnace of nowhere. A body without a mind, heart, or soul, destined for pure damnation. The dinosaur was dark and gloomy in his lair. It was a horrible and slimy serpent, coiled up on board skeletal bones that lay around it. Its fierce wind and scaly head frightened them. A wisp of smoke curled up from the dragon's nostrils. It stretched out its wings and flew away. Suddenly, the sound of wings flapping in the wind approached them. They were raging gargoyles. The enchanted priest and the others flew off as fast as they could out of the black hole of bondage. They found their way home and escaped from the deep sea of enslaved zombies and a world that will soon be forgotten.

Entering the church chapel, Father Time limped into the tub of warm bathwater, and Sister Claire wiped his forehead with a cold wet rag.

"How do you feel?"

"Not good. Are we safe for now?"

"I think so. He's beautiful, isn't he?" she said, holding their son in her arms.

Time glanced over at him and smiled. "He should be. He's mine."

Mary laughed and got up to lay their son down in his crib.

Oblivion kept an eye out for the gargoyles' return, gazing out of the window. Janice sat on the balcony of the patio, which faced the bright moon miles away into space. She shivered upon the concrete floor. The tights on her legs had runs, and her skin was as pale as a white sheet. The bottom of her eyelid was teary, bloodshot red. Anger ran deep. Vengeance was an honor to welcome. She had visions of the horror that lost, hopeless souls endured, succumbed. She could taste blood and enjoy the sweetness from whom it came from.

Oblivion walked out onto the paio, and gently placed his hand upon her shoulder. "Are you all right?"

"I lost everything, Oblivion, everything!"

"You didn't lose. I did."

"What do you mean?"

"I lost my chance of living an everlasting life in paradise. An angel seeking a way back home and not knowing quite how. Time is my chance of finding that out." He fell to his knees and began to cry.

Janice crawled over to him and passionately wrapped her arms around his neck. Their lips locked as she kissed him. It meant nothing to them at the time, but the urge was too great to overcome. The world was different. A menace had plagued the earth and was soon to return once more to finish the job.

Mary kissed Time's shoulder and leaned her cheek upon it. "I missed you, Time. I missed you so much and don't know what I would have done without you."

"We may not be able to stay here long, Mary. The church diocese will replace me soon, but in the meantime, let's enjoy the moment we have together with our son."

"I agree, Time, I agree."

Four people marked for death and destined to be together forever. Dozens of demon bats, winged creatures, flew into the sky in search of the chosen two. Two immortal lives were put on earth to make a difference, to warn the world about the coming of Christ.

Time's wounds took time to heal. The sun rose, and there was the sound of birds chirping in the morning dew. Janice awoke on a cot and ran into the bathroom. She loosened her brown hair and turned the shower knob on, having warm tap water. Gazing into the mirror, it was evident that she was changing—changing into one of those lost beasts she had seen lurking in total darkness. Her eyes were different this time, and her hairline carried strands of gray. She'd aged five years ahead of her time and began to be frightened—frightened of what she'd become. She immediately searched the bathroom cabinet and found a bottle of coloring solution and colored her hair. The warm water ran over her body as she washed her face. She felt unclean, dirty. She began scratching her back and felt small open lesions on the surface of her skin.

Janice got scared and jumped out of the shower to take a look. Her flesh was slowly deteriorating.

Sister Mary Claire walked in on her and gasped. "What . . . what is happening to you?"

"I-I'm turning into one of them things." Tears ran down her cheeks.

Sister Claire used hydrogen peroxide on cotton swabs to clean her wounds. "We'll have to get you to a doctor."

"No, I won't see one."

"Janice, you are a very sick girl. Let us help you, please."

"No one can help me, don't you understand? I don't want to be made out to be some freak!"

"You're not a freak, Janice, but you are sick. I'm afraid that if you don't get help soon, we'll probably lose you."

"The only way that I can be helped is to find the demon who made me this way, and that I will do." Janice got back into the shower and sat down in the tub. Sister Claire left her alone to herself and left the church guesthouse. She heard the door shut and closed her eyes. When she opened them, a flame flickered inside her pupils.

Time lay down onto the bed, and the news was on.

"Hi, I'm Barbara Tyler, and this is *Hot News*. No, it is not an UFO, but unidentified objects have been spotted on the radar, and the military—"

Father Time cut off the tube and dimmed the lamplight. He closed his eyes to nap. The next day was church services, and he wanted to be rested up.

Sister Claire sat in a rocking chair and kept an eye on their son, Jarnigan, nursing him from her breast.

Oblivion stood on the patio, gazing over New York City. The sound of emergency vehicles echoed in the air. They waited for their return, the return of the damned and the destruction that was inflicted upon mankind.

The winds blew heavier than ever. Trees were uprooted from the soil, and leaves cluttered the air. The sky attracted a black cloud heading toward the church chapel. People ran indoors and locked their doors. Others found shelter elsewhere.

"They're coming! Lock the doors, and pull the shades!" Sister Claire grabbed their son and hid inside the closet.

Janice got down on her knees and prayed, "Dear Jehovah God, deliver us from evil, and protect us from harm's way. Give me the strength to endure and the will to go on." The will to go on was all she'd thought about. Another fight to combat, and another day wondering if she'll ever live again. Once she stood up, the room got dark, and she transformed into Cutter, the Lost Soul Avenger.

Time and Oblivion secured the doors with locks and boarded up the windows. There was a heavy knock on the front church's door. It wasn't your ordinary knock, but it demanded someone to open it. Oblivion walked over to peep out the window.

"Don't look at it!"

"Why?"

"The evil one's returned."

"What are we to do, Time?"

"Let him knock. I must think."

"Please, we must do something!"

Time and Oblivion held their crucifix, and it transformed into swords. Glass windows were kicked in, and the fearsome two stood their guard. They hid within the church. The main door was kicked in. Wood shattered, and a fierce wind came in. Lucifer approached the podium. Christ, hanging on the crucifix, faced him.

"You came to save the whole world from destruction, but you forgot one thing: me! I know you two are here, and I will be back." He laughed and walked out of the house of the Lord. Time shivered and came from behind the podium stand. He then knelt down on his knee and prayed silently to himself, "Show me a sign, dear Jehovah God, show me!" He closed his eyes, and he opened them to another realm: the year 33 CE, Jesus of Nazareth.

Suddenly, he had visions of Christ stumbling through a mob of angry people spitting at him while he was carrying the wooden tree and the crowd was taunting him. Some were whipped, arrested for intervening. Rocks were thrown, and some shoved him to the pavement. Once he arrived at his destination, the guards crossed both his hands and feet and nailed him to the crucifix. Nails were being driven deep into his hands and feet. A crown of thorns was set on his head. The crucifix was raised high into the air for display for all to see. One of the guards cut the side of Christ's rib cage. The guards laughed and shrugged their shoulders, standing at Christ's feet. His blood dripped upon their shoulders.

"Forgive them, Lord, for they know not what they do." Other inmates who were persecuted on the crucifix next to him cried, for they too knew the truth.

A sudden earthquake erupted. Onlookers ran, terrified of what they have done. It shook the earth, the clouds darkened, and the sun disappeared. The tomb opened and released those who were once forgotten. The dead rose and walked again. Hail the size of rocks tumbled to the ground, and the rain showered the earth. Knees bowed for forgiveness of sins, and Mary Magdalene knelt at his feet to pray.

"Remember me."

Time came to his senses and rubbed his eyes. "Thank you for showing me the truth, dear God." Crossing his chest, he said, "The Father, the Son, and the Holy Ghost. Amen."

Trees were bent as though a great storm was present. The wind whistled, and Time nailed the doors to the church.

"We'll wait here. We'll fight here. Woven into legends, we were honored and feared. Where we once ruled a planet became unsurpassed. We must make them all remember. In some way, we must reveal that our spirits will live on forever, for we are warriors, and this fight is real."

Good and evil passed was on by ancestors. In a world full of hate, without hope, without reason, humans no longer acted human anymore but like soulless victims left for the slaughter. They had no conscience, no remorse—just a piece of flesh that lived with no purpose. Time saw that it was sad, watching the legion outside the church chapel. Suddenly, a dark cloud hovered over the chapel, and the rain came down harder than ever. A loud roar echoed into the night. The zikisaurus had returned once more, but this time on earth. Time and the others stayed within the church and plotted their next move. Mary was too weak to fight anymore and decided to stay with her child. Cutter and Oblivion bowed down before the huge statue. A crucifix hung on the ceiling that was displayed above the pulpit.

Horrible sounds came from the legion, who were waiting. The zikisaurus stalked the city of New York, killing anything in its path. The air force shot off rockets. The army shot at it and threw live grenades, and the navy launched missiles. The creature toppled over vehicles and destroyed buildings. Time stood in front and pointed his finger at the crucifixion statue.

"Would you die for him?"

They paused and nodded their heads.

"Yes, I will die for him," Cutter sobbed.

"Yes, I will give my life for him." Oblivion smiled.

Time grabbed his crucifix, which transformed into a caliber sword. "Good, then we'll die together."

Dying together was their fate, but God wasn't ready for them yet. The serpent dragon torched the city of New York. Time and his friends fought off the dark forces that invaded their city. Time could hear angels singing. It was one of the most beautiful sounds he'd ever heard. He paused for a moment and listened.

"Hear them? They're singing, and they are singing because the Son of God is coming back. Can't . . . can't you hear them?" Time's eyes glistened all around the sanctuary. His hands began to tremble with fear.

"Their voices are loud." Time's nose bled. "Jehovah God releases them upon us. The wicked will be removed, and good against evil will be put to the test. Wars will cease to exist, and the Son of the Father will be on the right cloud, coasting from the heavens. There will be no more sickness, famine, or tears."

Time raised his hands up toward the ceiling. "Just love."

There was a hard knock on the church chapel door, a visit from an old friend. Cutter placed her hand upon Time's shoulder and startled him. "I'm sorry, Time. There's someone here to see you."

Time glanced over at the front entrance as Oblivion welcomed the man in. What came through that door was frightening. His pupils were pale white, and his skin was extremely scarred. He was smothered in brown age spots, and his teeth were chipped and decayed. A foul odor came from his breath—the smell of a dead man walking. The old man's walk was slow. He walked with a limp, sliding on one leg. He was wearing a brown cassock.

"We meet again."

"I'm sorry, we know each other?"

"Oh, I'm afraid so. My name is Academus. You still don't remember me?"

"I'm sorry, I don't."

The old man sat down and crossed his legs. He took out his cigar pipe to smoke. "When I found you, you were wandering out in the desert. You had no clothes on or identity. A lonely wolf looking for its mother. I took you in just like you were my own. Where you came from was irrelevant. Your body was covered in blisters, deep sores. I tended to your wounds and taught you all that I knew, sending you to the best schools this country could offer, and this is how you repay me? You don't remember?"

"Academus, yes, I remember. What happened to you?"

"I was in a very bad accident, which left me crippled. The vehicle that I was in exploded upon impact. This is what's left of me."

"I'm so sorry that happened to you, my friend."

Academus got up and walked over toward Time. He stood in front of him and blew tobacco smoke into his face. "And now, you owe me."

"I owe you, I'm sorry, but you are sadly mistaken."

"You talk to your father like that?"

"The last time I checked, Jehovah God is my real father!"

"No, your real father is I, Academus! I invested my wealth into your well-being. When I found you, you had nothing!"

"And I appreciate your precious generosity, Academus."

"I left something out. When I found you, you weren't quite human. You had what looked like burned feathers hanging from your shoulder blades and, the most shocking, a tail. Like some fallen angel from heaven. Your skin was a beautiful color gold. It shined just like fourteen carat. Of course, you were only a child then. You probably don't remember all that."

Time fell to his knees and wept. "Wonder what happened to your feathers?" Time gazed up at the old geezer who used to be his earthly father. "Where are they now?"

"I took a pair of scissors, and I clipped them. I then took them and hid them away from the world. As for that tail of yours, don't worry, I left that." Time continued on weeping. "Well, now, I'm glad we'd spent this time being acquainted."

"You monster!"

"You're damn right I'm a monster. I earned that reputation. Let's not run it in the ground, shall we?" The old man put out his cigar on the wooden bench and smiled gleefully. Time glanced out the stained glass window, and the legion was gone.

"Academus, you are not welcome here, and I would like it if you left."

The old decrepit man spat in Time's face and grunted. "I made you what you are, you fallen angel from hell!"

Time glanced at him sadly and wiped his face with a handkerchief. "How did you ever find me?"

"Finding you wasn't easy. So you're a priest. Interesting. You never did acquire the taste for females."

"I have a son, Academus."

"So you managed to do that, eh. I'm a grandfather, how sweet. What is the boy's name?"

"Jarnigan."

"Who is his mother, if I may ask?"

"That doesn't concern you, Academus. Will you see Academus out, Oblivion?"

Oblivion approached the entrance doors and escorted him out quietly.

"I'll see you in."

"Believe me, Academus, hell is no place for any man."

Academus left, limping his way to his limo. The chauffeur got out to open the back passenger door. Before getting in, he glanced over at the church chapel. A tear fell from his cheek, and he smiled entering the vehicle. The wind blew hard, and Academus's hat flew off into the lawn. The limo had driven off. A hand picked up that

hat, and a man stood there, watching the vehicle leave. That man was Time. He remembered, all right—the beatings down to the unnecessary abuse he'd encountered over the years. Academus was no father to him but a past nightmare he had hoped to forget. Forgetting was the hardest, but going on with his life was easy. Sister Claire came outside, holding their son, Jarnigan, in her arms, and stood by his side.

"Who was that guy, Time?"

"No one, Mary." Time glanced at his hat, and inside was a note. The note read as follows:

I have to see you. I don't have long to live.

Pops

Time went to visit Academus, and the home felt eerie inside. A huge gate separated his home from all the others. It was an eighteenth-century home aligned with broken and missing shingles. Long green vines and moss had grown all around it. Some windows were cracked. Rats crawled across the dusty porch. Time approached the home and knocked on the front door. The butler answered it and gazed at him.

"He never told me that you were a priest."

"I suppose he didn't. Is he here?"

The butler welcomed him in and guided him to the den. "Would you like a cup of coffee?"

"No thank you." Time had seen odd African and Sahara Desert artifacts displayed on shelves across the room. He paced across the room, glancing at the pictures on the wall. They were pictures of him and his father on expeditions across the continent.

"So you came."

"How could I not? You left me a very disturbing message back there."

Academus poured wine into two wine glasses. "Would my son like a glass of wine?"

"Okay, cut the games, Academus, and tell me why you want me here!"

Academus sipped on his wine and sat on the sofa. "I'm dying."

"From the way you've lived, it's no surprise to me."

Academus laughed and coughs up a little blood onto a white handkerchief. "I tried to be a good father to you, boy."

"By locking me in the basement like a stray animal? By forcing me to eat—"

"No, by loving you, Time."

Time got up in his face. "If that's love, Academus, you have given it a whole new definition."

"Your words frighten me. You hate me, don't you?" Academus drank and smokes on his lit cigar pipe. "All I tried to do was give you everything, and I see I've failed."

"Academus, I appreciate all that you have done for me, but I cannot and will not forget the abuse that you have put me through over the years that I grew up. All my life, I have felt like nothing, until now. I have finally found my calling. I have a son now, who have two loving parents that love him."

Academus got up from the sofa and leaned into Time.

"A priest raising a child. Haven't you've broken your vows, boy? You became a priest before the eyes of God, and now this! Who is the mother, a nun?"

"Yes, yes, she is a nun, and I couldn't stop these feelings I've felt for her inside."

"Well, you little whore, you. You're just like the rest of us out here. Once you've smelt it, you never forget it. It stays up in your nose for years. You can't stop thinking about it. So every woman who crosses your path has the word *fuck* written on every ass. Yeah, you're just like the rest of us, all right, Priest?" Academus spat in a cup and burst in laughter.

"I see now why I left!"

"Time, you forget, I too practiced as a priest myself. I lost my eyesight finding you!"

"I'm nothing like you, Academus. I'll never be anything like you."

"A child born out of wedlock is a child born in sin."

"You're right, but it's also a child of God."

Academus put out his cigar. Time began to feel uncomfortable and headed for the door to leave. His black cassock flowed while exiting the home. Academus grabbed his shoulder.

"I'm sorry, boy. I'm so sorry for all that I have done to you. I hope you find it in your heart to forgive me someday."

"Forgiving you is easy, Academus. Forgetting what you've done to me is very difficult at this time."

Time continued to walk off and overheard the door slam from behind.

He whispered to himself, "In time, Academus, in time."

The earth took on another shape. The sound of wolves howled, and the leaves blew briskly in the wind. Time got into his vehicle and drove back to the church, only to confront an angry crowd outside. Protesters stood outside with signs. The signs read "Get out of our community, Priest!" Others held lit torches as though they were planning a lynching. Sister Claire and her friends kept the doors secured until Time got back. They shouted angry messages and threw rocks at the building.

"They're here because of you! Get out!"

"Demon priest, leave our community!"

The legion returned and scooped up as many humans it could find. People scattered the streets, running toward shelter. The screams made Sister Claire sick and their newborn cry. She sat down on the floor and covered her ears. Cutter and Oblivion nailed wooden boards across the doors and stained glass windows. Time scooted down in his seat, not to be seen.

The living became food for the legion. Body parts were ripped in half and thrown across the wayside. New York City streets were painted in red blood. The demon beasts tore into the citizens of New York. Decapitated bodies were thrown so many feet into the air.

A child hid beneath the vehicle, escaping the horror—a young oriental boy named Ying Wu. He'd seen his mother taken by one of the legion. His eyes sparkled while he was shivering underneath the vehicle belonging to Time. There was the sound of flesh slapping on top of the vehicle until they all left and deserted the streets once more. Ying Wu crawled from beneath the vehicle and banged on the car window. Time rolled down the window.

"Are you all right, son?"

"I think so. I have a scratch on my arm."

"I have peroxide inside. We'll take good care of it."

"There are others. Seems like everybody out here are dead, including my mama."

"They took your mother?"

"Yes, sir."

Time got out and grabbed the boy up in his arms.

As they entered the church, Oblivion secured the main door again, and Mary handed him a hot cup of coffee.

"Whose child is he?"

"He was hiding underneath my vehicle. I don't know. He claimed his mother got snatched also. What is your name, son?"

"Ying Wu. I want to go home."

"Looks like this is home, son. Sorry about your mama."

Ying Wu had vowed to avenge his mother's death. Time allowed him to stay at the chapel. Ying lay down on the cot and cried himself to sleep. Short memories of his mother kept popping up in his dreams.

"I'll always love you, little caterpillar. No matter what happens, we will always be together forever."

Memories of his parents fighting over the custody dispute came. "You've got him on the weekends, Jack. Now it's my turn!"

He thought about that same reoccurring incident that took place on the corner of Merchant Street, where he and his mother were shopping for groceries. A gargoyle abducted his mother. Visions of that tragic day repeated itself in his mind like a recorder.

"Stay alive, little caterpillar!"

"Mama!" Ying Wu reached out to help his mother escape the creature's grip.

"Please, stay alive for me!" Coughing blood, she fainted, and the gargoyle snatched her up in thin air. Trickles of blood smacked his face while Ying Wu gazed up at the sky and saw the demon beast raise his mother's helpless body into the thick clouds. A teardrop fell from his chin as he whimpered over her sudden passing.

He sat there for fifteen minutes, waiting, wishing for her return. The minutes had gone into hours sitting there. She never returned, and he realized that she wasn't coming back. He got up and wandered the streets alone, leaving behind what they had come for. Little caterpillar had seen the savage beast kill and kill again. Hidden behind a dumpster, he saw a woman murdered before his eyes, and he stayed there until the gargoyle was done and left. New York became a feasting ground for hunters claiming victims and devouring their flesh and souls. Little caterpillar wasn't sure if he would find a safe haven again but ended up at the church chapel. Something grabbed his shoulder.

As he awoke in the middle of the night, the sheets were damp from the sweat of his body. It was Sister Mary Claire.

"Would you like a glass of milk?" she said, handing him a glass of warm milk.

"Sure, thank you."

She smiled at him and sat down on a chair. "Are you all right?"

"Yes. I'm sorry. I miss my mama, that's all."

"You had a bad dream, didn't you?"

"Yeah. How did you know?" Sister Claire had transformed into a gargoyle and reached out to grab Ying Wu. Ying Wu had once more awoken in the middle of the night, panting, and no one was there. He glanced around the room, and the area was vacant from anything evil residing there. His heart beat rapidly as he slowed down to relax.

He got up and stood at the windowsill. The moon was bright, buzzing with man-eating gargoyles. His eyes gleamed and sparkled. Home was no longer home anymore. The earth had been invaded, and his only hope of survival. With his newfound friends, the Magnificents, Ying Wu had a special gift. He could see things before it happened. He had a sudden premonition of a mosquito landing on his arm. He was not sure if it would occur or not. He lifted his arm and saw the tiny insect land on it. It punctured the epidermal layer of his flesh and drank. Ying felt strange and was happy to oblige it and smiled.

Once it got done, it flew away off to its nest. It left a drop of blood sitting on his arm. A sudden urge came over him to glare at it, and he got hungry and sapoed it up. It tasted sweet, and it was that moment that he himself knew that he was changing. He removed the Band-Aid from his wound. The wound was infected.

His heart felt heavy with excitement as he pushed open the window. His eyes had evolved into a cat. His skin got hard and scaly. An animalistic growl came deep from within his lungs, and huge wings extended from his shoulder blades. He became a gargoyle.

Sister Claire entered his room unexpectedly and saw a dark shadow standing at the windowsill. She immediately put on the light switch, and the figure disappeared. She gazed around the room. Ying Wu was gone. She approached the window and yelled, "Ying Wu, Ying Wu, where are you?"

Above, on top of the church chapel's roof, sat two statues of gargoyles. Two weren't realistic. The other was Ying Wu, squatting in front of the bright moonlight, waiting for the legion to return. The sign of the beast had taken on new shape, and its name was called Implants.

Implants were tiny microchips implanted into the bloodstream, a special tracking device for humans. It was put into law in certain states for all residents of that state to get one. Law enforcement agencies, AMBER Alert, and the National Center for Missing Children from all over used the chips. Every newborn that came into the world was automatically approved for them. The world was infested by human microtechnology, and Time and his friends prayed for mankind to be spared—spared from eternal damnation and destruction. Thousands of humans voluntarily became infected. Those who did not were cast out of society, not able to eat or work. It was them who carried on God's word, and it was them who were saved.

The news media headlines exploded with Implants ad commercials and advertisements. Americans from all around became victims of a free society, a world where there were no struggles to achieve anything. All because of a tiny microchip inserted into their bloodstream, a sign of the beast. The National Director of Implants aired a commercial ad on television that reached out to millions of household Americans.

Implants Commercial

All across America, Implants has changed people's lives. You'll qualify for a new home, a car, going back to school, or even getting a business loan. Implants is a tracking device that finds you wherever you are. One visit to your doctor's office is all it takes. It's a special microchip inserted right beneath the surface of your skin. Then all you do is scan and go. There aren't any limits on what Implants has to offer. Here are some of the ways Implants works for you.

A man pulled up in his vehicle. "Come on, hop in, kid, and I'll buy you an ice cream."

"All right!" the child got off her bike and hopped into the backseat of this stranger's car.

"What's wrong with this picture? You've guessed right. This little girl was not his. In fact, he's a predator lurking on your streets. With Implants, you are monitored 24/7 on a daily basis. Implants tracks you down and your assailant too. You can rest assured with Implants, because wherever you are, Implants is there."

An obese woman was interviewed at the supermarket. She had five children. "I don't know what I would have done without my Implants. I have five children, and there is no way I could have fed them all without it." She scanned her arm at the register.

A man entered the hospital with his cane and checked in at the information desk. "Without my Implants, how am I supposed to continue my health care?" He scanned his arm at the desk.

A woman bought an SUV at the car dealership and began to drive off the lot with it. "Thanks, Implant!" Holding her arm up, numbers were inscribed on her skin.

The commercial ads ran all over the country, and Time turned off the tube. "It's the sign of the beast, and many Americans fell weak to the system. Jehovah God would have to intervene in order for the new government to overcome it."

Time and his friends were shocked at what happened to the country and sat down at a conference table to discuss it. It was a new time, a new age, and Implants was now the new wave of America.

"It's just a matter of time that the Antichrist will reveal himself to the whole world." Sister Claire gazed down at their newborn son and smiled. Jarnigan blew spit bubbles with his mouth and eventually fell fast asleep. Mary felt a sense of peace. "You haven't spent much time with your son, Time. Wouldn't you like to hold him?"

"Not right now, Mary!"

Mary felt offended and got up to leave the room with their son. Janice and Oblivion held their heads down in disbelief, while Time went after her. He followed her into a room.

"We have to talk, Time."

"I know."

"Look, I know we are living in critical times right now, but this is your son as much as mine. You are his father whether you like it or not!"

"I know, Mary, I know, and I'm sorry. When this is all over, I will find time, okay? Can't you see what's happening, sweetheart? The Messenger's prophecy is fulfilling itself. We are all affected by this."

"And our son, Jarnigan, is in the middle of this too. Our son, Time. He's all I have, and I can't . . . . I won't let him down, not now. How are we gonna fight them, Time? There are so many of them that it's almost impossible."

"Is your faith so weak that you are losing sight of God'? Jehovah God will win this, Mary. You have to hang in there a little longer, okay?" She placed their baby into Time's arms, got on her knees, and closed her eyes to pray. "Our Father, who art in heaven. Hallowed be thy name. Thy kingdom come. Thy will be done on earth as it is in heaven. Give us this day our daily bread, and forgive us our debts as we forgive our debtors. And lead us not into temptation and deliver us from evil. For thine is the kingdom and the power and the glory forever and ever. Amen. I know you are there, Jesus, and that you will never forsake us. Protect our son. Protect us."

The clouds in the sky got dark, and the thunder roared across the sky. A storm was coming, and they all went to bed. Mary laid their son down in his crib, and she slipped into a white nightgown. Time was snoring, and she got into bed to lie next to him. His tail slithered up to her head, and she giggled.

Implants were forced upon those who rejected it. Some decided to flee their homes and took refuge in the forest. The average person couldn't make a living without the chip. For those who got caught without a chip were either executed or banned from society. The journey was long and hard.

Escaping the nightmare was almost impossible to imagine. Losing your soul was inevitable. Colonies of people had moved on toward higher grounds and disappeared off the face of the earth, assuming new identities and images. Bibles were set on fire and being destroyed by the thousands. The Antichrist tried to gain control of the government, imposing ridiculous laws into order.

Thousands were damned and had to settle for the New World Order. Father Time and his colleagues stayed put and decided to fight back. Technology had advanced, and they spent money on new artillery. Others took shelter inside the church chapel. The Magnificents continued the fight until many of the Legion of the Damned were killed off by numbers. The military shot down as many of the demons that came from the storm and built fenced-in barricades to guard themselves from other attacks to come.

The demon bat gargoyles kept coming and coming. Bullets clipped off wings, and blood splattered in the air. A 5100(1)' battle took place, an Armageddon that was supposed to last for eternity. There were those who stayed at the chapel and prayed.

Time embraced her. "I now know why I fell in love with you. You're strong and beautiful. You're also the mother of my child."

The next day, Time spent time alone, knelt on the pew, and prayed. Gazing at the ceiling, he cried for salvation. A stunning bright light appeared from behind—an angel named Gabriel. His skin was like fourteen carat, and he had huge feathery wings that glittered in the night. The angelic being spoke to him.

"You must not give up the fight, Time. This war is not yet over. Jehovah God has unfinished business with the prince of evil."

"What would you like for us to do, Gabriel? We are outnumbered by the thousands."

"Continue to do the will of God, and he will be your shield."

The angel left, and Time was overjoyed and smiled. He had never seen anything so beautiful in his life and went to tell the others about his experience. Oblivion, Mary, Jarnigan, Janice, and Ying sat at the breakfast table and ate. A bowl of grits, eggs, and fish were served with a hot cup of coffee. Ying sat at the table and fumbled his food with a fork. Mary ate and fed their son in her arms. Time sat with them and made an announcement.

"I would like to make an announcement. Sister Claire and I have been seeing each other for some time now. During that time, she gave me a son." He looked into her eyes and got down on one knee. "Mary, out of all we've been through, I know in my heart that this is right. Would you marry me?" Time had taken out of his pocket a one-carat diamond ring and placed it on her finger.

She smiled. "Yes, oh yes, Time, I will marry you!" Tears ran down her cheeks as they kissed passionately before their company. "What brought this on, Time?"

"I had a visit from the angel Gabriel."

"Are you . . . are you serious, sweetheart?"

"I've never been more serious in my life, Mary. God's watching over us and doesn't want us to give up the fight."

Oblivion, Janice, and Ying congratulated the couple, while Mary stood there, amazed at what she'd heard.

They were married inside the chapel, and Janice held their son during the whole matrimony. Oblivion was their best man, Janice was their matron of honor, and Ying was the ring bearer. It so happened that a minister was present to marry us; he visited the chapel quite frequently. They smiled at each other and knew in their hearts that they belonged to each other. Their son, Jarnigan, was growing, and this was the seal to a new family.

At night, they could hear the wolves howling and rustling through the leaves and bushes. Mary checked in on Jarnigan and closed the door. Suddenly, she heard a crowd of people outside the church chapel. Gazing out the stained glass window, she could see lit wooden torches and a burning cross inserted into the lawn. It was evident that the Antichrist wanted to do away with all churches. They were wearing white sheets over their heads. They spat, threw garbage onto the lawn, and tried to climb over the entrance's gate. Time approached them, and Mary ran to his aid.

"Is there a problem?"

"Yeah, priest, you need to vacate. We're taking over this church here!"

"Is that so? May I ask why?" Mary stood at his side.

"No, you just need to follow orders!"

"I see. Who is in charge here?"

A slender tall man approached them in a business suit. "I am!" His walk was smooth, his voice was deep, and he was a strikingly good-looking guy in his forties. Time felt slightly uncomfortable as he approached the gate. He had documents and blueprints concerning the church and acted like a developer. Time remembered that face—he'd seen him before.

"I'm sorry, we haven't met. My name is Klaus Heimrich. I'm a developer. And your name is?"

"Time, and this is my lovely wife, Mary. How can we help you?"

"We have jurisdiction to shut this cathedral down, sir," he said, handing Time documents through the gate to look over.

"Who sent you here?"

"Never mind who, sir. You have three days to vacate these premises or else."

"Young man, this must be some kind of mistake. This isn't a US seal."

"That's a New World Order seal, sir."

"This land and church was founded by one of our founding fathers, young man. This can't be legal."

The Antichrist's follower got angry and tore the pages in shreds before Time and his wife. "I'll see to it that you die, Priest, and by the way, I'm not a man." He left them wondering.

"Who is Klaus Heimrich Time, and what does he want from us?"

"It wasn't long before Jehovah sent his son to save the world from destruction. For God so loved us that he gave his only begotten son to pay the debt for our sins. Klaus was the demon who gave the orders for the government to place chips in every newborn who came into our world. He will stop at nothing to have our very souls as well. He's right: A beast he is. A man he's not. He's not done with us, and his interest is shutting down every church in America. It won't be long before the Antichrist and his followers will attempt to have us all killed. In the meantime, we would have to find a safe haven for our son and then return here to protect the church."

"Where? Nowhere is safe, Time!"

"I have an aunt who lives in Jacksonville, Florida. We could go there for a while until things die down here and then return, okay? Her name is Aunt Betsy Rowens, my earthly father's sister."

"Are you two close?"

"Not really . . ."

"Then why go there?"

The crowd in front of the chapel left the burning wooden crucifix on the lawn. Oblivion and Janice ran outside the gate to dowse it out with buckets of water. Ying Wu stood over their child in his crib and smiled. Jarnigan smiled back and grabbed his fingers playfully. Suddenly, Ying Wu's fingers transformed into a beast, and the child cried out in horror. Ying Wu heard footsteps and transformed back into his normal self.

He then gave Jarnigan a ruby crystal that was tucked inside his pocket. Jarnigan gazed at it and laughed. The crystal lit up like a Christmas tree, revealing secrets of his past. Ying Wu had a tale to tell, while Jarnigan listened.

"Once upon a time, there lived a little boy named Zinsu. Zinsu was different from all his peers. He had a wish. His wish was to become whoever or whatever he wanted at any given moment. He would visit the library often and read many books on legends, dragons, demons, knights, and gargoyles. Zinsu had a fascination to be a dragon and would create wings to fly. He then had a fascination to be a knight and would dress up like one from time to time. His last wish was simple: gargoyle. He always wondered what it felt like to actually be one, to really be one, only this particular book was different. It had spells, magic, and couldn't be checked out. At midnight, Zinsu went by the library, and the doors were all locked, except one. Once inside, he immediately started searching for it and found it. It was a curse. The spell read 'Once the curse is read twice, there isn't any turning back.' Zinsu laughed. He thought it was a joke. So he read it, and—"

Sister Claire entered her child's room and lifted him to change his diapers. "Ying Wu, could you hand me the baby powder over there, please?"

"Sure." Ying Wu skipped across the open floor. His loose shoelaces were gliding across the rug, and he was wearing tinted-color eyeglasses. He was wearing a funny-colored hat. Its colors were purple, yellow, blue, and orange, touched with a farmer's denim-blue pantsuit.

Sister Claire glanced at him and giggled. "Young man, did you brush your teeth?"

Ying Wu handed her the baby powder. "No."

"You need to march back into your room, mister, and brush your teeth."

"All right." He finally felt like he was getting his life back on track. Once he got in front of the bathroom mirror, he ran warm tap water onto his hands and rubbed it into his hair, slicking his hair back. Jet-black hair was glazed over his forehead. The heat from the water fogged the mirror, so he rubbed the palm of his hand over the glass. Something or someone was watching him from behind the stall. It was tall, black, and eerie. His fear grew, and he slowly walked over to the stall to check it. He pushed the door open and noticed that no one was there.

Turning back around, there it was. A gargoyle somehow came in through an open window. It just stood there, staring him in the face. Sweat ran down the side of his face, and he shivered. The room felt cold, and all he wanted to do was get out of there in a hurry. It ran its nose across his neck and chest. Slime dribbled from its head and onto Ying Wu's face.

The fear he felt made him stiff and close his eyes. The creature backed him against the wall and blew smoke into his face. Its wings were astounding. Ying Wu trembled and slid toward the ajar door. A weird noise came from it, and Ying Wu opened his eyes, glancing back at it. The gargoyle didn't attack him and flew back out the open window. Ying Wu could hear himself breathing hard.

Sister Claire held Jarnigan in her arms, and the crystal fell upon the rug. The rock was rare and worked like a crystal ball. Visions of creatures could be seen inside it. Her eyes were fixated on it, and she bent down to grab it. "Where did this come from, young man?"

She left the room and immediately went to show it to Time. Time was standing at the windowsill, drinking a hot cup of tea.

"Time, can I have a word with you?" she said, closing the door from behind.

"Sure. What seems to be the matter?"

She handed him the rare ruby.

Time got upset and yelled at Mary. "Where did you get this?"

"Why, Time? What seems to be the problem?"

Pacing the floor, he realized that the ruby wasn't from this earth. "This rock isn't from here."

"What?"

"It's an abomination, and I don't know how else to tell you. It could have only come from one place, and it needs to be destroyed."

"I found it in Jarnigan's room. Ying Wu was the last person in his room, Time."

"Ying Wu!"

They sought out to find him. Ying Wu was found sitting in an Indian-style position, levitated over his bed. His eyes were closed while in meditation. Time and Mary walked into his room and slowly approached him.

"Who are you?"

"I am who I am." It wasn't his voice but another entity's. Time knew then that the boy's body was possessed and taken over by another being. Something was definitely different about him.

"What do you want from us?"

Ying Wu's pupil's rolled up into his head, and he began to spin around in circles. His hair follicles sunk into his scalp, balding him from above. Janice and Oblivion walked into the room and sat on another bed to watch. Thick, heavy purple smoke came from his lungs, and his veins pushed up to the surface of his skin. His fingernails grew longer than normal, and his ears extended upward. Bat wings shot out from his shoulder blades and flapped in midair, holding up his body weight.

The Magnificents gazed in horror at his disfiguration. Janice began to scream at the extreme change in him. They both got up from the beds and grabbed their crucifixes from around their necks. Their crosses immediately transformed into swords.

The demon spoke, "No need to be afraid. I'm not going to harm you."

"Why are you here?"

"I'm here to forewarn you all about the holy war that is to take place. Prepare yourselves for the coming of the great one, for he is to be on the right hand of the Father. We're living in a prophecy between good and evil . . . Jehovah will win this war, and Satan's defiance upon God isn't good. I will help you win this. I want to be your friend."

"How do we know for sure that you won't change your mind to destroy us?"

"You don't, but you can rely on me."

"Why are you using this child's body?"

"This was the only way I could reach you, Time. You had destroyed most of the legion. I had to find other avenues without fighting you."

A storm kicked in through the curtains, and Sister Claire had closed the windows from the draft coming in. Time glanced over at the window for a second. By the time he gazed back at Ying Wu, he became his normal self again. He passed out on the sheets, shivering, sweating, and shaking. Sister Claire covered his body with a blanket until he fell asleep.

"There's nothing more we can do for him, Time."

"I know, but in the meantime, we need to keep him at close watch."

Tree branches could be seen flying into vehicles and streets, and stray dogs ran into abandoned homes. Human voices whispered in the night. The clouds pushed across the sky. Janice stayed in the john, holding a razor against her wrist, deciding whether she should end her life or not. Oblivion and Sister Claire sat in the room with Jarnigan while Time tied Ying Wu down onto the bedpost.

Late at night, Ying Wu furiously shook the bedpost, trying to free himself. Janice slept on the closet floor. Oblivion had walked into her room and found her. An unused razor blade sat next to her arm. He carried her to the bed and laid her down. Janice woke up, staring him in his sexy eyes. Oblivion attempted to walk away as she jumped up from the mattress to kiss him. He gently pulled away.

"I'm saving myself for someone, Janice. I'm sorry."

"You don't want me? Look at me. Most guys would kill to have a chick like me in bed with them."

"Maybe, but not this one." He left her.

The anger she felt inside made her sick. She wondered what the woman looked like or was like intimately. While Oblivion slept, Janice snooped through his wallet and found the other woman's address. She decided to invite her to the church.

Hi, love.

Missed you a lot, and would love to see you again. How's the kid? I hope everyone is fine. The world is in chaos, and my friends and I are doing everything we can to save the human race. I'm

MELVINA HAWKINS-PATTERSON

staying at Saint Hosea Cathedral in New York. If
you have time, come and see me, okay?"

Love,

Oblivion

She had written the letter short and sweet.

The next day, Meredith ran out to the mailbox to pick up the
mail. Shuffling through the letters, she saw his envelope and was
extremely excited. It was addressed to her mother. She ran into the
house and gave it to her.

When school let out, Regis waited outside for Meredith, deep
emotions of hatred shown on his forehead. Meredith came out chat-
ting and laughed with a few classmates. Her best friend, Alisha, was
present.

"Jeez, Meredith, how did you get so strong?"

"Yeah, Meredith, I've never known you to fight."

"You put the fear of God in him, gal. He knows not to mess
with you now."

Meredith smiled and tightened the straps on her book bag. It
was fall, and the leaves sprung off the branches of the trees. She took
out the rare crystal from her pocket to look at it once more.

"Hey, where did you get that?"

"A friend gave it to me. Isn't it beautiful?"

"A gem. You want to sell it?"

"Are you kidding? There's a story behind it. The story is whosoever claims the emerald stone claims the world beyond its wildest
dreams."

Regis was hiding behind an oak tree and overheard them
speaking.

"Wow, I wish it were mine. Anyway, your mother picking you
up?"

"Yeah, see you tomorrow, guys!"

"You get any stronger, I'll have to be your agent." Alisha's mom
pulled up in her Lexus, and she ran toward it.

"Bye, Alisha!" Meredith sat on the concrete steps, waiting. Regis had suddenly appeared out of the blue and stood over her head holding a brick, until her mother pulled up in her Jeep. He immediately vanished in thin air. She ran to her mother's vehicle and got in. Her mother sped off down the road.

"How was school today, kiddo?"

"It was fine. I had trouble out of one student though."

"Oh, what happened?"

"There's this boy . . ."

"Oh, a boy. What's his name?"

"Regis, but there's only one problem: we're not friends, Mom. In fact, I think he hates me."

"Now why would anyone want to hate you, Meredith? You have the most likeable personality I've ever seen, if I might say so myself. Because you are my daughter, I would know."

"Thanks, Mom, but this boy gives me the serious creeps." Meredith chewed on a cherry liquish candy.

"Okay, then I'll go by the school tomorrow and speak to your teacher. We'll get to the bottom of this, okay?"

Meredith reached over from the passenger side and kissed her mom on the cheek. "Thanks, Mom. You mind sharing with me on what your friend has written?"

The two of them were happy to know that Oblivion wanted to see Meredith's mother. Julie smiled and had driven by a small restaurant in the suburbs. Meredith glanced at her books and decided to read a little. Another storm was coming, and Julie had turned on the radio, turning up the volume.

"Hail the size of golf balls and heavy rain will head your way. A funnel has been spotted. We urge you to stay indoors or seek immediate shelter due to dangerous lightning and thunderstorms in the forecast."

"Sounds serious, huh?"

"Think we ought to head home, Mom. We can always come back some other time."

"Maybe you're right."

Julie had taken the expressway home. The storm brought in extremely heavy rain. Hail plummeted from the sky and onto the Jeep. Julie became afraid and parked her vehicle along the side of the interstate. Dirt and debris blew into the windshield. Julie turned on the window wipers, and both pieces of metal broke off. Dangerous winds sent them flying deep into the woods.

Tornadoes are the ultimate manifestation of extreme weather. Julie and Meredith had seen a funnel farther out in the area, and they immediately got out of the vehicle.

"We need to find a ditch!"

Large tree trunks and trash flew past them. Rabbits, squirrels, and birds ran and flew in the opposite direction. Julie and Meredith found a ditch, and Julie covered her daughter's body by getting on top. The fear was intense and frightening. The severe storm sounded like a freight train was heading their way. Meredith cried out for help, and the earth shook from beneath them. Julie whispered in her daughter's ear, "If I never told you, then I'm saying it now. I love you, and I always will, no matter what happens."

"I love you too, Mom."

The sky got dark, and the storm passed over.

The tornado ripped through the heart of the forest, killing thirty residents. The storm was deadly, and the area was densely populated with poorly constructed housing and buildings. Devastating hail fell from the sky, destroying vehicles escaping the severe storm.

"Mom, Mom, are you all right?"

Meredith pushed up from the wet soil, and her mother wasn't moving. She felt for her pulse, and she didn't have any, nor was she breathing. She then tried giving her cardiopulmonary resuscitation. Her reflexes were weak, and she wasn't responding.

"Mom?"

A flash flood occurred, and Meredith tried to awaken her mother, with no luck. She remembered the amulet and placed it into her mother's hand, closing her fingers tight over the stone. The stone had suddenly lit up like fire. Her mother's body began to swiftly shiver and shake. Meredith checked her pulse again, and she was alive and well. The sun came out, and Julie's eyes slowly opened to a new day. Meredith had taken the stone away from her and placed it back into her pocket.

"You all right?"

"I think so, sweetheart."

Meredith hugged her tight. As she lifted her head, she could hear birds chirping. When she glanced over at the vehicle, the Jeep was totaled beyond recognition.

"Well, there's our ride home."

"Glad to have you back, Mom."

"Back? I never left."

Meredith figured she didn't know that she was deceased a while ago and decided to keep it to herself. The power of the amulet had wiped out her memory. Julie got up and smacked the dirt away from her slacks. She felt a little dizzy and stumbled while walking, but Meredith held her up. They had passed by uprooted and bent trees on the road. Flies were devouring dead carcasses. An antique baby doll lied near a tire. An elderly couple was holding each other up with tree limbs. They limped along the side of the road.

"You okay, sweetheart?"

"I think so, Mom."

A little boy at the age of eight walked down the expressway, searching for his parents. Meredith and Julie immediately noticed that he was alone and offered him help.

"Hi. Lost?"

"I can't find my parents. I think they got lost during the storm."

Meredith quickly glanced at her mother. "I know what you mean. You've got a cell phone?"

"Why? I'm not a tweeter!"

"You mean Twitter."

"What's your name?"

"Brandon. What's yours?"

"Meredith, and this is my mother, Julie."

"Nice to meet you, ma'am," he said, wiping his watery eyes.

"I know how you must feel, Brandon. Would you like to come with us? Maybe we'll find your parents for you."

"Sure, thanks!"

It was a long walk, and Brandon's parents were never seen. They'd walked for miles, and the sun beamed down upon them. An old, abandoned house sat off the side of the road. Julie, Meredith, and Brandon ran toward it. Julie banged hard on the door, and no one answered. She then checked the windows and found one cracked open. Pushing up on the ajar window, they both crawled through it and checked the phone lines. There wasn't any dial tone. Julie and the kids walked through the house. One room was a child's room. Toys were scattered all over.

"Now this is my kind of room, Brandon. What about you?"

"Mine too."

"Why don't you two stay here while I search the whole house, okay?"

Brandon, wearing a baseball mitt, tossed up a baseball. Meredith tried on a pretty hat, standing in front of a floor mirror. "Okay!"

Cobwebs cornered the ceiling walls. Julie tried putting on the lights, but all the power throughout the house was out. Rats ran across the hallway steps, and Julie had walked into the restroom to use it, stocking up on toothpaste, toilet tissue, and unused toothbrushes. Sitting down onto the commode, she had finished and reached for the toilet tissue. On it was a huge tarantula gently crawling up the tissue. Julie had reached for the tissue and noticed it. Shaking it uncontrollably off her hand, she immediately jumped up from the commode seat and pulled up her panties. A slight noise was coming from the kitchen, and Julie walked over toward it. There, baby raccoons climbed over the kitchen counter, eating scraps from the top of the stove. Julie checked the cabinets for food and stuffed the pockets on her jacket. She laughed and proceeded to search the home.

A damp, moldy smell engulfed the air as she slowly eased the place out. Another smell captured her attention as she opened the doorway that led to the cellar. Something was feeding off something in the basement. Julie found a candle and lit it. Stepping down into the basement, she had found the couple that lived there. The family dogs were feeding on their deceased bodies. The tornado sent glass from the window at them full force, killing them both on impact.

Julie closed her mouth from regurgitating and ran up the steps to look in on the kids. She also checked the closets for sleeping items. Meredith and Brandon joyfully played cops and robbers. Make-believe bullets flew at them in a fictional crime fight.

"Come on, we're leaving!"

"But we just got here."

She grabbed both their hands and lead them to the front door. "I know, sweetheart, but we can't stay here, okay?"

"I'm hungry."

"Me too."

Julie glanced around her surroundings. "There should be a creek not too far from here. We can check it for crawfish."

"Yuck. I hate crawfish!"

"What's a crawfish?"

"Don't worry, I have food on me." She disclosed canned goods, crackers, three cans of sardines, chocolate bars, marshmallows, bread, and peanut butter. "I also found these: three sleeping bags, back-packs, and a small tent."

The journey home was longer than what they expected. They were searching for fish in remote areas and finding crawfish to cook. They built a small campfire in the woods and lay down in their sleeping bags under the stars, singing. Julie had finally found happiness in the comfort of Brandon.

"Brandon, I always wanted a son named Brandon. I'm so sorry for your loss, sweetheart. I wish I could help, but I can't. After I had Meredith, the doctor told me that I could no longer have any more children. I wanted a son, but he gave me a beautiful little girl that I shall always cherish. Then suddenly a storm came, and there you were, in the midst of a catastrophe. In a way I'm sad but sorta happy." She turned to face him. "I would love to be your mother if you gave me a chance, Brandon. I think God brought us together for a purpose, don't you think?"

Brandon embraced her tight in his arms and smiled. The next day, they hiked up cliffs and mountains, crossing over streams and ponds. Hours gone by, and Julie had seen an abandoned vehicle covered up in hay in the pastures. Cows, sheep, and horses were grazing in the vicinity.

"Okay, we've got company. When I count to three, I want all of us to jump out. One . . . two . . . three!" The doors swung open, and they leaped out onto the hay. A rattlesnake eventually slithered its way out of the vehicle and disappeared. Julie and the kids jumped back into the car and locked the doors. She grabbed two wires and connected them together.

"Here's nothing," she said, then the vehicle started. "All right, we've got a ride home!"

"Go, Mom!" It wasn't much, but it got them on the road home.

At the chapel, Janice polished her toenails and peeped out of the boarded-up window. Oblivion meditated in midair. Sister Claire knelt down on the pew in the sanctuary, praying, while Time stood out on the balcony, staring at the bright blue sky. He paced the floor continuously until he received a message from God. He was thinking to himself about the future of this country and what lay ahead. His black cassock blew in the cool breeze. He could feel the warm sun penetrate his skin as he gazed down upon the city. Most of the residents of New York were scanning their arms and hands to purchase items and enter facilities. Sadness filled his heart as a new nation was born into turmoil.

Atheists protested on the streets, banning Holy Bibles from churches, libraries, and any other organization teaching the word of Jehovah God. Implants became universal, and they set up blood drives across the nation, implanting chips into the young and old. Time cried as he watched children stand in line with their parents to have chips injected into their bloodstream. Missing children around the world were found in ditches, landfills, and sometimes in pieces. The chips monitored their wherever they were about. Some chips were designed for destruction. Humans were called out by numeral chips instead of names. If a chip betrayed the Antichrists, cyanide would automatically be released into the bloodstream, terminating its traitors on spot.

The Magnificents stayed put and shared the Word with whoever wanted to stay in the realm of God and learn his Word. Time and his friends walked the streets, passing out fliers and literature. The Antichrist's followers followed them and monitored their actions on camera.

For those who wanted to follow Jehovah and got caught were tortured beyond recognition and sometimes killed. The Magnificents rescued others in the line of fire, and for those who weren't spared, died, praying on their knees. Churches were destroyed, and more victims fell by the wayside. Time was a target, and saving the chapel was more difficult than he could imagine. The chaplain pounded on the chapel door, and Janice opened it.

"Father Time, boy, am I glad to see you. It's just a matter of time that this here cathedral will be under attack!"

"They want me, not the church, Chaplain."

"How are you so sure, Father? New World Order has been enforced upon the world!"

"Have you lost faith?"

"No, I haven't, but if you don't . . ."

Time never lost faith and continued his crusade saving mankind against infliction. The main monitoring station was located in the outskirts of New York, keeping track of the citizens of that particular state. Armed guards walked along the fenced-in facility. The chief's name was Jake Orsell.

"Chip number 30986 is apprehended. When you receive the okay, terminate him."

"Yes, sir."

"Chip number 01563 has been found alive?"

"I'm afraid not, sir."

The Magnificents' plan was on sabotaging the center and destroying its records and everything in it. The guards who were there were like clones. Their jobs were to follow orders and not ask questions. They were expendable humans without a reason to live. Time knocked out all the power to the facility. Oblivion and Cutter flew over the fence. The motion alarm system automatically checked the area for trespassers, but there was no sign of them on the site. Time kicked a chained door in with one powerful kick, knocking the door off its hinges. The chain flew into a glass door, shattering it in pieces. The alarm sounded loud, and the armed guards searched the area.

"What seems to be the problem, chip number 28579."

"Sir, seems like we have company, sir!"

Chief Orsell pulled out his pistol. "If I'm not back in twenty minutes, call our leader immediately to have my chip terminated."

"Yes, sir!"

Time and his friends slowly walked through the corridors of the hallway. They split up, and Time went into a room containing files. Inside was personal information describing people who were next in line to be chipped. One file had his son's name on it, Jarnigan. When he opened it, an infant picture of him was inside. He clenched his fist in anger.

"This is war!"

Cutter went into an empty lab where they make the chips. There, she encountered a roster of unused numbered chips. There were millions of chips lodged in tiny plastic vials. Oblivion discovered a place where they keep their lab rats—captured humans, those who either refused or had given unto temptation. There were those who were behind cells, dying to be freed. His body temperature lit up like a hot, burning furnace, melting steel metal. Oblivion placed his hand upon the cells and released them. The people were appreciative and overjoyed and embraced him. He then led them quietly out of the room, down the emergency steps, and out of the entrance they came in.

Guards came down hallways with guard dogs sniffing out every possible lead they could find. Cutter toppled them over onto the floor, took out a small can of kerosene, and set them all on fire. She just stood there staring through the flames. The fire set off the water sprinklers throughout the building. Cutter managed to get out safely while Time stayed behind. Chief Orsell saw Time's shadow in the hallway and pointed his weapon at him.

"Well, well, well, what do we have here? Batman, I presume?"

"My name is Time, Demon Slayer!"

Chief Orsell laughed at him. "Demon Slayer? You really think that you can kill a demon?"

"I'll take my chances. You see, I don't like your kind. The world would be better off without humans like you."

"Oh, we know each other?"

"No, but you are behind the destruction of every child who wishes to see the face of God. Those chips are the sign of the beast. I was sent here to destroy them, and you too, Chief Orsell."

"Have you've ever swallowed a bullet, Time? Because when I'm through with you, you'll wish you had."

The two of them paced the hallway in circles. Time kicked the weapon from his fingers onto the marble floor. Chief Orsell threw a couple of quick punches and missed. Time blocked his moves and kicked him into a glass case. Glass shattered as Chief Orsell slammed into the wall. Chief Orsell got up, wiping his bleeding mouth.

"This fight isn't over yet!" The chief punched Time in the jaw and stomach. Time punch-kicked him over the information desk, into a case of medical supplies. Chief Orsell shook off unconsciousness and got up, holding a syringe.

"I'm going to chip you, Priest!" The crazed man began viciously swinging the syringe at him. Time avoided the needle by ducking, jumping, and flipping. Time managed to grab the syringe while Chief Orsell held it and jabbed it into his own eye. The syringe hung out from his eye socket. Blood trickled down the chief's face, and he fell to the floor. Time stepped over his corpse and proceeded out of the building. While leaving the building, the guard dogs ran after him and leaped high in midair at Time. Time shook them away from his arms while the beasts bit deep into his flesh. The dogs strenuously tugged him to the floor but couldn't. Time stood still and closed his eyes and spun in circles at high speed. The animals rapidly spun off him and slammed at full speed into the walls. It killed the wild beasts on impact. Time's friends grabbed both sides of his arms and helped him out of the building.

"I'll be okay. Are you?"

Cutter and Oblivion smiled at him. "You know we will. Let's go home, Time."

At the chapel, there was a loud knock at the door. The Magnificents had made it home safe and sound. Oblivion and Janice held Time up to take a look at his wounds.

"Is it serious?"

Sister Claire bandaged his wounds with hydrogen peroxide and gauze. "You'll live. We may need more ammunition, Time. I have a feeling they'll be back. We'll have to isolate our son from society just until this blows over."

"I know, but in the meantime, we'll have to protect the church. This is a place of worship. I can't turn my back on the church, and I can't turn my back on God. Prophecy is fulfilling itself. The sign of the beast has risen. We have to stay strong. We have to stay tight. A rain of evil is upon us, and this church is all we have."

"Time, Jarnigan is all we have too. Don't let him down, please."

"As long as warm blood runs through my veins, I will help Jehovah God complete his mission."

"And I too, Time, I too."

The night air was warm, and Time went to lay down in bed next to his wife. A gecko ran across the patio's handrail. The lizard suddenly vanished under a foot—something scaly and huge with long nails. It stood five feet tall with wide batty wings. Its pupils were as jet white as the moon, and it had lesions all over its face. Its teeth was badly decayed.

There were more than one demon. They hopped from the handrail to the patio floor. Some walked like decrepit old women, and others like soldiers. They were angry. Vengeance ran through their veins, and the taste of death was sweet. Dominated lost souls had entered our world, seeking Time the Demon Slayer. Time and his wife slept peacefully. He dreamt of Pilate.

"Who is this messiah they call Jesus?"

"He's in Bethlehem, my lord."

"I want you to find him and bring him to me!"

Time awoke to a loud noise in the middle of the night. He sat up in bed and gazed at the window. He noticed that it was ajar. Heavy footsteps slightly shook the floor. Time immediately went into the restroom and came back out as the Demon Slayer. He hid behind the bedroom door until the creatures passed. Damned and blinded, the demons could smell him out and walked into the room. Sniffing the room out, Time drew his sword slowly upward while Mary slept quietly under the sheets. The creatures never even knew she was there. They left. Time swiftly swung his sword at it and decapitated its skull. Just before the creature fell, Time grabbed his son from it and placed him back into his crib.

The child was still sleep and never budged. Something stood behind him, breathing hard. Time could feel its hot, warm breath, and the odor from its mouth was intense. Time immediately covered his son with a blanket and turned around to face his enemy.

"Hi, Time, remember me?"

"How could I forget? What exactly do you want, Satan?"

"I want time. Can you give me that? I want what should have been mine. Your soul, Priest, and all of your followers. You cheated me, and now it's time to pay!"

"The only thing that I'm going to give you is a hard time, beast." Time closed his eyes. "Get behind me, Satan, in the name of Jesus Christ!" By the time he opened his eyes, the enemy was gone. Time searched the whole church, and it was safe again.

She awoke to a soft touch, grabbed his hand to kiss it, and slowly rolled back over to passionately kiss him. His hunger filled her inside as he pushed her against the sheets. She grabbed the bed railing. The rush was a ride to remember.

The next morning, Sister Claire was in the shower, bathing herself. The aroma of hot coffee was in the air as she got out and wrapped a towel around herself. Stepping out onto the patio, she inhaled the fresh air. Father Time was in the chapel, praying.

"Hail Mary, full of grace. Blessed art thou among women. Blessed is the fruit of thy own Jesus. Holy Mary, mother of God, pray for us sinners for now and the hour of our death. Amen."

He repeatedly prayed those words over and over, kissing the rosary from around his neck and pressing the crucifix upon his forehead.

"In the name of the Father, the Son, and the Holy Ghost. Amen."

The baby began to whimper, and Sister Claire checked in on their son. She changed his diaper and breastfed him.

A group of angry protesters gathered around the church, yelling profanity and spitting at it. Some on the opposing side sacrificed their lives, standing in front of it and holding hands in a locked position, protecting the house of the Lord. Top secret agents of the New World Order watched the protest closely. The sign of the beast engraved into their scalps as they snarled in disbelief. Others carried bottles of alcoholic beverage, setting them on fire and tossing them at the church chapel. Janice and Oblivion once again doused out the hot flames with a water hose and watched the chaos in the streets.

The world was slowly changing around them. A new breed took over while the Magnificents fought to keep God's word alive. Janice went back in to check on the others. A young boy kneeling on the pew was crying. His clothes were torn, and his eyes were bloodshot red. Sister Claire sat next to him and comforted him.

"Are you okay?"

"No."

"What's your name?"

"Jimmy Lee Hutchins."

"Where are your parents, Jimmy?"

"Dead. They are atheists. I was like them at one time, but something very special happened to me. I had a friend who was dying from cancer. I would visit him from time to time, and he would teach me to pray. He knew he was dying, but he wasn't afraid to die. For some reason, he knew that there had to be something more powerful than all this. His faith was so beautiful. He hardly fussed nor holler. We would often go by the lake. Every day was a struggle, but he never gave up. I looked up to him as a brother."

"Oh yeah? What was his name?"

"Zackery. Zackery Adams. He died two weeks ago."

"I'm sorry to hear about that. How old was he?"

"Twelve. I'll never forget him, never!" Jimmy leaned his head against his arm and wiped his eyes. Sister Claire rubbed his back and went to check on her son. She opened the door and gazed at the crib and realized that her son was gone. Time came up the hallway without their son.

"That's funny, I thought you had our . . ."

Time hysterically searched the chapel. He swung doors open and searched closets. His son was nowhere around. Finally they walked out onto the patio, and Ying Wu was holding their son, Jarnigan, against the patio railing in a dropping position. Sister Claire begged him not to.

"Please, Ying, don't, please," she said, sobbing.

Time slowly walked up to him and held his hand out. "Why are you doing this, son?"

"He's not your ordinary baby. He's been prophesied here."

"What are you saying?"

"You don't understand. The stars will cast down upon him. The earth will stop moving upon its axis, and the sun will explode because of him. This child is Armageddon. He must be destroyed!"

"He's our son, Ying. You must stop this insanity." Sister Claire reached out for her son to be handed to her. Ying Wu raised him high in the air to throw him to his death.

"Ying, please."

He handed him gently to his mother. The child never knew what was going on and smiled. Sister Claire looked down upon her son and smiled back. Time grabbed Ying by the arm and led him into the conference room.

"Just what do you think you're doing, young man?"

"I looked into his eyes, and they spoke to me. I'd seen the end, and it wasn't pretty. Your son was born for a reason."

"And that gives you the right to kill him?"

"I tried and did not succeed. I pray you do, because if not, that child of yours will destroy us all."

"How can you be so sure, huh? He's just a baby. We don't even know him yet."

Ying snatched his arm away from Time and walked away. A hurl of rocks came smashing through the stained glass windows. Time and his friends got down on the floor and waited for it to stop. Time and his friends immediately stepped out front.

"This place is the house of the Lord. Whosoever is without sin, throw the next stone."

A group of prospectors glanced at a view, ashamed of what the people have placed upon the house of Jehovah God. Some cried in disbelief. The crowd left, and Time got down on his knees and prayed.

"Thank you, dear Jehovah God. Thank you for removing those who choose not to serve you from this place."

The clouds gathered about and got dark. A storm was coming. Lightning struck a tree, and the branch fell to the ground. The Magnificents went back inside and waited for it to pass. Sister Claire gathered up all the blankets and passed them out. Ying Wu stood at the door, staring at the doorknob. Something was turning the doorknob on its own. The crack of thunder roared, knocking out the power throughout the chapel. He shivered in the dark. His knees jittered, and his lips trembled. He wondered what could be on the other side of the door. It suddenly got quiet, and the door was kicked open, breaking the lock in half. He wiped his eyes and realized that nothing was there. Maybe it was an illusion or something.

"Who's there?"

Sweat fell from his chin as he slowly walked back over to close the door. A gargoyle grabbed his hand and held on to it tight. Ying Wu tried pulling his hand away.

"Join us. You're not one of them. You're one of us."

"No!"

"Who are you really fooling, kid?"

"I said no!"

The creature released his hand and disappeared. Ying glanced over at the window and noticed that thousands of ants crawled along the stained glass window.

Sister Claire grabbed his shoulder and startled him. "You okay, hon?"

"Yeah, I guess." He glanced back at the window, and the ants were gone.

"Ying, can we talk?"

"Sure."

Ying sat down on the bed, while Sister Claire sat beside him. "You said that our son was Armageddon, and why would you harm him, Ying? Jarnigan loves you. I thought you loved him. What happened, Ying?"

Ying Wu began to sob. "He's not a child. He's something else."

"What are you saying, Ying? He's just a baby, for Christ's sake!"

"And I hope he stays one for our sake."

"What is it you see, hon? Tell me! You must tell me!"

Ying pulled away and left the room. Sister Claire sat there puzzled about what he had said.

Time went into his son's room and glanced at him. The moment he'd spent with him was quiet. He picked up his son and held him in his arms, smiling. It was the first time he ever felt loved. He kissed him and sat him down in his crib. Rubbing his head by the palm of his hand, Time spoke to him for the very first time alone. "I know I wasn't acting like a concerned father, son. Forgive me. Although I think it is time for you and I to get to know each other a little better, though. I tried to say I was sorry once before, and before I knew it, I ended up here with you. I don't know if I'll make a great dad or not, but I'm sure gonna try, little tyke, because I love you. You are a part of me, a part that I always wanted to be." A tear fell from his cheek.

The harrowing winds blew harder than ever, knocking down power lines. Sister Claire, holding a candle, walked into her son's room to comfort him. Ying Wu stood at the doorway, smiling at the baby. He walked over to it to apologize to Jarnigan. "Can I hold him?"

Time glanced down at him and nodded his head yes. Ying Wu picked him up into his arms and smiled. "I'm going to look after you from now on. Maybe that'll save the earth."

Oblivion tried calling Julie but with no luck. Janice came up from behind him.

"Why are you running after her? She doesn't love you the way I do!"

"You don't understand anything about her, Janice."

"I-I hate you!"

Oblivion grabbed her by the arms. "Listen up, because I'm only gonna tell you one more time, hon. I am in love with someone else. I don't know any other way to tell you, Janice. You are a sweet girl, but I'm in love with someone else, okay?"

"Is that all I am to you? Sweet?" Janice began to sob.

Oblivion attempted to walk away but stopped. "I don't know how else to tell you." He stepped out on the balcony to take a smoke. Took out a pack of Drop Dead cigarettes, lit one, puckered up on the butt, and blew smoke into the air. Gazing up at the stars, he smiled. Something wet and gooey slapped his leatherjacket from above. He peered up into the clouds but didn't see anything.

"Maybe another storm," he said as he attempted to walk back in. Something swooped in, hard and heavy, hitting the pavement from behind him. It landed on both feet, creeping up from behind him and snatching him by the shoulders. Oblivion flew into the air and smashed into the railing. The force bent the metal in half. The grotesque, winged humanoid continued throwing Oblivion into the concrete wall. The ground shook. A helmet hinged its penetrating, bloodless eyes. Its figure had a gaping suit of armor. Each and every time Oblivion landed into an object, he bit his lips. Blood gushed from his mouth. The creature overpowered him, and he grunted in anger. It had empty, unblinking eyes filled with hate. It had no love but had one purpose: to destroy mankind. His helpless body tried to get up onto his feet but couldn't. Dirt, rocks, and debris fell to his jacket.

"You think you've won this fight, but Jehovah God will prevail!"

The demon bat creature spoke. "I've been wanting to meet you, human."

"What . . . what exactly are you saying?"

"My name is Zocai, leader of the Fifth Wing. I was sent here by the enemy to forewarn you all."

Time and the others stepped out onto the patio and noticed the mutant gargoyle standing there.

"Who sent you here?"

"I am a legion. Anyone who crosses me will perish."

"My name is Time, and this is my wife, Mary."

"We know all about you, Time and Oblivion. Join us, and quit your pack with God."

"Never. I will never do that!"

"Then you will die, hybrid!"

Time, Oblivion, and Janice grabbed their crucifixes, and it transformed into shiny, caliber swords. Janice stood in front of Time and Oblivion and drew her sword, and the tip of her sword touched the gargoyle's chin.

"Time, take your wife and son and leave this place! Oblivion and I will finish this once and for all. We'll guard this ship while you're gone."

"This church is my home, and this war is my fight."

More demon bat angels descended from the sky. Their chest were covered in armor, and they had piercing deceitful, fiery eyes. Their claws were keen and deadly. The lords of the air shrieked in the night with frightful a scowl and grim expressions on their faces. Their hearts filled with much bile. A malodorous and vile smell came from them. A fight ensued. They fought like men, like heroes. Cutter ferociously slashed at their wings, cutting them across their shoulders and face. Time and Oblivion slashed at them. Blood gushed from their veins. The night was red.

Sister Claire gazed out the window and noticed the chaos and immediately grabbed her son to hide him. Ying Wu gazed out and smiled. From the long dark night came engender terror. Their flinty wings swooped down upon them, scratching the fearsome three against their eyes.

Cutter punch-kicked them over the balcony, while Oblivion viciously swung his sword, decapitating their dreadful skulls in a whisper. Time closed his eyes and prayed for deliverance. A teardrop fell from his cheek. "My cup runneth over."

When he opened them, he was suddenly surrounded. He kissed the tip of his sword and swung it. Slashing into their flesh, blood splattered onto the concrete floor. Time levitated off the patio floor and went onto the roof. The beasts followed, drooling from their jaws, snapping at Time with their foul, rotten teeth. They could taste his flesh. Their tails cut like razors, smacking like a whip against his raw flesh. Time flipped high in the air and triple kicked them off the roof, impaling them on a sharp, pointed, splinter-spiked iron fence. Their eyes glowed like the color of the moon. They died slowly with their mouths hung wide open.

The evil beasts eventually vacated the church premises, leaving the fearsome three restless and tired. Time jumped high, landing back onto the patio floor. Cutter wiped the blood off her forehead.

"Is everyone okay?"

"I-I think so. What about you, Time?"

"I don't know."

Oblivion had trouble walking, dragging his body upon his riddled leg.

"They'll be back, I know it."

Ying Wu stood in the front of the patio sliding doors.

"You're right." The Magnificents immediately gazed at him. Time lightly leaned his sword into the child's chest.

"And when they do, there will be many. They will come as the legion, demons damned into eternity. Some will have three heads, others with the plague. They will spread a virus into the air, killing millions, all for the sake of destroying the chosen two. They want you, Time and Oblivion. They want you, and they won't rest until they do so."

"And how are you so sure of that?"

The child smiled a grim expression on his face. If looks could kill, they would have been dead in an instant. Time knew that the boy wasn't your average, normal child. He was one of them, warning them of the signs. At some point, he respected it, and on the other, he wanted the boy dead. He knew that in the back of his mind. He had to keep the boy alive so that his people could live.

"You know, you are very lucky that I like you."

"You mean blessed, don't you, Priest?"

Ying Wu walked away and headed up to his room. Oblivion and Cutter gazed at the boy in a strange sort of way. Mary ran out onto the patio and embraced Time and kissing him passionately.

"Are you okay?"

"I'll manage. How's our son?"

"He's sleeping, sweetheart. Would you like to see him?"

"There will be plenty of time. In the meantime, we need to be ready for the next attack. I have a feeling that it will be soon."

"I want to fight by your side, Time."

"I'm sorry, Mary, our son needs more of your time than we do. Besides, we'll be okay on our own, in the next hour or so," he said, facing the pitch-dark sky.

"Who knows what to expect? The night has an appetite, and we are the morsel."

Sister Claire continued on holding him in her arms and caressed his chest with her bright pink cheeks. "I'll never let you go, my love, never. Please, don't ever leave us."

CHAPTER FOURTEEN

Ying Wu had set out to kill Time even though Time was generous enough to take him in. He followed his heart as a gargoyle instead of a human. Time felt very uncomfortable with the child around him and his new family. He'd finally had enough patience with him, and the Magnificents held a private meeting. Time paced the floor.

"I've made my decision and decided that Ying would have to leave the cathedral."

"Think about what you're saying, Time. He's just a child. He doesn't quite know his actions."

"He's one of them, Mary, for God's sake. A gargoyle. A demon bat child capable of destroying us both!"

Oblivion agreed. "I agree. He's weird!"

"Oh, Time, I wish you would look at this another way. We need him. If he leaves now, he won't survive out there alone."

"Think about what you're saying, darling."

Time held her arms with both hands. "That child in there is not quite human."

"He may not be, but he can help us. He can let us know when the next attack will take place and when they'll return."

"All right, then, we'll vote on it. If the boy stays, raise your hands. How many of us say the boy leaves?" Time raised his hand. "The boy stays?"

Sister Claire, Oblivion, and Janice raised their hands.

"Okay, I guess I'm out-voted."

"Oh, sweetheart, I'm sorry."

"I pray that you're right, I truly do. 'Cause if you're not, God help us all." Time left them standing, staring.

In the suburbs of New York, a house party took place. A group of misfits pumped up to the music, dancing and drinking. A guy by the name of Charley stumbled, falling over furniture, too intoxicated to stand up straight. Two of his buddies sat around, waiting for company to show, passing around weed, and getting high. No one else showed up, except those who were there, and Charley got very angry. He smashed empty beer bottles against the wall.

"Fucking pricks, I knew they weren't coming!"

One of his homies inhaled on some weed. "Hey, Charley, maybe next time, man. Besides, who gives a damn if they show up or not? We've got a party here, man, smoking this wild shit."

"Yeah, you're right. Who cares if those stuck-up bitches show or not? Hand me that ghost, man."

His friend passed him the weed.

"Sure, you're right," he said, laughing. "Next time we see them hoes, they'll wish they'd come. I was about to pay for some, but since they didn't come, more money in my pocket, man!"

"You got that right, homie. Hey, pass me over some of that ghost, man. Don't try to hog up that shit yourself!"

"Okay, okay." Charley handed him the weed, and his friend sucked on it so hard that he accidentally swallowed it down his windpipe. His friend began to violently choke.

"Hey, man, you okay?" There was a loud knock at the door, and Charley answered it. "Well, it's about time . . . What the—" A gargoyle snatched him and flew off with his body from the front door.

Charley's other partner sat in front of his aquarium, drinking, watching the goldfish swim by. "Hey, Charley, man, is that them?"

Loud footsteps came from the front door and approached him. His friend didn't pay any attention, and the creature immediately snapped his neck, pulling his head clean off and tossing it to the floor. The next day, detectives combed the area and found nothing but bloody footprints and alcohol embedded into white carpet. The story made headlines all over the news. A panic surfaced, and everyone stayed indoors. New York became a ghost town.

The fearsome four secretly visited the home where the crime took place. Time could smell the aroma of death in that house as he walked through the dining room.

"I can tell they were here." Time held an eyebrow clipper and pulled up a hair specimen from the white carpet.

Mary rubbed her finger through something slimy on the rug. "Ew." She swabbed some of it from the carpet into a vial. "I'll run some tests on this."

Oblivion found a fresh, dirty footprint and poured a white heavy solution into it to match. "They were here, all right, and it looks like they cleaned house too. Look at the carnage they left behind."

Cutter began to shiver from the sight of it and ran into a room to lock herself in there.

Splattered blood marks on the walls, skin tissue, and bone fragments scattered all over the room.

Sister Claire got sick and ran into the restroom to regurgitate. Time went to see if she was okay.

"You okay, sweetheart?"

She leaned over the commode seat. "I think . . . I think so." She stood up to wipe her mouth with a white cloth from the sink. "Time, we may have to relocate. Have you ever thought about that?"

"Yes, yes I have." He leaned against the other side of the door. "They'll keep coming until they've eventually killed us both, but I won't vacate the church chapel, Mary. It is my home. It is God's home. I was raised in the church, and I will die for it."

"You say that, but I hope that when the time comes that you are prepared to do so, 'cause those things out there aren't going to give up until we stop them."

Cutter slowly gazed around the room. Crack pipe bottles and narcotics were on the dresser. A family photo sat on the mantle.

Oblivion went up the stairway and checked the bedrooms. There, a foul odor came from one of the rooms. He sensed danger and snapped his holy rosary from around his neck. The crucifix immediately transformed into a sword. Oblivion slowly pushed the door open with the tip of his sword. The door creaked open as he entered. Sweat poured down the side of his face.

"Anyone there?" The room was quiet. He could hear the others' footsteps down below. The odor was strong, unlike anything he's ever encountered. He paced the floor in circles, pointing his sword in the wind, until Sister Claire came up from behind him and startled him. He gasped in horror. "Everything okay?"

"I'm sorry, but you stunned me for a minute. Find anything else downstairs?"

"A lot of hair samples. We know for sure that they were here, but where could they have gone?"

"I don't know, but one thing is for sure: if we don't stop them, they'll wreak havoc all over New York City. By that time, it may very well be too late."

"I hope not. I have an idea who can help us locate their resting grounds."

"And who may that be?"

"There is this underground society, a place long forgotten. I've only been there once. Where there are those who were born extremely deformed or disease ridden. They've resided there for centuries, shunned away from the world. A place where men don't roam and loneliness has plagued the hearts of many who remembered them. We called them Wee people. Some were born with three arms, eyes in the back of their heads, and missing limbs. It's been years since I've seen them. One of them is a friend of mine. His name is Zachariah, a warrior by heart. He can help us."

"What happened to their parents?"

"Their parents lived in a small town high up in the Arizona Valley. The United States Government was about to use that site for nuclear missile testing. They had given the people there ample amount of time to evacuate the area. The people refused to leave their homes, in which caused a serious population to be infected by the radiation testing. Their parents had abandoned their infected babies totally after that. Many had written them off for dead. Society no longer had a place for people like that. So the only way to keep them alive was to find a home. I know where that home is. I can take you there."

Oblivion transformed his sword back and checked the closets. No life-forms or gargoyles were present.

"What good are these . . . these creatures you speak of if they are sick?"

"They're humans, Oblivion, flesh and blood. Besides, Zachariah was known as a renowned psychic at one time. He could foretell future and past events. People taunted him and called him a freak. When he was a little boy, he used his gift and found several missing children. Some were found maimed, tortured, and deceased. God only knows how their parents felt."

"I want to share something with you. If it should ever come down to any of us still around, I should hope it's you. Take the child and get away from here as far as you can go. Make a real life for yourself, Mary, not this one. This life is no way for a woman like you to live. You're too good of a person for this."

"We would all have to leave together, Oblivion. That is the only way. In the meantime, I'll contact my friend. Maybe we can stay with them for a while."

A commercial jetliner pulled into Arizona. Sister Claire, the baby, and Oblivion got off the aircraft with their luggage. The others stayed behind. A 4x4 Jeep Wagoneer pulled up in front of them on the runway. A man by the name of Steve Post greeted them.

"Hello, I'm glad you've made it here safe. Don't worry, I'll take that." Steve grabbed Sister Claire's bags. The three of them rode in the Jeep up into the mountains. "You may want to carry a doggy bag when you see them."

"Why do you say such words?" Sister Claire frowned upon him.

"Their children's children came out even worst. We tried to keep them from mating, but that was almost impossible. Some came out with more than one genital. Others, three faces on one skull. I don't know what to say about them, except they are different."

"How long have you known them?" Oblivion gazed out of the window into the sunlight.

"Known them?" Steve stopped the vehicle and turned his head to face them in the backseat. He opened his mouth, and a reptilian tongue smacked the thin air. Steve then closed his mouth and smiled.

"Okay, keep driving." Oblivion gasped in shock.

Sister Claire snickered as the vehicle continued on toward their destination. "You're right about the different part." Sister Claire laughed.

"My father's name is Zachariah."

"Your father's name is Zachariah? He's a good man, your father."

"Thank you."

"Your father and I go way back. He was a professor at Inman State University, before the accident, of course. I was one of his favorite students."

"Wow, he told me a lot about you, Sister. What is your baby's name?"

"Jarnigan. His father's name is Time."

"Are you married, Sister?"

"Yes, yes I am. His father's a priest."

"You said I was different, I see you are too. The ones who were most infected had to be quarantined."

"I'm . . . I'm so sorry."

A destitute, impoverished nation of people in need of plastic and reconstructive surgery. A nation so badly deformed and cast out of society, only to squalor in filth. Zachariah worked long, hard hours to find cures to help his people.

"One group of people are called the Moles, 97 percent of their body is fully covered with huge tumors. Severe cancerous growths planted all over their flesh.

"The Spyder Family, family members born with more than one limb. Their youngest son was born with eight eyes on his facial area. Somehow, his mother was bitten by an insect the same time before radiation contamination. The boy has never been to any educational institution. He's being homeschooled. Those eyes, those awful-looking eyes . . ."

Sister Claire sobbed. "Father God, bless that child. Take me to him."

"Say what?"

"I want you to take me to him, the boy."

Lights surrounded an underground cave that led to a forgotten nation of people. The fearsome two followed Zachariah's son into the darkness until they came to a dead end.

"When I open this doorway, you will see how fortunate you really are."

Zachariah opened that door, and what stood before them was shocking. Men born with more than one head greeted them at the entrance. A woman with two breasts fed their babies at the same time. An old man's face was so badly deformed he drooled at the jaws. Some didn't look human at all. Others managed to survive on their own without medical help. Oblivion couldn't help but stare, and Mary cried at the horror of it all. Zachariah led them to the little boy's room. He pushed the door as it creaked open. The child literally hung from the ceiling wall on a giant web like a spider, a human spider with eight eyes. Mary knew then that he was very, very special and confronted him. She held onto her son while entering.

"Hello, my name is Mary, and this is Oblivion, and yours?"

"Buzzzzzzzzzz."

"Why, hello, Buzz. We came here on a mission."

"What mizzzzzzzion?"

"I would like to ask you some questions about the legion, if you don't mind. You've heard of them, yes?"

"Yezz."

"I need to know where we can find them and where they will hit next."

The boy was quiet and never spoke a word. He just hung there in silence. A fly buzzed around him, and in an instant, his tongue rolled out from his mouth and immediately grasped the fly, devouring it. The Magnificents watched and clutched their mouths from vomiting. The boy's eyes twitched, and his hands were shaped like a prey mantis.

"My God, what you must have gone through."

"A great earthquake will come and unleazzzh the damned upon you. Thouzzandz of unzzaved zoulzz will wreak famine and havoc upon the earth. You will know when that time will come. A full moon at twelve o'clock midnight izz when it all beginzzz."

"Tell me, how do we fight them?"

"The power iz within the cruzzzifix you are wearing. It izz holy when uzzzed. It shall protect you."

"Thank you, thank you so much for helping us, and I hope that whatever you're searching for, you'll find it."

The child just stared at them. He couldn't take his eyes off them, and for that moment, a tear fell from his cheek. Mary's heart went out to him. She immediately darted out of the child's room and gasped, trying to catch her breath.

Oblivion followed her and the baby out into the dank hallway. Jarnigan was fast asleep, wrapped around her belly.

"You all right?"

"No, but we can't leave until I talk to Zachariah."

"Very well."

Oblivion calmly grabbed her shoulder as they proceeded toward his laboratory. The aroma of strong, dangerous chemicals in the air guided them to him. Zachariah worked long, tiresome nights without rest. He was passed out at the table.

"Zachariah?"

He awoke slowly, saw them standing at the entrance, and smiled. "Mary, my dear, it's so good to see you again, and who is this little fighter?"

"This is my son, Jarnigan."

"Jarnigan, that's a nice name, Jarnigan, and you are?" he said, shaking Oblivion's hand.

"Oblivion."

"Nice to meet you too. Please, do have a seat please. You are all here as my guest."

"Thank you, Zach, but we can't stay. We are here to find out something."

"Oh, and what might that be?"

"How do we fight the legion?"

Zachariah paced the floor and gazed out from an open window that led out into the dark sky. "You fight them with all you've got. I've seen this before. They're not one to wreck with. You mustn't fear them, never fear them, or you will lose this battle."

"I fear for my son, Zachariah. I fear for his life. Please, you must help us. We need to know how to stop them. The child here who crawls like a spider has helped us a great deal. We would like to hear from you."

"The power is in prayer. Pray for mercy, Mary. You already know the answer. You just need to use it to your advantage."

Oblivion, Mary, and the baby stayed for a while and observed their way of life. The mountain was beautiful during the fall. Green grass and the sweet smell of pine left us speechless. The natives there accepted the Wee people as though they were family. This was their home. Oblivion and Mary had decided to return home and packed their things. Zachariah and his people said their good-byes. They will always be remembered for their hospitality.

An airplane pulled into the airport, unloading passengers. Sister Claire, the baby, and Oblivion got off safely. A limo pulled up, and the chauffeur got out to open the back passenger door. They got in, and it rode off.

"I can't wait to see my husband. I miss him dearly."

"Yeah, I can't wait to see my old friend myself. How's the baby?"

"He's still asleep. Darn, it's almost feeding time." Mary lifted her blouse and exposed her breast to feed her son.

"Oh, oh, okay." Oblivion covered his eyes with his arm, turning away from her.

"Is he drinking the milk?"

"Yes."

"Good."

The sky got cloudy, and the winds pushed debris into the streets. A storm was coming and fast. Time awaited the return of his friend, wife, and child. Mary gazed out from the window of the moving vehicle. Pedestrians scattered the streets to find shelter. Oak trees swayed side to side. The baby began to whimper as she covered his head with a blanket.

"Don't look, my dear child. Before you know it, it will all be over."

Traffic blocked the limo in at the red light. There was the sound of cars hysterically honking their horns and emergency sirens shooting down the busy streets of New York. Mary and Oblivion grabbed their crucifix in case of trouble as the light changed green, allowing the limo to proceed toward its destination.

They had finally arrived at the church chapel, and the rain came down harder than ever. Sister Claire held her son close as Oblivion swung open the door to let them out. A black umbrella fanning away the raindrops protected their heads, and they ran toward the side door of the chapel and knocked. Time immediately opened the door to allow them to enter. Sister Claire gently embraced and kissed him. Oblivion smiled, and Janice came in behind them. Her hair and clothes were soaked and wet. She was shivering like she had a fever. Time was more concerned about her whereabouts.

"Where were you, Janice?" They had just argued about something, and Janice was furious with Time.

"None of your business!"

"You were supposed to have kept an eye on Ying."

"Ying, Ying, Ying. Don't you think it is about time that we dismiss him from this church?"

"Janice, what are you saying?"

"The children won't even play with him. They call him some kind of beast. Look at him, he's a gargoyle, for God's sake. He's not like the other children. He'll never be like the other children, Time. He's this monster living in human flesh, just waiting for a chance to destroy us all, and all you can do is watch him. Well, I'm not going to sit around and wait to be slaughtered. The first chance I get, I'll kill him if I have to." Janice ran toward the back of the guesthouse.

Sister Claire rubbed his shoulders. "Time, do you think it is a wise decision in letting the boy stay here?"

"We need him, Mary. He is our only hope of knowing where they'll hit next. Through him, we'll be better prepared."

"I hope you're right, Time, I really do, because that storm out there is another sign. Did you know that?"

Storms hit, and earthquakes struck simultaneously on every continent. The earth was changing by the minute. Around the world, gargoyles attacked and devoured their victims while demons ruled the night. The Magnificents secured the church in hopes of keeping

God's home alive. Feet ran down sidewalks, jumping over barbed wire fences were heard. Those who wanted to be saved fought to get in.

Janice sat on the sofa, holding a teddy bear, crying, and wishing she could open her door. But she didn't want to come in contact with the infected. Her eyes were tired, and she closed her ears from the screams at night, shattering the wind.

"When will this all end?"

A razor blade sat on the coffee table. She glanced at it, and her hand shook reaching for it, but she didn't touch it. This time, she scooted down under the blanket while the fireplace was still burning and prayed for deliverance from Christ. The sound of broken glass screeched. Ying Wu stood at the window and growled. Once a gargoyle, always a gargoyle. The child danced in circles and chanted, stamping his feet hard upon the wooden floor. His eyes burned fiery red, like hot coals. He felt like he was held in captivity, wanting to be with his own. Time, Oblivion, Mary, and their son knelt on the pews in the chapel, praying. Clouds rapidly moved across the sky.

The holy fight has begun. Good against evil and an unfulfilled prophecy of Revelations. Time kissed his rosary and bowed before the cross. Sister Claire got up and stood at his side, holding their child.

"Soon, it will be time for us to give our lives for him."

"I'm . . . I'm so afraid for our son, Time. What will happen to him?"

"We will put him in hiding until the moon is free from all sin. The demons fly at night, searching for new victims. Jarnigan will be our new leader. He will help save the planet and destroy all those against it."

"He can do all that?"

"That's why he's so, so very special, Mary. You must protect him for the time being."

Mary glanced down at her son and smiled, rubbing his fine red hair and kissing the top of his head. She felt a sense of warmth. The child spat bubbles and clung to his mother's bosom. He could feel the beat of her heart and fell fast asleep. Mary closed her eyes and prayed along with her husband. There was the sound of fists banging upon the church door.

Oblivion got up and ran to it, allowing those who weren't infected to enter, not those who were. Some asked for forgiveness and bowed for the first time in their lives. They had no beliefs in the Almighty and, for the first time, saw their souls at the hands of his mercy. Once they entered the house of the Lord, they sprawled over and fell to the floor screaming. Time walked over to them and placed his hand upon their forehead, praying.

Sister Claire felt happy about them wanting to be saved and joined her husband in prayer, passing out Bibles and warm blankets. They slept through the night until the screaming stopped. Time no longer wanted to fear the unsaved and opened the front chapel door. He walked out into the darkness, extending a wooden crucifix out in front of him, sprinkling holy water onto suffering souls. A sea of the undead gazed up at him. Their pale faces spelled death, fresh, open lesions all over. Sister Claire followed Time, holding a lit candle into a place unknown to them.

The church sat on a tall mountain, like a castle facing the ocean shore. Forest fires had swept the city of what was once the Big Apple. The earthquakes had destroyed the streets. Gaping holes surfaced into hills. Those who survived tried climbing toward the church and got swept away from the angry beast. The lost and blind victims of the storm gripped the earth, climbing nowhere in a strange, new world.

Janice fell asleep on the sofa, holding onto her warm teddy bear. Oblivion walked out onto the patio and shivered at the sight. He began thinking to himself about the safety of Julie and Meredith.

"I hope you're both safe, my love," he whispered to himself.

Flying gargoyles encircled the cathedral like giant pterodactyls. He gazed up at the full moon that overshadowed the earth. Sister Claire grabbed Time's shoulder.

"Don't go too far."

An icy chill froze them in their shoes while the earth got colder. The lost followed the blind, the blind condemned forever. Heavy footsteps shook debris beneath them, and Time and Mary stopped. They were surrounded by the Legion of the Damned. Time and Mary immediately reached for their crucifix, evolving into the Magnificents. The legion lashed at them full force. Sharp claws tore at their flesh. Sister Claire swung her sword, and amputated their limbs piece by piece. Time impaled some flying at him from above. Blood gushed from their veins. A gargoyle suddenly lashed at Time's back and knocked him off his feet.

"Time?"

Mary cried out to him. They kept coming and coming, leaping on top of Time, cutting off his oxygen. Time managed to get up and fought back even harder. Blood rolled down his head and shoulders until help arrived.

"Hang on, Time!" Oblivion came to his rescue, swinging his sword.

The flying beast tore into his back, ripping his black cape into shreds. The agony of razor-sharp claws caused huge gaping holes of blood. Time helplessly fell to the pavement. A gargoyle snatched his body and threw him twenty feet into the air, slamming him into the concrete wall of the cathedral. Sister Claire raised her hand in front of their deformed skulls. A bright, warm light came from her hand, and some disappeared into thin air.

Her eyes caused hallucination to the point of her kicking them hard with her feet, wisting their heads backward and snapping their necks. Cutter never awoke, and she slept through the madness. A claw caressed her face, adoring her beauty.

"Such a beautiful gal. I think I will take you as my princess."

The beast immediately grabbed her from underneath and flew away with her into the pitch-dark night, leaving her door ajar with broken hinges. Ying Wu hid on top of the roof behind statues, naked, wondering if he should join them. His little body shivered and shivered. Too afraid to kill and still having a heart. His arms were crossed across his chest, and his black hair was slicked back. The awful sounds of gargoyles howled, and Sister Claire stood in front of her husband to protect him. The fighting had suddenly ceased, and their leader confronted them. "You think you can stop us, nun? You think you can destroy us? But you can't. For we are the legion, and we have killed many. You dare attempt to fight me, and I will be forced to rip you limb from limb. Woman of the cloak, step aside, and let us take what is ours. We came for the chosen two!"

"You come near my husband, and I . . . and I will be forced to destroy you, I swear!"

"Don't make me kill you, bitch. I'm tired of a woman like you testing me. The last nun who did lost her soul trying."

The beast approached them, and Sister Claire raised her sword up to its chin. "I will tear your head, clean off you. Now back off!"

"We will soon meet again, and when we do, I'll kill you first."

The demon bat angels flew away, and Sister Claire tried helping Father Time up onto his feet. He wasn't quite coherent.

"Time, Time, are you all right?" Oblivion grabbed him by the shoulders and lifted him to his feet and into the church chapel. He slowly walked him into a room and onto a cot. Those who were there crowded around him and sobbed. Sister Claire had gotten a wet rag, wiping his forehead.

"Has he woken up yet?"

"No, but if we don't tend to his wombs, he will die."

Oblivion had gotten herbs and coffee grains. Packing his wounds with it, Father Time began to sweat out the infection, and they covered his body with plenty of blankets. Sister Claire had taken his temperature.

"We're losing him. We need to get him to the tub. We need ice, now!"

Oblivion ran down to the kitchen, to the refrigerator, and grabbed all the trays. He filled the tub with water in the tub. They both gently lowered his body into the water.

"Oh, God, no!"

Time fainted and awoke the next morning on the sofa. A new day had come, and the wind blew gray clouds across the sky, making room for the reflection of sunrays to enter the chapel's stained glass window. Time felt the heat penetrate his face and opened his eyes.

"Where am I?"

Sister Claire came and sat by his side with a hot cup of coffee. "You're here, here with me."

"Is it over?"

"No, not quite. They'll be back soon, and when they do, they're coming after me and the child."

Time grabbed her arm with his hand. "Why?"

"I'm in the way, that's why, and the only way to get to you is through me. Jarnigan and I are the last of your bloodline, Time."

"I have to get well fast to help you and the baby." He tried to stand but was too weak to.

"Besides, I had searched the church and the guesthouse. Janice is gone, Time. I believe she was abducted by them."

"What about the others?"

"They're safe for now. In the meantime, we are gonna need lots of ammunition, just until you get well, sweetheart. Do we have enough artillery?"

"I believe so. We'll need everyone whose taken refuge here at the chapel to participate, Mary." Time took her hand and kissed it.

"I'll get on it."

CHAPTER FIFTEEN

The army moved in and waited for their return. One of the officers proceeded to enter a tent to notify the lieutenant of his findings. The officer saluted him, entering.

"At ease, Private. Find out anything?"

"Sir, we've spotted them flying over our target, sir."

"Good, alarm the others."

The army wasn't ready. In fact, the legion had destroyed their main post and slaughtered and devoured many of their soldiers. The world was now at the hands of the Legion of the Damned, and the Magnificents had to react fast. Sister Claire stood before the saved and had given her speech.

"We won't go down without a fight!"

The crowd of believers clapped before her.

"We will not allow the enemy to win this war, nor will my husband and I leave our newborn son to fend for himself. Time needs you now. I need you. Will you all join us in battle and help us to protect our home from the beasts? It's just a matter of time that they'll soon return, and if we're not ready, it may very well be the end for all of us. Please, let's bow our heads and pray."

Weeks went by, and there was no sign of the legion. Sister Claire had gathered up the flock, and the flock was prepared to die. Men, women, and children prayed for strength and hope for a new world, a place where men could roam without being harmed. They had to fight for that and possibly lose their lives trying. Even if it meant giving their lives to him. They were heavily packed with serious artillery. Magnums, AK47s, a grenade launcher, and homemade bombs. One man stood before the congregation and spoke out.

"Are we prepared to die? Are we prepared to give our lives to him? is the question. Now is the time to test our faith. Revelations is here!"

"Praise the Lord!"

"Praise God!" The church body danced, yelled, clapped, and held their fists up high. Victory was not far, and Time overheard everything that was said. He knew then that he was not in this alone and smiled. Time managed to get up and walked over to see his son, and he sat down beside him. Jarnigan gazed up at his father and smiled. It was a sense of peace that took place there. In that room, in that sanctuary they called home. Lifting him in his arms, Jarnigan fell asleep on his tired shoulders. Time always spoke to him as though he understood. "Such an innocent little boy. If anything would have happened to you, I don't know what I would have done, but I do know that I wouldn't be in my right mind. All I know is that I am proud to be your father, and I don't want to live my life without you."

Time held his son out before the cross. "I give my son to you, Lord, and only you. Amen."

A halo encircled the child's head. His body glowed, a luminous bright light in the dim-lit room. Time held his son in his arms and rocked him silently to sleep. He placed him back into his crib. Oblivion entered the room.

"I'm going after Janice."

"And risk your life for her? You're needed here at the chapel, Oblivion."

"If we don't, they'll kill her."

"She may already be dead, but we do know that she is a Magnificent, Oblivion. She's perfectly capable of taking care of herself."

"What, being held in captivity with one of those things?"

"Oblivion, I'm sure wherever she is right now, Jehovah God is looking after her. All you've got to do is trust him."

"I'm going after her, and you're not stopping me."

Time gently placed his hand on his friend's shoulder. Oblivion grabbed it. "God will always be with you, my friend. Wherever you go, in light and darkness."

"Thank you, Time. I'll always remember you and all you've done for me."

"I haven't done anything, my friend, but be there when you needed me."

Oblivion smiled at him, and Time smiled back. The two parted ways, while the other searched for Janice. A heavy cloud of fog engulfed the air. ~~The sound of~~ an owl hooted, and he stepped off into the darkness. Oblivion packed himself with weapons in case of a sudden invasion. *or hoofing*

Janice awoke in a dungeon. Her eyes were heavy and tired. Weeping and wailing noises came from the cell next to her. The beasts stood at her cell, sniffing her scent. Janice realized that she was in danger and had to find a way out. She managed to stand on her shackled feet. Dizziness blurred her vision and thought. Her wrists were bound and handcuffed. Their shadows reflected on the wall of her cell. She could see the shape of their hideous figures. Their eyes were hooded with lazy reptilian torpor, and their feet were like gators. Janice got a little closer, and she could see the ghastly expressions on their faces. She began to tremble with fear in her sweat-drenched pajamas.

Gripping the bars of her cell, she said, "Hello, is anybody out there?"

A sharp claw smacked against her hands. The legion marched like Hitler's regime. Their feet shook the earth with every step, and Janice tried to free her hands from the cuffs. A member of the legion approached her cell.

"Hello, my pretty one."

"What?"

"You are mine, and I am yours."

"Pardon me?"

"Our royal highness has just married us."

"Say what? What . . . what exactly are you talking about? I just woke up here in this God-forsaken nightmare!"

"I am yours now, how should I say this, your husband, and you are now my wife."

"You've . . . you've got to be kidding me, right?"

Oblivion walked into the darkness and found a cave leading into a deep black hole. There, flickers of flame heated the stone walls, scorching his hands. Janice felt around her neck for her crucifix; it was gone.

She thought, *My holy rosary must have fallen off somewhere in this cell. I must find it if I am to save myself.*

The beast smiled at her. "I will be back to join you."

Janice gazed around the cell and saw it where she was lying. She managed to scoot down to retrieve it. She gently placed it underneath her tongue. "I never forget old habits." It came back to her during her youth, when she used to store razor blades into her mouth before a fight. The gargoyle came back and released her from her cell, only to escort her back to his chambers.

An army of demons scoured the area while Oblivion stayed hidden. Janice saw slaves slumped over, beaten to death, carrying hot coals up a mountain. The legion whipped decayed flesh off their backs, and she gawked in horror. The quick snap of whips smacked at their open wounds. Some managed to keep walking, while others gave up to be tortured.

A soldier approached them. "What brings her here?"

"She's not one of them. Step aside, Legion!"

"Are you talking to me?"

Bad blood among the two brewed, and a brutal fight ensued. The gargoyle shoved her to the ground as the two swung swords at each other, one hoping to decapitate the other. The intense heat cut off the oxygen, causing her to hyperventilate. The fight went on for minutes, minutes into an hour. Oblivion heard the cries of those who were condemned from grace, their voices loud enough to break eardrums. The gargoyle had suddenly won the battle of decapitating the other and led her into a small cave, shoving her against a boulder.

"This is your home!" he said, grabbing her by the collar.

"This ain't no home, and you ain't my husband!"

"We'll see about that!" He shoved her.

She wasn't the only female there. Women were held in captivity in cells, their flesh burned and charred. Janice covered her nostrils from the stench. It was enough to make her vomit. The beast grabbed her by the hair and dragged her across the dirt. Janice spat the crucifix into her hand, then the beast came back and bound and gagged her with duct tape. It dragged her into a room, slamming the door. The beast had taken off its armor and ripped her robe off, exposing her body. Janice screamed out loud and pushed herself away from it. The gargoyle slowly approached her.

Oblivion climbed down from the mountain and walked among the enslaved, blind demons that walked there. He saw a woman in bondage, shackled in chains.

"Did you see a young lady who didn't quite belong here?"

The woman didn't say a word.

"Lady, where do they keep you when they bring you here?"

The woman opened her mouth. Her tongue was missing, and she couldn't speak. Oblivion gasped at the sight and immediately ran down the hill to find Janice. Hot coals were thrown into the lake of fire, while souls surfaced from the lake into the sky. He heard the angry voice of the enemy yelling.

I've got to find her before it's too late. Before we can't leave this place.

Janice reached out to strike it, and the gargoyle grabbed her wrist, noticing the scars on her wrist. "You're a cutter . . . a cutter!"

She cried and snatched her arm away from its grip. "And you're a freaking monster!"

The beast smacked her face, knocking her unconscious.

The intense heat was enough to melt flesh. Oblivion had walked down a corridor of cells. Souls were forever trapped behind bars. Oblivion searched for his friend. Janice awoke, saliva hanging from her bottom lip.

"Help me! Somebody help me!"

A blind little girl had suddenly touched her shoulder. "Hello, what is your name?" A hybrid, half-human and half-gargoyle.

207

"Where . . . where did you come from? I didn't know you were here."

"My name was Alicia. Alicia Parker. That thing you called beast was my father."

"Your . . . your father. You've got to be kidding me, right?"

Alicia shook her head. "No, I'm not kidding. Are you going to be my new mommy?"

Janice stood up on her feet, loosening the duct tape. "Sorry, kid, but hell no."

She managed to free her hands and had taken the crucifix, transforming it into a sword and herself into a hero. The locked door was kicked off its hinges and into the dirt. The beast had awaken from resting and proceeded to kill her. Janice ejected razor blades into the air, slicing him open, knocking the beast out with a few kicks. She proceeded to run.

Oblivion gazed up and saw her running in his direction.

"Hey you. Where were you?"

She smiled. "Right here, waiting for you."

"Come on, we better get outta here before we can't."

"You're right about that."

Levitating off the ground, the Magnificents pound into demons flying at them in all directions. Cutter cracked necks, knocked out fangs, and diced them into pieces. Oblivion spun around at full speed, knocking out his assailants with his fist. Blood gushed from their fangs, a carnage of lost souls. The Magnificents fought their way up the mountain, before the cave was sealed off from the world. Cutter embraced Oblivion and kissed him one last time.

"I did that to say thank you."

"No problem. I wasn't going to leave you there like that. You're like a sister to me."

"I'm like a what? Then why did you kiss me?"

"I don't know, but you are welcome."

Time embraced his wife in bed while they slept. Jarnigan began to weep. "Time, Time, our son is crying."

"Isn't it your turn to check on him, sweetheart?"

"Okay, I'll check on the little tiger."

Time got up and walked over to the crib. Suddenly the room began to shake. The tremors lasted for about a minute. Time immediately gazed at his son quietly sleeping in his crib. He had gently tucked his son into his crib and proceeded to walk off. He had a sudden premonition of his son grabbing his hand. A demon's voice shouted out at him, "Are you God's favorite?"

Shivers went down his spine, and he gazed back at his son again. The child was still resting in his crib. He wiped his eyes and got back in bed with his wife. Mary rolled over to cuddle up to him.

"Is he okay?"

"I think so. You know what?"

"What?"

"I really love you."

"Thank you. I really needed to hear that from you. What type of future do you think our son would have, Time?"

"I don't know. I suppose he'll find love in another galaxy perhaps," he said, laughing.

"I'm serious, Time. The world is different. The sign of the beast is everywhere. I'm so very afraid for him. We won't be here forever to protect him, Time. I think we oughta have another child. In due time, though."

"Are you serious?" Time smiled at her.

"Yes, I want our love to last forever, Time, but we'll have plenty of time to work on that."

"Yes, of course."

"What do you think will happen to us, Time?"

"We'll wait on Christ, Mary, we'll wait on him together," he said, embracing his wife. Time and Mary held hands, stepping out onto the terrace. Wolves howled in the pitch-black night. It was cold and gloomy.

"Oblivion and our friend will soon return. I want to be here when they do."

"Do you think they made it?"

"I would hope so." Time kissed her and swooped her up into his arms to the bedroom.

A lonely child stood at the windowsill, gazing out of the window. His cat eyes nocturnal and normal by day. Scaly skin surfaced, and he slightly became who he really was. Ying Wu scratched at the stained glass window and howled along with his furry friends. Time and Mary could hear him. It was hard to rest. Those who stayed in the sanctuary could hear the howling as well. Fear gripped their hearts. Time had taken cotton balls and stuffed his ears, while Mary placed the pillow over her head.

The aroma of hot gravel was in the air. Two heroes walked across it to get to the other side of a hill. Cutter was still a little in shock but managed to keep her sanity. Oblivion kept looking behind, checking for them to return.

"We'll have to hurry before they return."

"I'm looking for another fight. I hope they do."

The earth rumbled, and tiny specks of flying gargoyles squeezed through the cracks of the earth and into the atmosphere. Cutter felt the ground shake and grabbed Oblivion's arm.

"They're coming!" The Magnificents ran through the woods. The wind blew hard, and the trees swayed from side to side. It began to rain. "We'll cut across these woods until we get to the cathedral!"

"You think we'll make it?"

"Either that or prepare to die!"

They levitated and flew across the woods, casting their shadows among the trees. The storm came in closer and pushed the clouds across the sky.

"I can see it. Can you?"

The cathedral was near, until a gargoyle snatched Cutter by the cape and swung her into an old oak tree. Cutter blacked out for a second and came through. Sharp, clawed feet surrounded her. She got up and faced her enemies. Blood trickled from her lips. Oblivion had seen what had happened and flew to help her.

"Well, are you gonna just stand there or what?"

Their angry growls grew, and she slowly stood on her feet, facing them for a fight.

"Come on, bring it on!"

They fiercely clawed and tried leaping at her. Cutter slashed at them, tearing into their rough, charred flesh, punching into their skulls. They're suddenly surrounded by live skeletons, which came out of nowhere. Their charred bones worn torn, shredded clothing. They were dressed like old pirates, carrying swords.

"Where did they come from?" she whispered to herself.

Oblivion quickly flew over to her and scooped her up into his arms. Off they flew to the cathedral. The army of evil came after them. The rain came down harder, blurring Oblivion's vision.

"Don't stop. Whatever you do, keep going."

They finally made it. Oblivion landed them safely onto the balcony. Cutter passed out again as he carried her into the cathedral and laid her on the couch. He locking both patio doors. Sounds of feet landing on top of the roof penetrated the wood. The creatures crawled up over the building and onto the patio. Oblivion rubbed Cutter's head with a wet rag until she came through. +o

"How do you feel?"

She awoke frightened more than ever. "Please, don't let me go back to that awful place again."

"We're not out of danger yet. They're here. I better warn the others."

Cutter cried, mascara running down her cheeks. A torn sleeve clutched her fingers, and she grabbed his collar.

"Please, don't leave me here alone. I don't . . . I don't think I can fight them all by myself."

"You won't have to. Trust me, I'll be back, okay?"

She loosened his collar as he left. Being in the dark was scary enough. She was on the inside while it was trying to get in. Ying Wu entered the room and startled her. She put on a lamp. He walked over to the patio doors, gazing at the full moon. The rain trickled down the glass doors.

"Can you see them?"

"What . . . what are you talking about?"

"They want in . . ."

"Ying, step away from the patio doors, sweetheart."

"They're talking to me, see?"

"Ying, I want you to step away from the doors."

"No."

"Please, Ying, step away from the doors!"

Ying immediately unlocked the patio doors and opened them. A cool breeze blew into the chapel. Furniture blew onto the floor. Father Time, Oblivion, and Sister Claire ran into the room and saw what was happening. Oblivion grabbed Cutter from underneath and took her out of the room.

"Let's go into the other rooms. They're coming!"

The winds blew harder. Ying Wu stood there, smiling, while Sister Claire called him.

"Ying, Ying, come with us!"

Dark shadows with wings approached the chapel and sat on the railings of the patio. Sister Claire reached out to grab Ying, but the winds forced her back.

"Ying, please!"

He was grinning from ear to ear. His eyes pierced the moon, and he gazed up at the dark sky. Sister Claire managed to grab him and close the door. The glass doors had suddenly burst, sending chipped glass into their faces. Sister Claire dragged the poor child into the other room along with the others. Time got angry of the thought of having the beast-like child there.

"Why did you bring him here?"

"We just can't leave him there, Time."

"For all we know, they're probably after him, Mary!"

"He can help us, Time, I know he can!"

"He's a demon, Mary, for God's sake!"

"He's a child, Time."

"And a freaking monster!"

Ying Wu pointed at a map on the sofa. Time walked over to it and opened it. "What do you see, boy?"

Time handed Ying the map, and he scrolled down the map with his finger. "This, this is where they are."

Newspaper, pens, and Bibles flew at them in thin air. Something evil had entered the chapel, forcing its way into the room. Time got nervous and grabbed Mary's hand.

"Its time for us to become Magnificent!" The fearsome four had changed into heroes. Ying had decided to join them and changed into a gargoyle carrying daggers.

"That's why we need him, he'll blend in with the others, perfect!"

The door swung open, and dark shadows entered. The Magnificents didn't know what they were encountering, but evil forces had entered the chapel, smacking them down onto the floor and shoving them against walls.

"It wants you to lose your faith in Jehovah. Stay strong!"

The winds blew harder, and eerie and screaming voices echoed in the room. Demons crawled across the ceiling, snatching them by their capes, tossing them across tables and chairs. Time punched them through stained glass windows. Mary touched them, and some disappeared before her. Oblivion spun around into a funnel, sending them flying out of windows and onto the pavement. Cutter sent razors into their raw, burned flesh. Ying Wu leaped upon the demons and bit into them, tearing them in pieces with his claws.

The screams got louder as the Magnificents fought for their lives. The stench in the air made them gag, while the evil came in. Claw marks engraved deep into the ceiling, and pencils and pens flew at them like darts. Mary punch-kicked them into walls. The impact chipped the paint. They crawled on their knees, exposing three toes, and their yellow decayed teeth tried to devour them. Disease-ridden bodies from hell had entered a world long forgotten. Oblivion dislocated bones from tossing them out of the church. Time flew into the air and kicked one demon into the head, killing it instantly. The battle lasted for an hour until the Legion vacated. The Magnificents never claimed the victory but lived to fight another. Time and the others immediately boarded up the shattered church windows.

Janice cleaned up the blood upon the floor. While scrubbing the floor, she overheard a noise coming from the other room. She slowly pacing her steps over to the door. The door creaked open, and there was nothing. She suddenly felt a cold draft and entered.

"This room is awfully cold . . . Something evil walks among us."

The door had slammed closed behind her. Janice walked over to open it. It was locked.

"Hey, open the door, guys!" she shouted, banging on the door. No one responded, and fear gripped her soul. All around her, she heard whispering in the dark. Still, no one was there to help.

She felt like no one cared.

"I'm not afraid of you!"

The whispers started up again, and this time she heard what they were saying, "Cut yourself."

Razor blades slid across the floor in front of her. She remembered her first cut. Vomiting upon the floor, she retrieved the razor and gazed at it.

The Magnificents had finished cleaning, and Sister Claire searched for Janice. "Has anyone seen Janice?"

"She was here a minute ago." Oblivion got worried.

A razor leaned on a wrist, and there was an undecided addiction to give up. Janice wept, wiping her eyes, "I can't . . . I just can't do this right now." Oblivion checked the rooms for her.

"Leave me alone!"

The razor blades levitated from the floor and spun around in circles before her. Janice couldn't take her eyes off them. Oblivion tried to turn the doorknob, but it was locked.

"Janice, Janice, are you in there?"

"Wow, look at them glow, they're so pretty."

She smiled at them and grabbed one and placed it gently on her wrist, until Oblivion kicked the door open. "Give me your hand, Janice!"

"No," she said, cutting into her wrist. Her flesh popped open.

"No, don't do that! Please, please give me your hand."

"No!"

"Janice, Janice, please listen to me. You're one of us now, a Magnificent."

"Maybe you ought to forget about me. There's nothing magnificent about me," she said, raising the blade to her neck.

"Janice, please don't do this!"

Janice slit her throat. Blood gushed from her jugular vein onto the floor.

"Noooooooo!" He leaned over her frail body and applied pressure to her neck. "Please, please don't die on me."

The rain came, and the funeral was short and sweet. They were her only family, and they stood over her grave, paying respects to her death. Time spoke out, "She was part of our family, and now she's dead. Janice will always be remembered as a young, bright, beautiful girl. Full of hope and energy. She's saved my life more than once, and I will always remember that."

Sister Claire spoke, "You were like a little sister to me. A sister I never had, and I will never forget you." She was crying.

Oblivion wiped his eyes and spoke, "I wrote this poem. I hope you like it. It's titled 'Whatever Happened to You?'"

Whatever happened to you?

You were so full of life.

I thought you would never give up.

Whatever happened to your beautiful smile?

A smile worth waking up for.

You told me that you would never leave me.

You were so strong, I . . .

Anyway.

Now that you're gone,

A part of us lies deep within these rocks.

A Magnificent.

Whatever happened to you, Butterfly?

Whatever happened to us?

The Magnificents raised their fists up high, honoring her death.

"God be with you!"

"God be with you!"

"God be with you!"

Those words echoed across the sky. Ying Wu placed a beautiful rose upon her grave. A tear fell from his cheek onto a rock. The tear rolled down the side of the rock and penetrated the soil, which glowed a green neon color. A crowd stood around them in mourning. Time placed his hand upon Oblivion's shoulder.

"We better go inside, it's getting late."

"I need . . . I need a few minutes alone, thank you."

Everyone left and went inside the chapel. Oblivion stood over her grave and knelt down. "I will avenge your death, I promise."

The sound of wolves howled in the pitch-black night. A black nun by the name of Sister Lucci watched their child during the funeral. An older woman, her hair was jet-grayish white, and she was blind. Time entered the room, and she approached him.

"Yes, Sister Lucci?"

"Your child isn't like the average."

"What do you mean?"

"I tried breastfeeding him, and he didn't want my milk. He also bit down on my nipples until they bled."

CHAPTER SIXTEEN

"You're not his mother, Sister Lucci. Even you would understand that."

"I am aware of that, Father, but these are the end of times. What happens when we don't have any milk at all to feed our babies?"

"God will find a way for our son to eat, Sister Lucci."

Sister Lucci touched his face and ran her fingers across it. "You are a strong man, Father Time." Sister Lucci reached down to grab his manhood, but he immediately grabbed her hands to stop her.

"I'm . . . I'm sorry. I-I don't know what got into me, Father."

"I see."

"It's been a long time since I had a man come into my life. Behind these walls, nothing but darkness, Father Time. I have been blind for years, and sometimes a woman like me gets lonely. I'm not sorry for touching you, Father Time, but I am sorry that we haven't met early. Early before all this. The world now lies in the hands of the Antichrist and all his followers. You are a Magnificent, Father Time, and your wife is a very fortunate woman to have you. I'm sure you feel the same about her."

"I do. When Mary and I met, it was like a match made in heaven. When I first kissed her lips, I knew then that she was the one for me."

"You do realize that there will come a time when you two shall part and your child could very well be the last of the Magnificents?"

"I do realize that, but there's nothing I can do about that right now, is there? Mary and I will worry about that when we come to the end of that road."

"Whatever you do, Father Time, walk with God."

He left her standing there and entered his son's room. Jarnigan smiled at him, spit bubbles driveling from his mouth. Time lifted his son into his arms and held on to him tight. He walked out onto the courtyard. A blanket kept his son warm and snuggly. The cold temperatures of the winds dropped dramatically.

Sister Claire sat in the library, reading various books on untold prophecies. Oblivion joined her with two cups of hot chocolate and sat next to her.

"This should keep you warm, princess."

"Thanks. Anyone ever told you that you are a lifesaver?"

"Why, yes, you did." They chuckled at the thought.

She savored the hot chocolate and smiled at him. "Something on your mind?"

"I'm thinking about Julie . . ."

"Who's Julie?"

"The woman that I'm madly in love with. The woman I hope to marry. She has a beautiful daughter named Meredith, and I miss them dearly. I hope they're still alive. Just the thought of something bad happening to them kills me."

"Leave it in God's hands, okay? I'm sure they made it safely."

"I hope so too. I found this, an old diamond ring to place on Julie's hand in matrimony." Oblivion handed it to her.

Sister Claire smiled and handed it back. "Its beautiful, Oblivion. When do you suppose you'll ever see her again?"

"Real soon. I'm going out there tomorrow."

Sister Claire grabbed his hand. "Go with God."

A blizzard kicked in, and Oblivion hiked his way over the mountains to find them. He set up a campfire and a tent. The heat from the campfire kept him warm. Extremely cold winds shifted inward, and Oblivion slept peacefully in his sleeping bag, dreaming of finding Julie and Meredith. A white wolf sniffed his scent and tried to rip his tent open.

"Who's there? Whose out there?" The wolf whimpered and was hungry. He slowly unzipped his tent. "Why, hi there, my furry little friend. What brings you here today?"

"*Woof, woof!*"

"I think I can accommodate you with that. Beef jerky okay?"

"*Woof!*"

Oblivion threw him a piece, and the wolf lapped it up. "You were hungry, huh, little man?"

"*Woof, woof!*"

He petted the wolf. "You want to earn your food, boy, hmm? Come here and sniff this." Oblivion retrieved from his pocket Julie's parity and placed it under the wolf's nostrils.

"*Woof!*"

"Good boy. Take me to her. Help me find her, okay?"

"*Woof!*"

The journey was rough, and there were times Oblivion and the wild wolf thought they were lost. The lakes were frozen, and Oblivion placed his hand upon a block of ice and melted it into a jug. Drinking from it, he shared a little with his four-legged friend. He then gathered plenty of wood and built a sled.

"I haven't given you a name, have I?"

"*Woof, woof!*"

"I think I'll name you Sasha. You like Sasha, little man?"

"*Woof, woof!*"

"Great, Sasha it is."

The wolf was attached to the sled, leading Oblivion to Julie and the kids. "You can smell her, right, Sasha? I can relate to that."

Julie, Meredith, and Brandon never made it home safely and used the vehicle as shelter. "Well, let's look at it this way, kids. It got us there partially. I mean, we can walk the rest of the way home. What, a mile or two?"

"Oh, Mom, the sky could be falling in, and you would always talk as though we have nothing to worry about. You are so funny. You have anymore of those liquishes?"

"Sure thing, kid." Julie handed Meredith and Brandon a bag of cherry liquishes.

The blizzard covered the vehicle enough to see the headlights. Julie got out of the vehicle and scraped the snow from the window.

Oblivion set up tent and ate. He sat by the campfire and shared morsels of food with Sasha. His body glowed a bright-purplish color. Sasha was amazed and rolled in the snow. The next morning, Oblivion and Sasha were on their way to find Julie's house. Sasha got nervous and stopped.

"What's wrong, boy?"

The wolf scratched at the buried vehicle under the snow.

"What you find, boy?"

Julie and the kids were there sleeping. "What in God's name. Julie? Meredith?"

"Oblivion, is that really you?"

Julie jumped out of the vehicle and passionately kissed him. Meredith and Brandon smiled watching. Her mother was in love again, and she was finally happy. He was overjoyed and in love. The green emerald she held glowed in her hand, and she squeezed on to it tightly. They glanced into each other's eyes and smiled so sweetly.

"I thought . . ."

"Never mind that. I need to get you out of here. Come on, kids, this is Sasha."

"Wow!"

"Wow, a real wolf. Where did you find him?"

"Well, it's a long story. We sorta found each other."

"Neat."

"This is Brandon. Brandon, this is Oblivion."

"What kind of name is Oblivion?"

Oblivion stooped over and grabbed his chin. "A Magnificent."

"What's a Magnificent?"

"Come on, Brandon, we can ask questions later, hon."

Julie, Oblivion, and the kids stood on the back of the sled while Sasha pulled them over the slopes toward home. Time awaited the return of the legion. He and Mary gathered ammunition for a fight. Prayers went up as the Magnificents planned a state of active armed conflict. Church members boarded up the doors and windows, barricading themselves inside the chapel. A mob of angry protesters threw lit torches at the church, yelled extreme profanity, and demanded that the church be burned down. Suddenly the sky had wings. The

Legion of the Damned had returned, and the lost souls fled the area. Sister Claire and Time entered the rooms and came out like heroes. Sister Lucci approached Time.

"You need not to worry about your son, Time. I will take care of him. In the meantime, go out there and kick some ass."

Ying Wu stayed in his room and glanced out of the window. He could see them approaching the chapel. His eyes burned like fire. His head wanted to join them, but he didn't belong.

The demon bat angels flew at great speed. Their wings were extended out, and their feet were shaped like double-webbed toes. Saliva hung from their sharp jaws, and their voices screeched an awful noise. They came like killer bees in the pitch-dark night, and their target was Time.

Ying Wu smiled and pressed his nose against the glass window.

Father Time fell asleep in the rocking chair holding his son. Sister Claire walked in and pressed her hands upon his shoulders, caressing them. He got up and placed his son into his crib. "I know you want this." Sister Claire gazed into his eyes, and they kissed passionately. He pushed her against the wall, lifting her, propping her legs across his hips. They made love as he lowered her to the floor. She moaned in ecstasy and sat on top of him, riding him until they climaxed. Sister Claire laid her head upon his and closes her eyes. He kissed her cheek.

"I will love you forever, my love."

The gargoyles burst into the room unexpectedly. Father Time and Sister Claire immediately got up from the floor and snatched the rosaries from their necks, transforming into a Magnificent, their bodies fully clothed. The creatures walked like humans on crutches, breathing hot air.

The moon glowed like a crystal ball while a war pursued. The demon bat angels leaped at them, tearing into their flesh. Sister Claire touched as many as she could, and they disappeared. Father Time kicked some into the wall. Concrete smacked onto the floor. Father Time flipped high and double punched them out of the window.

Chipped glass shattered into the air. Sister Claire spun around in circles in a funnel-like position, kicking and punching them out cold. The demons kicked through stained glass windows into the chapel and attacked church members. The church members panicked and ran in all directions of the chapel. Some demons were doused with holy water and caught on fire. Church members fought back and spared their lives to save their children. The Magnificents drew blood and amputated skulls with their swords. The Legion of the Damned eventually vacated the chapel and flew off into the night. Father Time and Sister Mary Claire went to check on the injured.

Church members sprawled on the floor in pieces. Father Time and Sister Mary Claire covered them with sheets and prayed over their tortured souls.

"Time, I'm scared. I'm so very scared of what might happen to us."

"Don't be. Jehovah is on our side."

"I realize that, but look at the odds here, Time."

"And we shall overcome this."

"Oh, Time, I love you," she said, sobbing.

"Don't have doubt in your heart. We are going to get through this together. Now let's bag these bodies up and bury them."

Sister Mary Claire and Father Time buried the remains of their victims in the backyard of the church chapel. The church members that survived the attack were present. They eventually boarded up the stained glass windows that got destroyed. Father Time gave a speech at their burial.

"Right now, there are two of us. Sister Claire and I will do everything we can to keep you safe here at the chapel until our friend returns. We will need your cooperation in the meantime to stay here at the chapel and guard it as long as you can. It is all we have right now, and if you leave it, it may very well cost you your life."

One of the church members spoke out. "What if we can't?"

"Then we will all lose this battle. I need you to stay strong."

The church members got angry and spoke out. "What makes you two think that you can save us? Didn't you see what they've just done?"

"Yeah, they came right into the house of the Lord and destroyed it!"

"Mommy, I'm scared."

"They just killed my wife!"

"I can't find my dog. Do you suppose they have him?"

"What kind of people are you? You stood by and watched our friends die!"

Father Time spoke out, "Please, we are all in this together. What we have to remember is that this isn't our fight but God's fight! Those things out there want our souls, and we have to do everything we can to hold on to it. If you give up now, you have given up on all of us. The church is our home now. The church is where we stay!" The church members nodded their heads yes and returned to the chapel. Sister Claire smiled at him and embraced him.

"Thank you."

"You didn't have to thank me, Mary. I said what I had to say, that's all."

"And you said it well, my love, you said it well."

It's been weeks, months, maybe years since the storm had settled. They hadn't heard from the Legion of the Damned, and Jarnigan grew up to be a handsome child. He looked a lot like his father, Time. The way he smiled and walked. It was just a matter of time he would know the truth. They got their life back. The congregation grew, and they multiplied by numbers.

Children ran about a park and laughed. Oblivion and Julie were married, and Meredith started dating. A happy family indeed. Father Time hitched them, and they were present during their ceremony. Sister Claire had never seen such a beautiful wedding. The way they smiled at each other, it was love. Jarnigan was growing fast, and Time sat him down to talk to him about the birds and the bees. Not that he cared to know any of that. He was too much into his Bible. Another Magnificent to come. Sister Claire was baking cookies in the oven.

"Mother?"

"Yes, darling?"

"What does a vagina look like?"

She gazed at him and laughed. "Why do you ask such a question?"

"Dad keeps telling me to avoid that right now. I may want to explore."

Sister Claire shoved a large cookie into his mouth. "I'll leave that up to your father right now, okay?"

"But, Mom!"

Jarnigan gazed out of the church window and watched the lost souls walking by, the sign of the beast stamped onto their foreheads and hands. No one was exactly safe. The earth they knew was in the past, and a new dictator took over. Jarnigan felt sorry for them. It was as though they couldn't see—walking zombies. Their shells existed, but they had no insides. Jarnigan prayed each and every day to not fall into the hands of the enemy. They were able to find food and feed the children through the Colony, a group of scavengers that lived within the sewers, surfacing at night and looting the stores. Some were killed, while others survived and lived.

Father Time paid them, and they went on their way. The stench on their bodies would make a man croak, but it was God who sent them. They would share morsels of food with the Colony during Thanksgiving, but that was all. Jarnigan felt sort of sad; he wanted friends.

The other children within the congregation considered him different. He was just a normal sixteen-year-old boy, but they didn't see it that way. Jarnigan had a crush and fell for a young lady by the name of Anya, a beautiful Ethiopian girl. He talked about her all the time and just didn't have the nerve to ask her out. She had the gift for dancing and would shake her hips in front of him every chance she got. He knew then that she would soon be the one and promised her to wait, placing a ring upon her finger. She took it off.

"When the time is right, my love."

"I will wait, forever . . ."

"I will wait forever" was what he meant, and the two grew up together.

The day came for Time to talk to Jarnigan about who he really was. Jarnigan stood on the patio, drinking tea.

"Jarnigan?"

"Yes, Father."

"We need to talk." They sat on the wooden bench.

"What troubles you, Father?"

"I know you are probably wondering why we aren't extremely close, son."

"Yes."

"I'm a hybrid."

"A what?"

"Before the beginning of time, Lucifer defied God and was cast out of the kingdom of heaven. On his way to damnation, a multitude of angels followed, but two never went."

"Two?"

"Yes, my son, two. Oblivion and I are the chosen two, Jarnigan."

"Wait a minute, I don't understand, Father. You're human, flesh and bones, like I am. What do you mean, the heavens released two men from total destruction, and you expect me to believe that?"

"What I tell you is the truth. We are under attack. The Legion of the Damned won't stop at nothing to destroy us. They will soon return!"

"Where is this legion?"

"Deep within the crevices of the earth, a place of no return. I don't know how long it will be before they find you, but when they do, you must fight to keep the ones you love. The storm isn't over, my son. For when they appear, hatred lies in their hearts. They will do whatever they can to suck the life source from your veins and feed on your flesh. For they are like savages, carnivores. You must . . . you must fight!"

Time left Jarnigan sitting there on the patio alone. A storm came, showering the soil and the trees. Jarnigan leaned over the balcony and thrust his fist toward the dark clouds that passed by.

"When my father steps down and passes throne unto me, I will avenge his death. For when you return, I will be waiting. I will be waiting!"

ABOUT THE AUTHOR

Melvina Hawkins Patterson was born and raised in Pittsburgh, Pennsylvania. Her father was a salesman, and her mother taught choreography and drama at Pitt University and was an actress. She has eight siblings. Ms. Patterson's first novel published is *Children of Eden*, and it can be purchased at IUniverse.com or any major bookstore worldwide. Her mother, Kathy Grant, inspired this writer to become the author she is today. A screenplay is available for review and film.

CPSIA information can be obtained at www.ICGtesting.com
Printed in the USA
LVOW08s1300260316

480897LV00001B/11/P